KT-512-461

Nigel McCrery worked as a policeman, until he left the force to become an undergraduate at Cambridge University. He has created and written some of the most successful television series of the last ten years – his credits include *Silent Witness*, *Born & Bred*, *New Tricks*, *All the King's Men* and *Back-Up*. He is also the author of five internationally bestselling Sam Ryan mysteries. Nigel lives in London.

4721800051380 7

Also by Nigel McCrery

Core of Evil

Tooth and Claw

Scream

The Thirteenth Coffin

Flesh and Blood

NIGEL McCRERY

BLOOD LINE

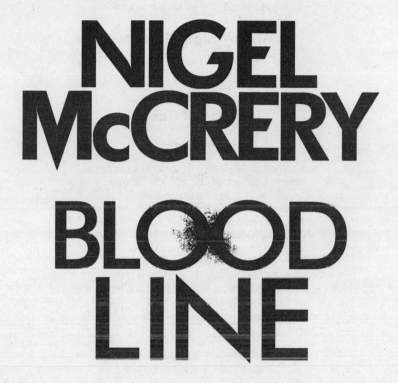

Quercus

First published in Great Britain in 2018 by

Quercus Editions Ltd
Carmelite House
50 Victoria Embankment
London EC4Y 0DZ

An Hachette UK company

Copyright © 2018 Nigel McCrery

The moral right of Nigel McCrery to be
identified as the author of this work has been
asserted in accordance with the Copyright,
Designs and Patents Act, 1988.

All rights reserved. No part of this publication
may be reproduced or transmitted in any form
or by any means, electronic or mechanical,
including photocopy, recording, or any
information storage and retrieval system,
without permission in writing from the publisher.

A CIP catalogue record for this book is available
from the British Library

PB ISBN 978 0 85738 238 2
EBOOK ISBN 978 0 85738 237 5

This book is a work of fiction. Names, characters,
businesses, organizations, places and events are
either the product of the author's imagination
or used fictitiously. Any resemblance to
actual persons, living or dead, events or
locales is entirely coincidental.

10 9 8 7 6 5 4 3 2 1

Typeset by CC Book Production

Printed and bound in Great Britain by Clays Ltd, Elcograf S.p.A.

For Abigail for just loving me

1

Isabel, then

Isabel Alarcon looked over the rim of her coffee cup as she took her first sip. 'Do you act as tour guide for all the young girls you meet on the bus coming into town?'

'Only the pretty ones,' Mauricio said jokingly, her sole companion at the table. Then he shrugged. 'And, of course, the ones named after the town itself.'

Isabel responded with a sly smile, unsure which category she fell into: the pretty, or those who carried the name of the town. Probably *both* from the engaging smile aimed back at her by Mauricio as he raised his cup in a silent 'cheers'.

They were sitting on the terrace of the only café overlooking Alarcon's Place Marie, the town's main square, named unimaginatively, Café Marie. Though the café owner looked as far from a Marie as possible, more like Bluto, Isabel thought to herself. Mauricio had informed her that the proprietor's name was in fact Ignacio. Thick-set, with three-day stubble, and the last inch of a fat cigar tucked in one corner of his mouth. She knew that Health and Safety rules had banned smoking combined with serving food and beverages in Spain yonks ago – but then Alarcon was one of those places frozen in time, in more ways than one. Opposite the café was a stone-built Town Hall with a clock above its main arched entrance, and at the far end a medieval church complete with a bell-tower.

It looked the sort of square that women and children would scurry from into hiding as Mexican banditos rode into town. Except for the solid stone cobbles – not exactly typical of a Western.

The same stone cobbles continued through the town to the menacing edifice of Alarcon Castle two hundred yards away. It was Alarcon's main tourist attraction.

The castle dominated the town with ramparts and interspersed turrets meandering down the steep ravine to one side, through which a tributary of the River Júcar flowed. The raised ramparts and turrets were like a mini-version of the Great Wall of China; the ravine the area's mini Grand Canyon.

It was a sight that was in equal parts dramatic and

daunting, and would have made a good stage-set for *Game of Thrones*, Isabel had always thought.

Although it was her first visit to Alarcon, she knew the landscape and some of its history from the various books on the town and castle which had held pride of place on the coffee table and bookshelves at home when she'd been growing up.

'And is it your family's connection with the town that has brought you here now?' Mauricio asked.

'Yes, more or less. My finals at uni are all finished and it was one of the first things I wanted to do – delve into my family's dark past.' She smiled and took a sip of her *café con leche*. 'Well, third thing to be exact. A week in Barcelona, two weeks in Valencia, then here.'

Mauricio lifted a brow. 'Isn't that the wrong way around – Barcelona being the more important city? There is more to see, no?'

'I suppose. But my godparents live in Valencia, and it's home now. I've lived with them since my father died eight years ago.'

'I'm sorry to hear that.'

'That's okay. It was as tough as hell to take at first. Sudden road accident in Kent. I'd just turned fourteen, and suddenly I'd lost my father.' She pushed a bittersweet smile. 'My godfather, Terry, was a big help in getting me through that. My mum fell apart, and so I stayed with him and his wife Barbara at their house in Marbella. Then my mum died too, a year or so later – she never really got over my father's death, I guess. So, Terry and Babs practically brought me up, got me into English school there. Then a couple of years back they moved up the coast to Valencia.'

Mauricio looked about to say something, then decided against it, perhaps deciding it was too light or inconsequential to interfere with her heartfelt family history.

She guessed that he was about four or five years older than her, dark-brown hair and light-brown, soft eyes, a total contrast to her own blonde hair and blue eyes. He was slim and quite attractive. But she suspected it was his outgoing personality that endeared him to girls – and she could imagine that his quasi-tour-guide chat-up lines had been spun with many a visitor as they'd approached on the bus from Valencia to Alarcon. She'd discovered that Mauricio was one of two regular bus drivers on that route, but his family home was in Alarcon – which was why he knew practically everything about the town.

'I'll fill you in some more of its history, if I see you around.'

'It's a date,' she'd said with a smile, flushing slightly as the alternate meaning of what she had said struck her. But then he was quite attractive.

Then on her second day in town, she'd bumped into him again as she'd come out of a shop and they'd arranged this café meeting now. Only three-hundred yards square – it was difficult not to keep bumping into the same people in Alarcon. On that second meeting, he'd discovered her Spanish was quite good – almost as good as his English from giving history snippets to visiting tourists – and so now they alternated between the two.

'*Los cuento,*' Isabel said. 'Here I am prattling away about my own personal history – when you're supposed to be telling me more about Alarcon's history.'

'Okay. Where do you want to start?'

'I don't know. You're the guide today. I'll leave it to you to decide.' She smiled at Mauricio as she leaned back.

Mauricio thought for a moment. 'So, let's start with the fable of the blood in the castle walls. Then, in comparison, the rest of the town's history might not seem so dark and macabre.'

2

Lapslie and Bradbury, now

'Sir. There's something I'd like to talk to you about.'

DS Emma Bradbury caught Inspector Mark Lapslie in the corridor shortly after the lunch break. She knew she wouldn't see him in the canteen, it was far too active and noisy, and the main local pubs and cafés were out for the same reason. Usually he'd either go to a couple of pubs half a mile from Chelmsford police HQ that weren't so busy and tuck himself in a corner, or have a quiet take-out soup and sandwich in his office.

'Yes, what is it?' Lapslie turned to her with a tight smile. Slight impatience in his voice, but over the years Emma Bradbury had learnt that this was his normal tone. Her boss had a condition called synaesthesia, which converted sounds into tastes and smells, and it grated constantly on his nerves – thus the quiet pubs and venues away from the throng, and he didn't do social graces well either. Many of her colleagues thought he was just difficult and anti-social, but she was one of the few on the Chelmsford force that had known him long enough and well enough to know different.

She glanced each way along the corridor. 'Might be a bit difficult here, sir.'

'Ah, yes . . . of course,' he said, finally picking up that it was a private matter, something she didn't want to discuss openly. He gestured towards his office. 'Come in.'

Emma waited for Mark Lapslie to settle into the seat behind his desk and let a brief silence settle. She knew his concentration would be better then. 'It's something Dom mentioned to me last night.'

Lapslie's brow knitted. 'Not problems with him again, I hope?'

'No, no. Everything's fine on that front.' Emma knew that Lapslie didn't approve of her boyfriend, a retired gangster, and felt that the association would impinge on her work. Then last year when she'd admitted seeing someone else on the side, Lapslie had shown real concern, worried that Dom might react violently if he found out. 'In the end, I took your advice and stopped seeing Peter.'

'The college lecturer?'

'Yes.' She'd told Lapslie about Peter, started to explain how his softer, more intellectual side had appealed to her, then stopped herself short. She wasn't even sure how and why it had answered a need within herself, let alone explaining to anyone else. But Lapslie's basic concern was simply that Dom was being cheated, and how he'd react; who she was seeing or *why* was by-the-way. 'I haven't seen him for over six months now.'

Lapslie pushed a tight smile. 'That's good to hear.'

'Yes, I suppose.' Emma bit at her lip. *Good to hear.* So, while Lapslie still might not approve of her relationship with Dom, he at least appeared to be taking solace in the fact that his advice had helped her avoid an incident with Dom. 'It was more to do with an old friend of Dom's, Terry Haines. Or, more specifically, his goddaughter, Isabel. She disappeared six days ago. Nobody's seen hide nor hair of her.'

'How old is she?'

'Twenty-one. Just finished her finals at university.'

'Twenty-one?' Lapslie smiled wryly. 'She's probably just gone off with some friends and forgotten to make contact. And *god*father, you said? So, he's not even her real father – even less reason that she should notify him.'

Bradbury shook her head. 'I went through exactly the

same routine with Dom when he first told me, and no, it's not like that at all. Isabel's father died in 2010, and her mother died a year or two later, after having been committed for mental health issues. So, rather than her being fostered out by social services, Terry and his wife, Barbara, stepped in – took Isabel in. They've been her main family since, she's practically like their own daughter. And Dom tells me that she was always very good with time-keeping and letting them know where she was. She would phone and tell them if she was going to be even a few hours late, let alone six days. You know the type of girl and arrangement.'

'Yes, I do.' Lapslie sighed. 'But you know how it works, Emma. We have trouble mobilising anything effective for even a fourteen- or fifteen-year-old – because most of them are runaways who simply turn up a week or two later. What could we possibly do for someone of twenty-one?'

Bradbury nodded solemnly. The intensity of any alert and search went down incrementally with age. A three- to seven-year-old and you could get half the nation's police mobilised. But by the time they reached fourteen and the number of temporary runaways increased drastically, those searches would be tempered accordingly.

Over eighteen, they were adults, so if they wanted to run away from their families and *never* make contact again, that was their choice.

'You mentioned she was at university,' Lapslie said. 'Was that a local one? Wivenhoe Park or Southend Essex?'

'No, she'd been at Cambridge. Trinity College.'

Lapslie's brow furrowed even more deeply. 'And Terry and Barbara Haines. Do they live locally – was she staying with them?'

'No. They live in Valencia, Spain. Moved there four years ago.'

'And previously? Were they local then?'

'No, they were in Marbella for another twelve years before that. They haven't been resident in England for sixteen years – though, yes, at that time they *were* local, lived in Southend.'

Lapslie started shaking his head. 'And the girl? Please tell me that at least she disappeared around here? That the last time she was seen was in Essex?'

Emma sighed. 'I'm afraid not, sir. She was last seen in a town called Alarcon, in Spain about a hundred miles from Valencia. She was supposed to go out there just for ten days, but she never returned.'

The head shaking continued, and now Lapslie closed

his eyes briefly – a *'give me strength'* expression – before opening them again. 'The girl isn't local, nor are her de-facto parents–guardians, and what's more she disappeared in Spain. It's clearly a matter for the Spanish police. We wouldn't be able to get involved.'

'Terry has been on to them already. They've been hopeless. That's why he's asked a personal favour through Dom to see if we might be able to help.'

'We'd still be tied by those same constraints. No link at all to pin it locally.' Lapslie gestured helplessly. 'And even if I did personally want to do something to help Dom's friend out – how on earth would I get it rubber-stamped by Rouse?'

Emma Bradbury nodded. Chief Inspector Rouse, their hawkish department head at Chelmsford HQ, was a stickler for protocol. 'Terry had a bit of a theory he passed to Dom that might help on that front.'

'Yes, *please* . . .' A tired tone, Lapslie's patience rapidly waning. 'Pray tell me this theory.'

'Terry is convinced Isabel's disappearance is connected with a run-in he had years back with another ex-gangster in Marbella. Part of the gang wars and feuds endemic back then, which was why Terry moved his family to Valencia four years ago.'

'And how would this possibly help with the specific situation we face with Rouse and Chelmsford force's involvement?' His patience was now completely gone.

'Because the man Terry Haines had a run-in with was no less than Vic Denham.'

'Vic Denham? Are you sure?' Chief Inspector Rouse looked keenly across his desk at Lapslie. 'Because that's not a name to bandy around lightly. Especially . . .' Rouse's voice trailed off.

'That was the name passed on through Bradbury.' Lapslie nodded solemnly. He knew that gap could be filled in with *'here at Chelmsford'* or *'with me'*, and they'd amount to the same. For over twenty years Vic Denham had been the bane of Rouse's life.

Tim Sayle, one of Rouse's fellow rookies when he'd first joined the Chelmsford squad, had confronted what he had thought was the last of a balaclava'd gang exiting a NatWest bank. But there'd been one more lagging behind that Sayle hadn't seen. The man knocked Sayle to the ground with two heavy cosh blows, which would have been bad enough, but the man then lashed out with a flurry of kicks to the kidneys and spine when Sayle was down. And it was those extra kicks which put

Tim Sayle in a wheelchair permanently when he came out of hospital two months later.

They had Vic Denham picked out from a photofit by an eye-witness who'd seen them changing cars two miles away, balaclavas removed, but that witness's reliability was tested on the stand due to their short-sightedness, and the gang got off.

But everyone internally knew that it was Denham because of his increasingly notorious MO. Rival gang whispers were circulating that Denham's stock-in-trade was almost kicking to death those who rubbed him the wrong way. '*Knock him down, so I can deal with him.*' A henchman would deliver a side-swipe, then Denham would move in with a pair of specially crafted shoes with pointed silver-plated steel toe caps on the outside. Victims would see those shoes glinting as they knifed towards them. As a result, he'd gained the gangland moniker of 'Vic the kick'.

Denham was linked to at least three other armed robberies in the area, but they'd never had enough to even get a case-file supported by the CPS. And when one case did finally heat up and start to look worrying for Denham, he high-tailed it to Marbella.

Tim Sayle had stayed with the force, but had to take

internal, deskbound jobs. Rouse had kept Sayle under his wing and got him the best promotions he could, but still it never seemed enough. On constant pills for the pain, Sayle suffered from severe depression and in the end had committed suicide six years ago.

It was the one soft spot Lapslie and others had seen in Rouse – his caring for Tim Sayle and how Sayle's death had finally affected him. Many ventured that was why Rouse had been so understanding and accommodating with Lapslie's synaesthesia; in Lapslie he partly saw a mirror image of his old friend, Tim Sayle. Soldiering on in the force despite an ailment.

'So, he's still down in the Marbella area?' Rouse now asked.

'Looks like it, sir.'

'I saw that he was active down there seven or eight years ago.' Rouse shrugged. 'But I must admit, I haven't checked since.'

Lapslie nodded, saying nothing. He wasn't sure if that was true, given what Denham represented to Rouse. He had the feeling Rouse would have kept regular tabs on Denham's activity.

'And you're sure it's not a ruse, simply to get us involved?'

'That's a possibility I suppose, sir.' Lapslie knew how much Rouse would love to have another shot at Denham, as did half of the Essex police and criminal fraternity as well. He shrugged. 'But the source it has come through I judge as reliable. And I daresay we can't possibly know unless or until we check it out.'

'True.' Rouse sank into thought for a moment. 'I suppose we have a sufficient number of unresolved cases against Denham on our patch to warrant following up. Especially now with this girl having disappeared.'

Another mute nod from Lapslie. Rouse didn't appear to need much encouragement. But Lapslie had hardly ever seen his boss so uncertain; normally his decisions were made stridently. Perhaps having this dumped back in his lap after twenty years, when he'd no doubt given up all hope of Vic Denham ever being brought to justice, had caught him off guard.

At length, a resigned exhalation from Rouse. 'Okay. This is how I feel we should handle it. Work the case from your desk for two or three days. Phone the Spanish police and enquire about their progress. Speak to the girl's godfather in Valencia too. If after that time she still hasn't appeared and the Spanish police seem to be dragging their heels – then catch a flight out there with Bradbury. Start making your own enquiries.'

'Thanks, sir. Will do.' Lapslie got up and started making his way out, looking back thoughtfully from the doorway. 'Obviously I'll keep you up to date on my progress – particularly anything new on Vic Denham.'

'First priority will be hoping this young girl shows up alive and well.' Rouse smiled grimly. 'Having waited twenty years for retribution against Vic Denham, I can wait a few days more.'

3

Isabel, then

'Curious, to say the least,' Isabel said, running one hand over the foot-square stone blocks and the mortar in between again.

The strange red and black spots were heaviest on the mortar, but some could be seen to have permeated into the stone blocks, giving them a pinkish tinge in parts.

Isabel looked back up at Mauricio from her crouched position. 'And it's meant to have been caused by blood, you say?'

'Well, so the fable goes.' Mauricio shrugged. 'Though to tell the truth, nobody knows for sure. Like most old fables, it is difficult to tell how much has been added or invented over the years since. And that is not helped in this case by there being *two* possible accounts of what happened.'

Isabel nodded, straightened up. 'Do you favour one?'

'Not really. They both end the same way, with murder and blood. But the way they get there is different.' Then his expression brightened, struck with a thought. 'Why don't I tell you *both*, then you can make up your own mind, decide which is the most likely?'

'Like Cluedo?' She watched Mauricio's brow crease, and was reminded that some things didn't translate, or were known by different names in Spain. 'It's an English murder-mystery game.'

'Okay. A murder-mystery game.' Mauricio nodded knowingly. 'Seems very "fitting", as you say. Is that the right term?'

'Yes, that's the right term.' She chuckled, thinking to herself that British TV had a lot to answer for exporting endless *Upstairs, Downstairs* and *Downton Abbey*-style dramas.

They walked along the cobbled path bordering the perimeter wall as Mauricio spoke.

'Both go back to one of the first nobleman-owners of the castle, Juan Alarcon, who had a very beautiful sister attracting other nearby noblemen, who were keen for her hand in marriage. One of those noblemen was particularly arrogant and aggressive, known for his bad ways, and his offer of marriage was rejected out of hand. In fable one, angry at the rejection, he returns to the castle late at night and rapes the sister, but is caught shortly after by the castle guards, and the brother orders the guards to kill him.'

'And in fable two?'

'The same approach and initial rejection. But in the second version, there's no rape – he returns instead to kill the brother, thinking that's the main obstacle to gaining her hand in marriage. The brother catches him out halfway through this plan, and the guards seize him and kill him.'

Isabel nodded. 'And how does that then connect with the blood marks in the castle walls?'

'As with their beginnings, both fables end the same way: once killed, his body is chopped up and mixed in with the mortar used for building the castle perimeter wall at the time.'

Isabel smiled tightly. 'Probably their only shot at getting him to finally be a solid, upstanding citizen.'

Mauricio's brow creased, and she held one hand out in apology. '*Sorry*. English sense of humour. So, only the middle of each story is different?'

'*Exactly*. Rape of the sister in one, intended murder of the brother in the other.' Mauricio's expression lifted as he looked at her more directly. 'Any preferences?'

'So, rape or intended murder?' As they'd come around a curve in the perimeter path the wind hit them more strongly, whipping at her hair. Isabel smoothed it back as she looked out at the view, as if for inspiration.

The rocky outcrop with the castle nestled into its summit was the tallest of those in the vicinity; the craggy mount with the village two hundred yards away was slightly smaller, and another smaller still to their side fell away with a sheer drop to the gorge below through which the River Júcar flowed. Beyond was a patchwork of rugged heights with rolling plains in between. It was a dramatic, awe-inspiring view but at the same time hostile and foreboding, as brutal and uncompromising as the tale Mauricio had just shared.

'I suppose rape seems the most likely scenario,' she said at length.

'Why's that?'

'Well, rape is a definite action that's already taken place, whereas "intended murder" involves some mind-reading. How could the brother be so sure that's what was planned?' She gestured. 'Also, rape is the sort of thing you'd like to keep quiet. Family honour and all that. Possibly that's how the second fable version came about – to try to divert attention, to cover that up.'

Mauricio smiled slyly. 'Seems like this Cluedo game has guided you well. Because supporting the rape, there were a lot of stories passed down of that time – the sister disappeared for a year straight after the incident. In fact, first concerns were that she might have been killed as well.'

The pieces took a moment to fall into place. 'What – you think the sister got pregnant from the rape?'

'Yes. That's the theory for those holding to the rape version. Strict Catholic country, abortion was a cardinal sin. The only option would have been to have the child, then have it spirited away to an orphanage. A year later she marries a better-suited local nobleman and the Alarcon bloodline continues as if nothing has happened.'

'Except for the red and black blood splotches in the castle walls – which CSI will have a lot of trouble tracing back after all this time.' She smiled. 'And what was the name of this fair maiden who brought about all this blood and mayhem?'

Mauricio looked at her more directly. 'I thought you already knew – one of the reasons for your visit now. All those books from your father on Alarcon's history you mentioned.'

'Those were mostly just general history and geography

and a lot of pretty pictures. They tended to avoid the blood and thunder fables.'

Mauricio's countenance darkened a shade, or was he blushing?

'She had the same name as you – Isabel Alarcon. Though spelt the Spanish way, with a double-L and A, Isabella.'

4

Lapslie and Bradbury, now

'You've heard nothing from her in the last nine days?'

'No, nothing at all. Not a peep,' Terry Haines answered Lapslie's question, his wife Barbara at his side nodding her accord.

'And you've obviously kept trying her mobile phone?'

'Yes. It went into message the first couple of days, then after that it just went dead, back to dialling tone.'

'Obviously hasn't been recharged,' Lapslie said, his expression grim. 'And did you leave messages on those early calls? She'd have known you were eager to hear from her?'

'Yeah, we did.' Terry gestured. 'Probably too many messages at one point. Two or three each of those first few days. And as many calls again in between where we left no messages.'

Emma Bradbury, a seat-space away from Lapslie on

the same leather sofa, interjected, 'So there would be little doubt remaining in Isabel's mind that you were concerned about her well-being?'

'No, none at all,' Barbara said. 'If you knew her like we did, you'd know how unlike her it is not to make contact, to leave us hanging like this, worried sick.'

Lapslie nodded solemnly. *Worried sick.* The same as many a concerned relative after nine days with no news. Lapslie had clearly seen that familial bond between them when Terry Haines had handed him a couple of photos of Isabel at the outset of the interview. 'That's Isabel at fourteen, not long after she first came to us. Then one only a couple of weeks back taken on the back terrace here, not long before she went off to . . .' Terry's voice had trailed off then. He'd cleared his throat after a second to compose himself. 'You'll need those to start enquiring about her, particularly the second photo.'

Thinking of the photos, Lapslie asked, 'And have you already shown the photos you gave us to the Spanish police?'

'Yeah. Scanned and emailed them to a guy in Madrid heading the case, Inspector Ruiz.'

Lapslie had himself spoken to Bernardo Ruiz just yesterday before taking the flight out. No progress or leads from Ruiz's side, not helped by the fact that, so far, the case clearly wasn't a priority for him.

The girl's age was one factor. 'So many teens go missing and turn up a few weeks later unharmed,' Ruiz had commented. Distance, another: Madrid was a hundred and eighteen miles from Alarcon. He'd visited twice already in those nine days, and it had became clear from Ruiz's other comments that he considered this more than enough given the substance of the case. Alarcon had only one part-time policeman, Hernando, who doubled as castle and town 'Guardian', showing tourists around the castle at set times each day. 'Hernando was sure that Isabel had already left the town. And that was supported by one of the local bus drivers who thought he'd seen her on the bus out to Madrid.'

'And did you speak personally with the bus driver concerned?'

'No, I didn't. He wasn't in town at the time of my second visit. He was out doing what he normally does – driving buses,' Ruiz snapped, his impatience at being pressed on the case starting to show.

None of Isabel's personal belongings had been left in her hotel room at the local Parador de Alarcon – no credit cards, wallet or mobile phone. So, on the face of it, it appeared that she'd taken those with her – but then she hadn't officially checked out of the hotel, either.

Ruiz had sighed. 'But that doesn't mean too much. She'd already given details of her credit card for her deposit upon checking in at the Parador, with the arrangement that any balances were then settled from that same card.'

Lapslie said that he'd phone again to arrange a time for them to meet in Alarcon after he'd spoken to Isabel's godparents in Valencia.

'You mentioned that you thought Vic Denham might have been involved in Isabel's disappearance and may intend to harm her?' Lapslie looked at Haines levelly. 'What led you to suspect that?'

Terry exhaled heavily, as if shedding in advance the burden that Isabel's disappearance might be connected with his own past ills. 'It all goes back to the gang war of four years ago in Marbella. One of the many over territory and drugs. Vic Denham was injured in an attack on his villa, but his son was killed.'

'How old was his son?'

'Twenty-nine. An up-and-comer in his father's enter-prises, and just as hot-headed and violent in his own way. Many suspected that's why he was targeted as much as his father.'

'And Vic Denham thought you were behind the attack?'

'Yeah. I told him straight I was out of that stuff now. Especially all the drugs nonsense – but he wasn't having it. Felt convinced I was behind it, just because we were old foes.'

Lapslie nodded. 'Who do you think *was* behind it?'

Terry Haines smiled gently. 'You know the way it works. We might be guilty of many things, but we don't rat. The most important thing is that it wasn't me.' Terry shrugged. 'I took the threat seriously, though. That's why we moved out here.'

Lapslie looked out towards the terrace and the pool beyond. The Cruz de la Gracia estate, four miles from Valencia and close to all the main beaches. From what he'd heard, Haines's spread in Marbella had been equally impressive. Haines had done well for himself.

At first Lapslie thought that the enquiry stemming from a 'buddy' of Vic Denham's might cool Rouse's ardour to pursue the case. But it quickly became clear that there was no love lost between Terry Haines and Denham. There also seemed to be a grudging respect for Terry Haines, not only among fellow criminals, but also within the Cheltenham force. Terry Haines had never got involved directly in robberies, only financed and organised them. And he wouldn't back anything that was clumsy or violent. As armed robbers went, he was seen more in the *Rififi* mould – a man of principle. 'Haines and Denham are completely different kettles of fish as far as I'm concerned,' Rouse had remarked, making it clear you wouldn't find Haines kicking victims half to death or putting them in wheelchairs for life.

Terry Haines had heavily receding brown hair and a slight paunch. If it wasn't for his stocky build and the snake and dagger tattoo on one arm, he could have easily been a retired accountant or office worker. While Terry had a relaxed, slightly slumped demeanour, taking in information calmly before responding, his wife Barbara, '*Just call me Babs*,' was keen and lively, almost on the edge of her seat as they talked, nodding with enthusiasm and concern.

'But why didn't Vic Denham target Isabel while she was here?' Lapslie enquired. 'Why wait until she was away in Alarcon?'

Terry Haines raised a brow. 'Have you seen this place, Inspector? There's a reason why I chose here when we moved from Marbella. One of the most secure gated estates in Valencia, and I've also got an extra video link to the gatehouse and entrance, plus alarms and dogs. Not the easiest place to break into.' His face clouded momentarily. 'There was a reason why I took Vic's threat seriously and moved out here. There was an incident while we were in Marbella.'

'When was this in relation to Vic Denham's threat to you?' Lapslie asked.

'Only a couple of months after, which was why I linked the two in my mind.' Haines grimaced ruefully. 'It made me concerned for my family's safety.'

'What happened?'

Terry Haines looked to one side, as if he was having reservations about saying more; or perhaps he was simply getting the order of events clear in his mind. After a moment he looked up and started speaking again.

It had been a hot night. Hotter than normal for July in Marbella. Terry didn't like sleeping all night with the air conditioning on; when they left it on overnight before, he'd often wake up shivering in the early hours. Combined with the natural cooling overnight it was too much; so he normally set it on a timer to go off an hour after they'd gone to bed.

But tonight, the heat was insufferable and lingered into the early hours. Terry found himself waking suddenly with it, his body soaked in sweat, his mouth dry. 3.22 a.m. on his bedside clock. He reached over to the glass of water on his bedside table and took a heavy slug. Even water became lukewarm with the heat. He pondered whether to put the air conditioning on, but that would simply chill the sweat on his body.

He got up, towelled off his body in the en-suite, then went to the kitchen to get some ice-cold water from the fridge. And, just after filling a glass and taking a sip, as he closed the fridge door, he heard noises from outside.

'*Qué estás haciendo?*'

He froze, listened more intently. Sounded like Eduardo, one of the security guards, asking what someone was doing.

'*Qué nada. Solo soy un amigo de visita.*'

'*Esta vez de...?*'

Eduardo's voice was suddenly muffled, cut off. Terry had already placed the voices as coming from by his entry gate. He quickly switched the kitchen light off and peered out of the kitchen window.

Nothing at first, then a faint shadow of movement, a rustling sound. Through the gate, he got a fleeting glimpse of Eduardo's slumped body being dragged to one side, down by the bins. Then a wheelie bin was being pulled across, but very quietly. Suddenly, the shadow of a large man clambered up on the bin and started levering himself over the garden wall.

Terry's heart froze. The man would be approaching the house any second. He rushed into the lounge, grabbed his Beretta M9 from a side drawer.

He thought at first of putting all the outside lights on in the hope of frightening the intruder off, but he would also bathe himself in light as he went outside.

In the end, he just put on the outside spotlight, then went out the kitchen door rather than front door, crouching low as he levelled his gun. The large man squinted and held one arm up as the light blazed on him, hardly able to see beyond it. But Terry could see in that moment the gun in the man's right hand.

Terry's heart was in his mouth. If the gun had been pointed his way, he'd have fired at the man directly. But the man was squinting more towards the front door.

Terry fired a couple of feet above the man's head. The man turned towards where Terry had fired from, startled. Terry tensed, ready to fire at the large man directly if his gun started swivelling his way. But Terry's position was obviously still in shadow, because the man, with a final uncertain glance in Terry's direction, turned and scurried away.

'So, a large man, you say?' Lapslie confirmed.

'Yes, pretty big.'

'What? Over six foot?'

'A good six three or four, I'd say.' Haines shrugged. 'But it was difficult to say exactly . . . it was pretty dark.'

'And did you recognise this man at all?'

''Fraid not.' Another shrug. 'Like I say, it was pretty dark . . . and when I put the spotlight on, he put one arm up to shield his eyes against it. Which also covered part of his face, obviously.'

Lapslie nodded thoughtfully. He wasn't sure if Haines was being totally straight with them over this element. Maybe it was someone whose identity he was keen to protect, or back again to the old villain's byword: *never rat on each other*. Or maybe, as Haines said, he simply didn't get enough of a good look at the man.

'And did you report this incident to the local police?'

'Nah. Didn't seem worth it. After all, in the end, nothing really happened.'

'Did you speak to Eduardo about the incident?'

'Yeah, of course. As soon as I knew the coast was clear, I went down to see if he was all right. He was just coming round, had a bit of a bash on his head – but apart from that he was fine. He seemed to be more concerned that me and Babs were okay. That the intruder hadn't harmed us in any way.' Haines grimaced. 'I put his mind at rest that the intruder had run off before he even got into the house.'

'And did Eduardo mention reporting the incident?' Lapslie asked.

'Only to his local security company that guarded the estate. I don't know if anything would have reached the local police.'

'Was Isabel in your house in Marbella at the time of this happening?' Bradbury enquired.

'Yes, she was,' Terry said. 'Her first summer break from uni in England.'

Barbara added, 'Just been with us ten days when it happened.' She smiled hesitantly. 'It was good to have her at home after not seeing her for a while.'

Lapslie nodded sympathetically. But the mention of Isabel reminded him of the other anomaly that had hit him about all of this. 'What I don't understand – if

Denham's beef is with you, why not just strike back at you? Why would he target Isabel?'

'Because Vic was a great believer in "punishment to fit the crime". If he found out someone had pinched off him, he'd have their fingers or hand cut off, bit like the Yardies' standard punishment – he wouldn't have them killed.' Terry smiled lopsidedly. 'Of course, if it was a sizeable blag, he would have them taken out. But in this case, Vic had lost his son rather than been harmed himself.'

Lapslie held a palm out. 'So, it was mainly a supposition on your part, based on Denham's past form?'

'No, it was more than that. Goes back to something Vic said at the time of losing his son, Leo.' Terry sighed, troubled shadows crossing his eyes. 'He said to me that one day I'd understand what it's like to lose someone close. Someone I loved.'

5

Isabel, then

'I hope Mauricio is proving to be a good guide,' Gabriel Alarcon remarked. 'Giving you the history of our town and answering all of your questions.'

Isabel nodded, smiling. 'Well, most of them. I suppose if it was *all*, then we wouldn't be here.'

'Yes. Mauricio mentioned on the phone some genealogy links you'd like to pursue. His knowledge goes quite some way, but beyond that you must "go to the horse's mouth" so to speak.' Gabriel Alarcon smiled, opened his palms out on his desk. 'So, in what way might I be able to help?'

Now his early sixties, Isabel noticed that Gabriel Alarcon's English was not only good, but quite formal. Probably from the two-year post-graduate course in history at Oxford that Mauricio had mentioned. There was a student year group photo too on his office wall from

Madrid's Complutense University, class of 1976, along with various diplomas, plaques and awards. Isabel had noticed similar displays before in various lawyers' and accountants' offices in Spain. It was something that had been prevalent in England fifty or sixty years ago – exhibiting your educational heritage and skills – but it still seemed to be a popular habit in Spain. One area of time-warp, as if they'd picked up the practice from old Ray Milland and Rex Harrison films and still thought that's how things should be done in an office environment.

'It was mainly to find out how I might have ended up with the surname Alarcon,' Isabel said. To her side, Mauricio nodded in support. When she'd first broached the subject with him, he'd offered a few possibilities, but said that the main source of information would be the Town Hall and Gabriel Alarcon, the local Marques: "*We have a saying is Spain: when you need to know something like that, you have to go to the Jefe.*"

'What past links my family might have to the town? What relatives I might still have here?' she continued.

'Yes, well, we can but look,' Gabriel said.

'My father in fact apparently visited you here some time ago to discuss the same subject.'

Gabriel's brow knitted. 'When might that have been?'

'Oh, eight or nine years ago now.' Seeing Gabriel Alarcon still lost in thought she added, 'He was a wine merchant, he used to visit Valencia and the South quite regularly talking to producers. And on one of his trips, he visited the town here. Became convinced we might somehow be linked to the town's founders.' She smiled, held a hand out. 'That you and I might indeed be somehow related. Albeit distantly.'

Gabriel returned the smile, though hesitantly, his mind still searching for a clear recollection. Finally, 'Yes, I recall him now. The wine merchant. He said he might visit again on his next visit to discuss the matter further – but I never saw him again.'

'No, you wouldn't have done,' Isabel said, her expression suddenly graver. 'He died only two months later. A car accident back in England.'

'Oh, I'm sorry to hear that.' Gabriel's face clouded. 'I didn't know.'

Isabel nodded. No reason why he should have. Prominent wine merchant, but obviously not prominent enough for such news to reach Spain. They had enough of their own car accidents to report. '*Numero uno en Europa*,' she recalled a Barcelona taxi driver boasting as he hit warp factor nine. She thought at first that he was talking about Alonso winning the Grand Prix, but in fact he was referring to Europe's car accident statistics.

After a moment more of silence and a grim nod in respect of the news of her father's death, Gabriel commented, 'From what I recall, I didn't find any connections with the names your father gave me. But perhaps he hoped to give me some other names or information upon his return – or you have some other names now?' Those hands opening out on the leather inlaid desk again; a welcoming, *here to help* gesture. *Especially in light of this grave news now about your father.*

Isabel passed across a sheet of paper, prodding. 'They're probably the same ones he gave you: Alberto and Maria Alarcon, left Madrid's Atocha district in 1886 to settle in London, where Alberto started the family's wine import business. The only other name I can think of is Fernando Alarcon, Alberto's grandfather, born somewhere between 1805 and 1810. He had a small vineyard in the Murcia region, which is what I understand led to the family starting out as wine merchants. Fernando had to bring his grape harvest regularly to a local distiller, then finally went into partnership with him.' Isabel shrugged. 'But my father might have already told you about Fernando, I don't know.'

'Yes, of course . . . I can't fully recall myself. After all, it was a while ago. But I'll check the records.' Gabriel took a breath. 'Though as I probably explained to your father, the chances of any noble connection to the original Alarcon family – the line from which myself and my younger brother are descended – are slim. You see, a lot of people ended up with the Alarcon surname, despite having nothing to do with my family.'

'I see.' Isabel's brow knitted. 'Why was that?'

'Well, as anyone will tell you, the population of this town hasn't increased in the past hundred years. In fact, it has decreased – particularly in the last forty or fifty years. But it isn't a new trend that the young of our town have left for the brighter lights and work opportunities of Madrid or Barcelona – it was happening in the Middle Ages as well. Although back then, everyone was known just by their first name and their trade. John the blacksmith, Jose the baker.' Gabriel shrugged. 'Except when they went to Madrid, Valencia or Barcelona, there would be a hundred blacksmiths or bakers. So then they became known more by where they came from. Juan or Jose de Alarcon. Then over the years the *de*, the of, would be dropped. And they'd just become Juan or Jose Alarcon.'

'And you think that's what has happened with my family name?'

'It's the most likely explanation.' Gabriel Alarcon smiled ingratiatingly. 'After all, we've had more people leave this town over the years than stay here.'

The room was like a large medieval banquet hall with an arched window at its far end looking onto Alarcon Castle. There were twenty-two seats around the long table at its centre, ten each side and one at each end.

'This is where the town council meets each week to discuss main events and legal issues concerning Alarcon,' Gabriel Alarcon explained as he led the way along the expansive room, Isabel and Mauricio just a pace behind.

'Quite a lot of people to decide the fate of such a small town,' Isabel remarked, having already done the maths: population of 220, that meant that 10% of the town would be sat here to discuss matters at any given time.

'Ah, not all the seats are filled each week,' Gabriel explained. 'Only six of us preside over the town's agenda each week: myself, my brother and son – who are the town's main lawyers and public notaries – the castle's curator and warden, the town's warden and the manager of the Parador, the town's main hotel.' Gabriel glanced at Isabel. 'Where I believe you're now staying.'

'Yes.' Isabel smiled. 'Very comfortable, thank you. And very cultural.'

Gabriel nodded. 'The hotel was remodelled in fact within the walls of the old castle, without any extensions. It's very important to us to maintain the history and cultural identity of the town. So we have strict rules on building. Hardly any new buildings, and those that do have to be renovated or built afresh have to use the same ancient stone to blend in. Our main draw is tourism, you see, and much of that is dependent on the visual continuity of the town.'

'Yes, and very effective too,' Isabel said. 'The six of you are doing a fine job. The whole town is like being transported back in history.'

Gabriel smiled graciously and cast his eyes towards the walls each side. 'You could say there are more of my ancestors present at every town meeting overlooking current affairs, than just the six of us.'

Isabel joined Gabriel for a moment in studying the portraits lining the walls each side: generations of Alarcons going back to the Middle Ages. Sharp brown eyes staring down at them, some more kindly than others, with a gentle mischievousness. Others harsher, more penetrating, eyes almost black, as if warning off. Though that tended to be on the older, medieval portraits.

Isabel could see the likeness to Gabriel in a couple of the paintings, and as he'd stood to show them around, she'd noticed that he was quite tall, at least 5ft 10in, when the average height of men in the town appeared to be a good few inches shorter than that. He loomed over them not just in property and wealth, but in height too.

Gabriel held a hand out. 'A few portraits are missing – but all the main Alarcons are here, stretching back to the first defeat of the Moors and the town's return to Christianity under Alfonso VIII.'

Mauricio interjected, 'The Moors – that's our term for the Arabs, by the way.'

'Yes, I know,' Isabel said.

'I'm sure Isabel's spell at Cambridge would not have gone to waste in that regard.' Gabriel smiled.

Isabel had informed him at the outset that she'd just finished her studies there, and they'd talked for a while about their personal preferences for Oxford or Cambridge.

'Sorry,' Mauricio offered. 'Just so used to offering that

bit of information on the town to visitors about the castle's history.'

Gabriel was hardly paying attention, still appraising the sweep of portraits. 'I daresay at one stage, many more people were sat around this council chamber table deciding the town's fate. Not only the fact that the town was more populous back then, but also its jurisdiction covered a wider area – a good twenty miles each way into surrounding provinces. Now it just covers the town of Alarcon and a few square miles surrounding it.'

At that moment, they were distracted by a throaty roar from outside, a red Ferrari turning into the road heading towards them. Isabel recalled seeing the same Ferrari the day before, speeding along one of the narrow streets in the lower part of the town, and she and Mauricio had to scamper across the road sharply to keep out of its way. She'd noticed Mauricio's eyes linger on the car for a moment after it passed, and she'd asked him, 'Whose car is that?' 'Nobody important,' Mauricio had commented.

'Ah, more family,' Gabriel commented absently, and Isabel wasn't sure at first what he was referring too. His eyes were still fixed on the portraits. 'And do you see a resemblance to your fair self in any of these portraits?' he asked Isabel.

It was hard to judge, Isabel considered, because there wasn't a single woman among any of the portraits. Though she noticed that a couple of the men in the more ancient portraits did have long, wavy hair touching their shoulders.

She pointed. 'I must say, the earrings on that one look familiar. I think I owned a pair like that once.'

Gabriel laughed. 'Yes, that was the fashion back then among Spanish noblemen. The French and Italians disapproved of it at first, but then it caught on among them also.' Gabriel tapped the table-top, as if a prompt to remind himself. 'But I will look up those names you gave me for any links. Alberto and Maria . . . and Fernando, Alberto's father.'

'Grandfather,' Isabel corrected. 'He preceded Alberto by a good fifty years.'

'Yes, sorry. Of course, grandfather . . . I have it written down. I'll–' Gabriel broke off as the door behind them opened and a young man in his twenties with dark wavy hair stood there in jeans and a white cotton smock-top. He was smaller than Gabriel, slim and compact, but the resemblance between the two was clear. 'Ah, my son Dario.' Gabriel said by way of introduction. Then as he looked towards Dario, 'Mauricio has brought us a new visitor all the way from England who happens to share the same family name as us. Isabel . . . Isabel Alarcon.'

If Isabel hadn't already guessed that Dario was the owner of the red Ferrari from his father's earlier comment about 'family', she'd have known it from the key ring tab hanging from his jeans pocket. Another habit that had largely died out in England but was popular among some Spanish men: their key fobs proudly displayed by their crotches, as if to announce, 'Look what I drive.'

Dario Alarcon smiled warmly as he approached and held his hand out in greeting, and she could see that same mischievous teasing look she'd seen among some of his ancient relatives. 'Very pleased to meet you.'

'Me too,' Isabel said, but with a shade of reserve. She hadn't made her mind up yet about Dario Alarcon. But then rather than simply shaking her hand, he raised it to his mouth and kissed it, and she felt herself blush. Not because she found him attractive – though he was – but because the action caught her by surprise.

As she took her hand back, she noticed Mauricio glaring. There was obviously some problem or maybe competitive jealousy between the two men. She made a mental note to ask Mauricio about that when the time was right.

6

Lapslie and Bradbury, now

Mark Lapslie had never felt so hot. They were parked in a pull-in on the N111, with the rocky promontory of Alarcon to their right. The air conditioning was on full-blast on the Seat Toledo Emma Bradbury had hired in Valencia, but still Lapslie felt his shirt sticking to his back, a trickle of sweat running down his forehead.

'Where *is* this Ruiz?' Lapslie snapped impatiently. 'He was meant to meet us here ten minutes ago.'

'There's one advantage of him being late, sir.'

'And what's that?' Lapslie didn't trouble to temper the indignation in his voice.

'While we're sitting here, at least we've still got the air conditioning. Out there it's even hotter.'

He eased a throaty grumble. 'Mmmm. You're being a great help, Emma. As usual.'

'Always glad to be of service, sir.'

Their love–hate partnership had been going strong for eight years now, DS Emma Bradbury being one of the few on the Chelmsford force who could put up with dealing with DCI Lapslie on a day-to-day basis. Everyone else thought he was a complete pain in the ass; mostly due to his synaesthesia. The condition made him anything from mildly cranky to openly abrasive and hostile. But she was one of the few that understood his moods and knew how to play them. Often mildly winding him up worked a treat; gave him something to direct his crankiness towards. Also, she knew that he enjoyed the banter – another diversionary target for his anger and frustration, rather than the alien smells constantly assaulting his sinuses.

'Besides,' Emma said with a fresh breath, 'working in Spain, that's something you'll have to get used to. People being fashionably late.'

'Will I now?' Lapslie's best *You've got another think coming* tone.

Emma Bradbury sighed. 'There's an old saying in Spain. One minute, *un minuto*, means ten minutes. Ten minutes means an hour. *Una hora* means much later, and *mas tarde* means tomorrow.'

'Tomorrow? Isn't that *mañana* in Spanish?' Lapslie's brow creased. 'So what does *mañana* mean?'

Emma's mouth twitched in amusement and she was about to respond but was distracted for a moment by a black Alfa Romeo Giulia speeding towards them. 'There are two answers to that. The first is "don't ask"; the second is "never".'

The car was going so fast that it looked sure to zip by them. But at the last minute, it swerved in and came to a sharp stop three yards ahead of their front bumper. Inspector Ruiz got out the passenger side, followed by a young detective who was driving.

'Ah, he's here.'

Lapslie checked his watch. 'Eighteen minutes late.'

Emma smiled tightly. 'For someone who told us *mas tarde*, that's actually quite prompt.'

Inspector Bernardo Ruiz was practically a chain smoker, which hampered his breathing as they made their way up through the town, all of its streets winding up sharply to the castle and Town Hall which dominated the surrounding landscape.

With the intense heat, Ruiz huffed and puffed his way up between heavy draws on Marlboros – two on his way up – alongside Lapslie, with Emma Bradbury and Ruiz's colleague, Antonio, just behind. Antonio's English was rudimentary, so he simply nodded and smiled at all the right moments; *and the occasional wrong moment,* Emma thought to herself.

'I've found out quite a bit more since we first spoke,' Ruiz commented as they climbed the hill.

'What? You've been back to Alarcon again in the meantime?' Lapslie quizzed.

'No.' Ruiz shrugged. 'As I said, there's the distance factor, with it being some way from Madrid. But I have achieved quite a bit on the phone. I've been able to map out most of Isabel's movements in the six days she was in Alarcon.'

'Most?' Lapslie raised an eyebrow.

'Yes. There are still a number of gaps. But hopefully those will be filled in over the coming days with our combined efforts.'

The subtle emphasis on 'combined' did not escape Lapslie's notice. 'How long are you planning to stay here, Inspector?'

'I have to be back in Madrid by tonight. So, I have the rest of today here – but can come back again later, if necessary. You?'

'We booked the Parador for tonight by phone from Valencia. But we'll probably stay another day or two beyond that – depending on how it develops.' Lapslie looked at Ruiz more directly. 'And from your enquiries, any prime theories on what has happened to Isabel?'

'Well, she certainly hasn't been seen again in Alarcon since the eighteenth, almost ten days ago now, if that's what you mean.'

'And Madrid or elsewhere?'

'I put out a national police alert straight after our first phone conversation. But nothing back as of yet. No sightings of her.'

Lapslie nodded. Four days since that alert. Probably too early to make a judgement call on her whereabouts. He'd meanwhile run an interbank check in the UK on her debit and credit cards. No movement on any of them since the eighteenth. It wasn't looking good.

Lapslie took a deep breath. 'Hopefully her movements in the six days she was here will give some clue as to what has happened to her.'

'Yes, I think they might,' Ruiz said, and Lapslie noted the more upbeat tone in his voice.

Ruiz went on to explain that apart from the time Isabel spent in her hotel room or around the town generally, she did see two people more than anyone else. 'Mauricio Reynes, local bus driver and part-time tour guide. And Dario Alarcon, son of Gabriel Alarcon, the town Marques and Mayor. Indeed, the café here is where she had her first main rendezvous with Mauricio, after meeting him on the bus into town. And the Town Hall across the street is where she first met Dario Alarcon two days later.'

They'd been meandering up through the town as they spoke, and as they came into the main town square, Ruiz held a hand toward the café ahead and the Town Hall on the opposite side.

'And you see these two men as possibly significant?' Lapslie pressed.

'Yes. Because from what I've heard, there appears to be some problem between the two of them, some rivalry – which Isabel might have unknowingly got caught in the middle of.'

'And what is the nature of this rivalry?' Emma Bradbury asked.

'Mauricio is twenty-seven, Dario just two years older. So they are of a similar age but there's a significant difference in wealth between the two: Dario is one of the richest young men in Alarcon; Mauricio isn't.'

'I see.' Lapslie followed Ruiz's lead as they took seats on the terrace of the Café Marie. Although they were now under a sun-umbrella, it was still insufferably hot. Lapslie could feel sweat trickling down his neck after their walk through town, and again felt the dampness of his shirt as it connected with the seat back. He felt his sinuses assaulted with a mix of burnt caramel and sulphur with the heat, and pinched at the bridge of his nose to ease it, and stop his eyes watering.

'Are you okay?' Ruiz asked with a look of concern.

'Yes, fine. Just that sometimes intense heat makes my eyes water.' He didn't want to go into detail with Ruiz about his condition. Most people found it difficult to comprehend, would just look at him oddly after the explanation.

He looked thoughtfully at the Town Hall across the square, then along the length of the cobblestone road running from the far side of the square to the castle and Parador at its end, a good two hundred yards away; but the castle was so dominant and imposing – it could be seen from practically any point in town – that now he felt he could almost reach out and touch it.

As café owner Ignacio approached with a cigar stub perched in the corner of his mouth, Ruiz appeared pleased that he no longer stood out as the only smoker present. After their orders were taken, Ruiz spent a moment longer talking to Ignacio, saying they'd talked earlier on the phone, then filling in some subsequent details. Lapslie's Spanish was limited but he had just enough to understand the basics of the exchange between the two men.

As Ignacio went back inside the café with their orders, Ruiz commented, 'It was Ignacio who in fact saw Isabel and Mauricio together at their first main meeting. Then, again, he saw them together only a few days later coming out of the Town Hall – at which time, things appeared far more strained and heated between them. An argument started, and Isabel walked off ahead of Mauricio in a huff.' Ruiz held one palm out. 'And only ten minutes beforehand, Dario Alarcon's red Ferrari had pulled up in front of the Town Hall. Ignacio thought that might have been part of the problem.'

Lapslie nodded. 'So, Ignacio is aware of some problems between Mauricio and Dario.'

'Yes. As are half the rest of the town. But my reason to suspect that they are connected to Isabel's disappearance goes much deeper than that. Isabel and Mauricio were overheard arguing a couple of times. Once in the

Parador restaurant, and another time walking through town. And Dario Alarcon's name came up in those arguments.'

'One advantage of a small town, I suppose,' Lapslie commented. 'A lot of eyes and ears to pick up everything.'

'Precisely so. Much of that could be put down to just small-town gossip, if . . .' Ruiz broke off as their drinks, a mixture of coffees and soft drinks, were brought on a silver tray and placed on the table. He waited for Ignacio to be a good few paces away before recommencing, 'if it wasn't for one particular witness's comment. Luciana, a cleaner at the Parador. She was just finishing a late shift on the 11th, and it was raining quite heavily. But even with the poor light and the rain and mist, she felt sure she saw Mauricio with Isabel out towards the far end of the castle ramparts. She remembered it in particular, because she thought it strange that they should be out there at night in the rain.'

'And the significance of that?' Lapslie pressed.

'That part of the castle rampart is the highest point, with almost a sheer drop to the rocks and the river below. And, in that moment, Luciana felt sure she saw Mauricio push Isabel.'

7

Isabel, then

'And having given him an invite, do you intend to go ahead and have dinner with him?' Mauricio demanded.

'I didn't exactly *give him* an invite,' Isabel said defensively. 'When he heard where I was staying, he all but invited himself to have dinner with me.'

'But you still could have said *no*.'

'Oh, right.' Isabel put one hand on her hip, glaring back. 'Tell him flat out in front of his father: if you see me in the Parador restaurant on one of your visits there, don't bother to come over to my table, because I'll tell you to sod off!'

Mauricio's face clouded momentarily with doubt. The argument had started when they were barely through the Town Hall's main door. When Dario had heard she was staying at the Parador, he'd commented, 'I dine regularly there. I might see you there one night ... perhaps you can even join me at my table.'

'You could have at least appeared uncertain about it,' Mauricio said. 'I thought there might be something special developing between us.'

'*Special?*' Isabel shook her head. 'I hardly know you. You're just a happy, smiley bus driver . . . who probably spins the same chat-up lines to every pretty girl who shows up in town.'

Isabel caught Mauricio's flinch at *bus driver*. Perhaps she had been a tad insensitive; Dario's red Ferrari was parked only five yards away. She took a breath. 'Look, I'm sorry. I was beginning to have the same idea . . . until I realised how controlling you might be.'

A gap of a few yards had grown between them, mostly due to Isabel being keen to get away from his rebukes, and Mauricio looked down uncertainly for a moment, eyes flickering, as if unsure of the next thing to say to help bridge that gap.

'There are some problems between me and Dario.'

'You don't say.' Isabel's hand was back on her hip. 'And do you intend to tell me about them at some stage?' Mauricio's eyes still showed uncertainty, and she left it a moment more before adding, 'Or is it going to take a dinner-date to pry the story from you?'

He stepped towards her, a smile rising on his face.

One gap closed, she thought. How many more to bridge?

'I can recommend the trout or partridge in pickle,' Dario commented as Isabel perused the menu. 'The La Mancha stew is also good, but it might taste little different to you to an English hot-pot stew or French Beef Bourguignon. Not so exciting.'

'Thanks. I had the partridge the first night here, so I think I'll try the trout. It says here that it's in season.'

Dario shrugged, swirled his red wine in its glass. 'Spring's the best time for it. But we're still good for it now, I suppose.'

'You appear to know the menu well.'

'I should do. I dine here or at the other main restaurant, La Cabana, practically every other night when I'm in town.'

'And how many nights is that?'

'Usually only three or four.' Dario smiled gently. 'With only two hundred people in town, our family *abogado* and notary practice isn't exactly run off its feet. My uncle deals with the general legal side of things, then I handle any notary duties . . . when I'm not in Madrid or elsewhere.'

They broke off as the waiter approached to take their orders, Dario recommending a local white wine to go with her trout, while he opted for the partridge.

'And what is it you do in Madrid?' Isabel asked.

'I'm partner in a small fashion business. Three shops in Madrid, one in Barcelona, and new ones just opened up in Ibiza and Miami.'

'Miami?' Isabel raised a curious brow. 'Is that where you learned your English?'

'No.' Dario chuckled lightly. 'I spent most of my time in South Beach, and everyone speaks Spanish there. My English was just from school, then a spell at Warwick University. My father had this desire for me to study history like him, but it was a disaster. I hated it, dropped out after a year. Returned to Madrid to study economics and law.' Dario held a palm out. 'No point in pursuing legal studies in England, if you want to practise in Spain. We mostly follow the Napoleonic code here.'

Isabel nodded. She'd been hesitant at first to join Dario for dinner, in part at least because she'd practically promised Mauricio that she wouldn't. She'd come down to the bar from her room and as Dario had spotted her through the archway from the adjoining restaurant, he'd approached, taking some papers from his inside pocket. 'Ah Isabel, you know those names you passed to my father? I think he might have found some information on them.' Then as they'd started talking, he'd gestured towards the restaurant. 'Look, if you'd care to join me, I can fill in the rest of the details.' And it had seemed rude not to accept the invite, to hold him back from his dinner while he explained. Also, whatever problems Mauricio had with Dario were Mauricio's, not hers. Having made the decision, she didn't now regret it. Dario was easy company, and he did know more about the Parador's menu choices than most.

Her only residual guilt was about the *timing*. She'd arranged to meet Mauricio for dinner tomorrow night, but in begging off until then she'd said she was too tired for tonight and was just going to grab a snack at the bar and head to bed early. But because she'd inadvertently lied, she found her subconscious occasionally prompting her to look over Dario's shoulder toward the restaurant entrance, as if afraid of getting caught there with him, before finally telling herself that she was being ridiculous. *How on earth would Mauricio know she might be here with Dario?*

'Fashion, eh?' Isabel took a sip of her wine. 'I didn't have you down as a fashionista.'

Dario held a hand towards his clothes. 'Does it not show?'

'No, I didn't mean it in that way. I meant . . .'

'It's okay. I don't pretend to be. My partner's the "fashionista", if you will. I just take care of the books and the business side of things. Besides, a lot of it is retro. Revived Ibiza styles from the 80s, a lot of costume jewellery and brocade on denim and cotton.'

Isabel smiled. Made sense. Apart from the flipped-over trouser pocket Ferrari key-fob, Dario's outfit was actually quite smart, if a little dated; white kaftan shirt with embroidered trim, his cream linen jacket now over his chair-back. 80s *Miami Vice*, if she had to pin down the look.

Isabel glanced back at the papers they'd started discussing at the outset, now on the table between them. 'So, you think that this Eduardo Alarcon, two generations before Fernando Alarcon, was the first to arrive in Madrid? He's the main link between my ancestors and Alarcon?'

'Yes. We have Eduardo listed in the Alarcon records as far back as 1742, with the last listing in 1767 – after which it appears he went to Madrid.' Dario leafed through the half-dozen papers and tapped the third page down.

'A cabinet maker, he'd have been known as Eduardo Fabricante in Alarcon, but then . . .'

Dario broke off as their meals were put before them. '*Buen provecho.*'

'*Gracias. De acuerdo.*' Dario paused until the waiter was a few paces away before continuing. 'As my father mentioned, in Madrid or Valencia, there would have been hundreds or thousands of Fabricantes – so originally he'd have been known as Eduardo de Alarcon-Fabricante. Literally, Edward of Alarcon, a maker. Then over the years, the "de" and the "Fabricante" would have been lost.'

Isabel chewed her first mouthfuls of food. She supposed this was the sort of thing a notary specialised in, so there would be little chance of error. But still she couldn't help but feel disappointed. Her father's claims over all those years had amounted to nothing.

'So, no links to Alarcon nobility?'

'I'm afraid not.' Dario smiled apologetically; an attempt to soften the let-down. 'You and I aren't related – even distantly.'

Still, she thought, *look at the upside: cabinet maker. Could have been worse. Her ancestors could have been tramps or thieves.*

She'd been lost in thought for a while, impervious

to her surroundings, and hadn't done her intermittent check towards the restaurant entrance over Dario's shoulder – so when she caught sight of Mauricio she wasn't sure how long he'd been standing there.

She jolted with surprise. Mauricio had already turned, red-faced, back towards the bar and the hotel entrance as she stood up and started after him.

'Mauricio!' Then a quick, 'I'm sorry,' back at Dario as she hastened in pursuit. She caught up with him only a yard from the hotel entrance. 'It's not what it looks like . . . Dario caught me by surprise, said he had some papers for me from his father about my family's links to Alarcon.'

'Did he now?' A flat tone. *Feigned disinterest*, Isabel thought. Mauricio opened the door and stepped outside.

She followed him. 'And of course, I had to find out about that. I had to know.'

'The ideal bait, I think is what they call it in English,' Mauricio said coolly.

'Yes, I suppose it was. And I'm sorry. I fell for it.'

'Yes, you did.' He was expressionless; Mauricio was clearly trying to deny that he might care. His only doubt was shown by the fact that he'd stopped moving away.

She started to wonder how Mauricio might have

known or guessed she was with Dario. Was he stalking her? Although it was almost impossible not to give that impression in a town the size of Alarcon, where you kept bumping into the same people every day. But then as Mauricio started pacing away again and she followed him the first few steps, the hotel car park came into view – with Dario's bright-red Ferrari parked at its end. In the raised forecourt by the castle, the car would have been visible from much of the town, a bright beacon announcing Dario's presence.

'Will I still be seeing you for dinner tomorrow night?' she called after him.

'I don't know,' Mauricio's voice trailed back.

Isabel tapped a finger on the bar. Eight minutes past the time they'd arranged to have dinner. Maybe he was still coming. She'd left two messages during the day on his mobile, the first not saying much: 'Hope to still see you tonight. Give me a call when you get the chance.' Then with no call back after three hours, she'd said more on the second message she left: 'Look. I need to see you again, if for no other reason than to discover what this problem is between you and Dario. For sure I'm not going to him to ask about it.'

That should do it, she'd thought. Make it clear that she'd rather share confidences with Mauricio than Dario. But with still no call back, she had no way of knowing.

She sipped at a Campari and lemon. She was obviously drinking faster than normal; it was a third of the way down already. Her father's favourite drink, according to her godfather, Terry: 'Said it was the only drink that was sharp enough to clear his palate before a wine tasting. But it also worked with food too: the ideal *apéritif.*' So, she guessed she was taking her father's advice many years after the event; or perhaps partly in homage to him.

'Ah, you're here!'

She suddenly jumped as Mauricio's voice came from behind. She hadn't seen him approach. 'For a minute, I didn't think you were coming.'

He frowned. 'Sorry. My fault. I went through to the kitchen to speak to Vincente, the chef, and got a bit carried away. We went to school together, you see, and our mothers are friends too.' He gestured towards the restaurant. 'But I did look through from the kitchen at intervals, and when I didn't see you there – I feared too that you might not be coming.'

'Oh, I see.' She smiled uncertainly. 'But I called you earlier – *twice.*'

'Sorry. I was on the bus run today, double shift. Only got in forty minutes ago – barely time to shower, change and get here on time.'

She studied him briefly. White chinos and an electric blue polo shirt. Smart but casual. 'Well, you've scrubbed up well.' Heavier frown from Mauricio. One English term that obviously hadn't travelled to Spain. 'You look good,' she said, touching his arm as she left her bar stool and they went into the restaurant.

As they studied the menu, Mauricio said, 'One reason I went to see Vincente beforehand is that he does a special now and then which isn't on the menu today – but he'll make it if we want it. One of the best Paella Valenciana's this side of Valencia, or any other side for that matter. With not just prawns on top, but three large langoustines.'

'Sounds delicious.' She smiled to herself. Mauricio knew he wouldn't be able to outdo Dario with money or knowledge of the Parador menu, so he was trying to do so with favours pulled behind the scenes in the kitchen. Something Dario wouldn't be able to do.

'So, do you want to try Vincente's paella?' He shrugged. 'Or you can just go for the normal menu, if you want.'

'Let's go for it,' she said with a mixture of triumph

and abandon. 'I think I've probably had enough of the normal menu, don't you?'

And she caught a hint of triumph on Mauricio's face too as he gave their order to the waiter. Her meal last night with Dario was being tagged as 'normal', whereas this meal now was being anticipated as something different and 'special'.

Mauricio didn't broach the subject of Dario until they were halfway through their paella. 'It's difficult for me to talk about, even now.' There had been some moments of awkward silence, as if Mauricio was building himself up to the subject; or perhaps he was still bothered by her meeting Dario the night before, only yards away from where they now sat. 'It's to do with my mother's house, our family home for many years, and a promise made to my mother by Dario's great-uncle, Luis, who used to deal with all notary and property registration matters – a promise which Dario decided to go back on when he took over that duty.'

Mauricio went on to explain that originally everything was owned in Alarcon by the ruling Marques and his family, with almost everyone in town working for them on a 'serfdom' basis. 'Hardly anyone owned their own homes,' Mauricio said gravely. 'And that situation has continued in Alarcon more than most towns. Still to this day, sixty-eight percent of the property in the town is owned by them, either on short- or long-term leases. My parents' house, where myself, my brother and sister were raised, was no different. But my father had worked as a servant in Luis's house all his life and my mother too, as a maid. And when my father died, Luis promised my mother that when the lease ended twelve years later, she could buy it at a nominal price. A figure of 400,000 pesetas, £2,000, was agreed, half of which my parents already had saved. My mother, together with my eldest brother who'd already started working, made sure to save the rest in the meantime. The house was worth ten times that at the time and was expected to double again when the lease was finished twelve years later.'

Mauricio took a sip of his wine, shadows darkening in his eyes. 'But Luis himself died four years before the lease ended and when Dario took over he refused to honour it, said that as far as he knew there was no such agreement.'

Isabel shook her head. 'Wasn't there any paperwork?'

'A lot of things were done on trust in those days. If the Marques and his family said something would happen, they usually made good on it. Besides, my mother couldn't read or write, so what help would paperwork have been? Even a simple X marked by her would probably have been refuted by Dario in any case.' Mauricio shrugged. 'We felt sure that Luis would have marked something on internal files or records to that effect, but Dario argued that no such note or record had been made. If my mother wanted to buy the house, she'd have to pay the full market price. To make things worse, the new lease price was five times higher as well.'

'And Dario's motive for doing that?' As she saw Mauricio's brow knit, she simplified, 'His reason?'

'Simply put, *greed*.' Mauricio held a palm out. 'The house was worth far more than anticipated by then. Families from Madrid had started buying up weekend houses and *fincas* here – and the local market had risen ridiculously. Dario thought he could make more by keeping the house for himself and the Alarcon family.'

Isabel grimaced. 'Rather like the pattern with Welsh cottages and London buyers. Locals find themselves pushed out of the property market.'

'It broke my mother. She felt like she was a non-person. That she'd worked all her life for nothing. She had nothing left to leave to her children.'

'I'm sorry.' She understood now the bitter antipathy

between the two men, the reason for Mauricio's anger over her meeting with Dario, which she could feel coming over in waves again now.

Mauricio attempted to shrug it off. 'It's okay. Life goes on. We survive – but that's all we do. My eldest brother rents a room with his wife above the *ferretería*, the ironmongers. And I've stayed on in my mother's house with my younger sister, working endless double shifts to pay the higher lease to Dario Alarcon.'

The silence was heavy for a moment.

'It's bad enough,' Mauricio said, 'but for something like that to happen *twice* now between my family and his.'

'Twice?'

Mauricio shrugged. 'It doesn't matter. It's a long time ago now – over two hundred years.'

Isabel nodded. But it clearly did matter. The shadows in Mauricio's eyes were more troubled; he obviously found the subject difficult to talk about.

They discussed general lighter things for a while: how she was finding things in the town; was she coping with the heat all right; anything interesting she'd bought herself in the local shops, the difficulty of 'avoiding the usual snowstorm castle souvenirs'.

He'd smiled easily, but she could sense the second family problem with the Alarcons hanging in the background between them – though it wasn't until they were finishing and settling the bill that Mauricio finally got around to it. Some rivalry between his family's ancestors, the Reynes, and the Alarcons in the early 1800s, 'All over a young and pretty servant girl, Margareta.'

Isabel had offered to go Dutch. But Mauricio had waved her off in any case, insisting on paying the bill.

As they got outside, there was an eerie, distant flash of light. As they looked to the east there was a sheet electric storm, lighting up the hills and valleys far into the distance. It was strangely beautiful.

'Let's go to the high point on the castle rampart – we'll get a better view of it,' Mauricio suggested. He led her by the hand. 'It will help illustrate my story too – you'll see why.'

They walked up the rampart surrounding the castle, Mauricio explaining that this Alarcon family ancestor was also called Dario and his own family's ancestor, Diego. Diego Reynes. 'They were both desperately in love with this same girl – but then one day she died tragically, with Diego accused of her murder. And where it was meant to have happened was just up ahead, at the highest point on the rampart.'

The view got more dramatic as they went. It was completely dark when there were no lightning flashes, but then it suddenly lit up for miles around when the next flash came. It was breathtaking.

'So, here you say – is where it happened?' Isabel asked, looking down at the almost sheer fall to the rocks and the river below.

'Yes, more or less. He supposedly chose the highest point, for obvious reasons, so that the fall would kill her.' Mauricio's face darkened again. 'But the other tragic part of it is that many in town thought Dario was guilty of pushing her over rather than Diego. At the time, the Reynes were cousins to the Alarcon family, and partners in much of the wealth in town. But because of the incident, Diego was executed by garrotte and an edict passed that madness ran in the family – so they were then stripped of all their wealth and property.'

Isabel nodded sombrely. 'That's terrible.'

It was a heartfelt moment, and Mauricio had placed his hands on her shoulders without her realising. He closed his eyes for a moment, as if in penance. The lightning flashed again then, lighting up everything around them, and a light rain began to fall. The storm was obviously moving closer.

'Uh, we should be heading back,' Isabel said.

'In a minute.' Mauricio opened his eyes, staring meaningfully into hers – then without warning leaned forward and kissed her. She abandoned herself to it, but when she pulled back again, his look was thoughtful, strange. The rain meanwhile became heavier around them.

'Do I look like the sort of person that would push a girl to her death? Is the madness that runs through my family so obvious?'

He gave a light push to illustrate, and she felt a sudden frisson of fear. Did Mauricio see the rivalry over her between himself and Dario as some sort of replay of what had happened with that girl? 'Of course not. But then, I . . . I hardly know you.'

'Yes, I recall you said something like that the other day.'

Mauricio's expression took a more pained turn, and Isabel remembered that her comment had come just before she called Mauricio a smiley bus driver. 'Yes, I'm sorry about that.'

'*Sorry?*' Mauricio glanced around for inspiration, his

face strangely lit by another lightning strike, streaked by the rain, which was coming faster now. 'Such an easy, throwaway expression.' His expression became heavier, graver. 'You shouldn't have met Dario for dinner the other night. It was wrong.'

'I know.' She wanted to avoid another *sorry*, fear gripping her stomach tighter. 'But I didn't know then about the problems between you.'

Mauricio shook his head, eyes closing again for a moment, as if he was struggling to gain strength. Then, as they snapped open again. 'So, I ask you again, Isabel, do you believe these age-old stories about my family's madness? Do I really look like the type that would push a young girl to her death?'

And on that last word, *death*, Isabel felt herself pushed again, far harder this time, and Mauricio's grip slipped from her shoulders so that she was falling backwards. There was nothing to stop her fall. There was only the abyss below.

8

Larry Gilbert, then

He felt hunched up driving such a small car, especially on a long journey. But for the sake of discretion he'd hired a compact Seat Leon in Malaga, rather than driving his larger, flashier Mercedes S-Class. More comfortable for a journey like this, he thought to himself, but it would have drawn too much attention and given too easy a plate-trace if anything went wrong in Alarcon.

He'd hired the Seat using one of his five aliases. He would pay cash in town wherever he could, but had three credit cards in the same name too – Tobias Mercer. One of those generic names that could be Spanish, English, German or French. It would keep them guessing if they started trying to trace him. His real name was Larry Gilbert and he in fact was half Spanish and half English, speaking both fluently, courtesy of his parents: Freddie Gilbert, one of the first wave of East End mobsters to settle in Marbella, and his mother, Anna, a local waitress his father had met four years later.

Now thirty-two, Larry had lost his father five years ago, and had only shown up to the funeral out of respect for Anna. He'd parted ways with his father years back, having witnessed one too many beatings of Anna. Though at least when he reached 6ft at the age of fourteen, his father's beatings of him had stopped.

He'd topped out at 6ft 3 inches and was never sure whether his nickname of *Largo* was due to his size or the mean streak he showed later in life as a drugs enforcer and hitman. One fellow hitman, shortly after Larry had garrotted their target, had said that Larry had a passing resemblance to Humphrey Bogart, with much of the manic intensity Bogart had displayed in *Key Largo* and *Treasure of the Sierra Madre*.

While his size and bulk helped him dispatch victims easily, it had its drawbacks; like now, in a small car with his knees raised high each side of the steering wheel and starting to cramp. But it had been preferable to appearing too obvious. A big man in a big flashy car, he'd have stood out like a sore thumb in a small town.

At least he was almost there now. *Alarcon 5 km*, the sign ahead announced. He started looking out for the turn off the main N111. But when he did finally see the exit for Alarcon looming ahead, there was a bus pulled in not far from it. He sped up, knowing he'd be able to swing past the bus and turn in. But at the last minute the bus indicated, pulling out, and, although he put his foot flat down to make it past, the angle to make the turn was by then acute.

He swung in sharply in front of the bus, the bus braking heavily and beeping its horn. He got a quick flash image of its driver waving one arm in protest. He was about to gesture back and give him the finger, but reminded himself not to draw too much attention. With a tight smile, gaze fixed ahead, he drove along the side road towards Alarcon.

Drawing too much attention. That obviously hadn't been too much of a consideration for his employer. Largo thought back to when he'd been given the details of the hit.

'You've got it clear where she is? Place called Alarcon, halfway to Madrid.'

'Yeah, all clear. But why somewhere so remote?'

'We thought it better it happens there, away from Valencia and the Costas. But no changes on any other front – take care of her your usual way.'

'Usual way' meant a quick bullet to the head. In the backstreets of Barcelona or between the rival drug gangs in Marbella that might not raise too many alarm bells, but a small backwater like Alarcon would be a different matter. They probably hadn't seen a revolver in the town since the Spanish Civil War.

So, he'd decided at the outset it would be best to make it look like an accident. The question then was how, where and when?

He'd been sent a photo of a pretty girl of only twenty-two. She had a Spanish name but was originally from England. She spoke both languages fluently. So not too different to his own background. He'd seen her in town a few times in his first thirty-six hours there and had casually followed her most of the way back to her hotel – but Largo still hadn't worked out the most opportune time. There were some high drops from the castle ramparts bordering the Parador, but she walked straight from the town square to the hotel entrance, and didn't at any point meander beyond that.

He realised that the odds of catching her doing that on the off-chance as she returned to her hotel were remote. The most likely time to find her there would be if she decided to take a short break from her room to get some air, or perhaps to take in the views from the castle ramparts. He decided that the only way to catch her in one of those moments would be to keep watch on her for a while, so he took his car from outside the Miramar, the hotel where he was staying, and pulled into the Parador car park, picking an inconspicuous space towards the back and slumping down slightly in his seat so that he wouldn't be too obvious. He could be someone waiting to pick up a friend from the hotel, or perhaps a local taxi driver who'd been called by a guest.

As the light began to fade, he checked his watch: 7.52 p.m. Already he'd been there almost two hours. What were the chances of her going for a stroll around the castle once it was dark?

He jolted as he saw a familiar face from the day before. The bus driver who'd waved a fist at him when he'd arrived that first day! Dressed smartly, so obviously seeing someone. Largo slumped down deeper in his car seat to avoid being seen.

He straightened up again after the bus driver had gone into the hotel. He decided to wait a little longer, taking out his mobile to play *Assassin's Creed*.

It was a habit he'd developed in the past year to kill time on long stake-outs. It felt somewhat like a busman's holiday – killing people on-screen as a prelude to killing someone for real – but Largo felt it relaxed him.

'You're weird,' his old sidekick had once commented when he'd started playing while they waited for a target. He'd smiled back dryly. 'I just prefer playing this game to your company . . . no need to take it personally.'

He sat up. He'd unconsciously slipped down in his seat as he'd played the game. Over an hour had passed without him realising. It was fully dark now. A few people came in and out of the hotel, but no sign of the bus driver or the girl.

Largo was about to start up and leave when he caught sight of an electrical storm on the horizon. Little chance of her coming out in this now, he thought; but the storm was quite beautiful and he found himself strangely transfixed by it, curious how it might develop: would it drift away or move closer?

And as it did appear to move closer, a stronger flash lighting up the car park and the vista ahead, he saw the two of them come out of the hotel – together, as a couple! The bus driver leading the girl by the hand, as if he was keen on showing her something.

They headed around the far side of the castle, and within twelve yards were out of sight. Another lightning flash followed by a crack of thunder struck only seconds later, and the rain became heavier, almost a deluge. He tapped his fingers on the steering wheel, sure that at any instant they'd reappear and take cover in the hotel entrance.

But when after another minute they still hadn't reappeared, he got out of his car to investigate. What on earth might they be doing on the castle ramparts in this torrential rain?

9

Lapslie and Bradbury, now

'But you're saying that this Luciana, a cleaner at the Parador, saw Isabel later that same evening?' Lapslie pressed urgently.

'Yes, maybe only fifteen or twenty minutes later,' Ruiz said. 'She initially rushed to the house of the town warden, Hernando, to tell him that she'd just seen Mauricio and Isabel on the castle ramparts, and that she thought Mauricio had pushed Isabel over the edge. But Hernando didn't answer.'

'How long did she try Hernando for?'

'She said at least five minutes – until she was sure he wasn't there.' Ruiz grimaced. 'It was raining heavily at the time.'

'What did she do then?'

'She rushed back to the Parador to tell the barman Benito what she thought she'd seen. She said she was frantic to tell *someone*. But Benito simply shrugged and said, "That's not possible. Isabel came back into the hotel a couple of minutes ago." Seeing Luciana was still doubtful, he got reception to buzz her room and Isabel appeared in the foyer a minute later.'

'I see. You mentioned a couple of times that she "thought"? Wasn't Luciana sure of what she saw?'

'It was dark. A lightning storm had come over and it was only in a momentary flash of lightning that she could see them, but she was sure she saw Mauricio push Isabel over the edge. Then it was heavy darkness again. In the next burst of light she could only see Mauricio further ahead walking on his own. She couldn't see any sign of Isabel.' Ruiz held a hand out. 'But don't forget, I was getting all of this in a statement the day after. Maybe with Luciana seeing Isabel for herself soon after, she realised she was mistaken, so used *thought* in her statement to me.'

Lapslie nodded. That seemed likely. He got an image of Luciana rushing and knocking on Hernando's door in the pouring rain, getting no answer, then running breathlessly to tell Benito at the Parador. When Benito told her that he'd just seen Isabel, she must have felt a bit foolish, so had adjusted her story afterwards to suit.

They'd walked from the main town square towards

the castle, then up the surrounding rampart to where Luciana had seen the pair. 'So, this spot here is more or less where Mauricio and Isabel were when they were seen?' Lapslie clarified. A faint nod from Ruiz. 'And where was Luciana when she spotted them? Thirty yards back, forty?'

'More like fifty or sixty. She was over a third of the way towards the town square, she said, having left the Parador just minutes earlier. She said she probably wouldn't have paid them any attention if it wasn't for the rain and thinking how strange it was for people to be out there at that time of night.'

'And she didn't see Isabel on the rampart after Mauricio seemed to push her?'

'No. Only Mauricio on his own.'

'And how long before that next lightning flash before she had a clear view?'

Ruiz shrugged. 'She wasn't totally sure. Fifteen or twenty seconds. Maybe longer.'

Lapslie looked the other way, further up the rampart. Thirty yards ahead it wrapped around the other side of the castle. Lapslie pointed. 'Could be that if she was headed this way, with Mauricio in pursuit, she might have been out of sight behind the castle by then.'

'Could be.' Another shrug. 'Certainly, there would have to be some explanation with her being seen so soon afterwards at the Parador. One thing she is sure of, Isabel wasn't heading back down the rampart towards her. She'd have seen her clearly if that was the case.'

Lapslie looked both ways, gauging distance and visibility. 'Yes, I daresay she would have.'

Emma Bradbury offered, 'Unless she went back into the hotel in that time gap.'

Lapslie nodded. The hotel entrance was about forty yards away, so the lightning gap would have to have been longer for that to be a viable theory. Thirty seconds at least, unless she was walking briskly. 'I suppose we'll know soon enough from questioning the Parador staff as to when exactly Isabel returned to the hotel that night.'

'Yes,' Bradbury agreed. 'But would they recall the exact time? The difference between her returning straight away or ambling on her own around the castle ramparts before returning would be only a few minutes.'

'True.' Lapslie was lost in thought again for a moment.

'Luciana was very precise with her timing and description.' Ruiz glanced briefly at Antonio, who had been the main one to interview Luciana. 'Not only about that, but about what else she saw that night. A man watching them not far from the Parador car park.'

'Oh, I see. Another man. Young, old, middle-aged?'

'Middle-aged. Light-brown hair, very tall. She wasn't sure at first that the man was watching them, because when he got out of his car she thought he was heading towards the hotel entrance. But then he passed it and went to one side, looking intently towards Mauricio and Isabel. And when she caught sight of Mauricio heading back down again, this man turned quickly and went back towards his car.'

'And had Luciana seen this man before?'

'Only once. Two days beforehand. He wasn't a local.'

The wind had lifted, catching them on the exposed high rampart. A pleasant interlude to the oppressive heat, Lapslie thought. Luciana's description seemed precise enough that she probably wasn't mistaken; and in fact, '*any new faces in town*' had been his next intended line of questioning.

Terry Haines had described the man trying to intrude at his Marbella villa as large. This 'very tall' man meant a bit more investigative meat on the bone.

As much as a lovers' quarrel with Mauricio over Dario might make it more of a simple open-and-shut case, it wasn't why Lapslie was here. The main reason Rouse had given his approval to pursue the investigation was the possible link to Vic Denham. So Lapslie had been concerned about making that first call to Rouse with just a lovers' tiff theory in hand. Rouse would have rightly said, *'It's just a local Spanish police matter now. I expect to see you and Bradbury on the first flight back here.'*

'Well suppose for a moment that this stranger is irrelevant, could be it was just a dry run for Mauricio,' Lapslie remarked. 'A prelude to the real thing happening a couple of nights later.'

Ruiz gestured. 'Is that likely?'

'More likely than you might think. Both victims and murderers often find themselves in a repetitive cycle of actions. All he needs is a good excuse to get her back here, perhaps even to explain some problem from that first night. And it's an ideal lover's leap, there can't be too many of those around here.'

'Oh, I don't know,' Ruiz said, indicating the surrounding hills and rock faces.

'Yes. But how many with the river running directly below? And a night with heavy rain would ensure that a body was washed out to sea quicker. Might be why we haven't found a body so far.'

'Except that we now know it didn't happen that night when there was a heavy storm,' Ruiz said. 'Isabel was seen later that same night, and for a couple of days after.'

But suddenly Lapslie was hardly paying attention, his eyes having fixed on some rocks jutting out fifteen feet directly below – the first point a body might hit before tumbling into the ravine and the river below. The rocks appeared to have a pink tinge.

'Am I eyeballing this right?' He beckoned Bradbury over, and she confirmed that the cluster of rocks he pointed to were the first likely spot that a body might land. Then he looked at Ruiz. 'And can you confirm what the weather was like in Alarcon the night that Isabel was last seen? Particularly any heavy rain.'

'I don't know. But I can check.' Ruiz went into his mobile's weather app. 'Dry for most of the night, but rain hitting at just before 3 a.m. the next morning. Quite heavy for three hours. Some local flooding.'

Lapslie nodded thoughtfully. A body leaving heavy bloodstains on those rocks for a few hours before being washed away might leave that pink hue. He tried to discern any further pink on the rocky outcrop eighty feet below that, the next point a body would hit before finally tumbling into the river. But it was too far down to see clearly. Lapslie took out his mobile. One last call to make.

It answered after only three rings. 'Jim Thompson.'

'Jim. Mark Lapslie. Got a job for you in Spain. Just tell Rouse it's linked to the Vic Denham case – you'll get approval in a jiffy.' Lapslie was struck with an after-thought. 'Oh, and Jim. Didn't you once tell me that one way you relaxed outside of the forensic lab was rock climbing in the Lake District?'

'Yes, I did. Why?'

'Nothing. Just that I think you're going to love this one.'

10

Isabel, then

It had probably been no more than a second that Mauricio let her fall – but it had felt like a lifetime – before his hands reached out and clasped her back, his legs braced for leverage to hold her falling weight. He was strong and pulled her back in easily.

Her breath was still gone in shock, and as she caught it back, she hissed, 'Are you mad?'

'No,' he said flatly, nonchalantly. 'If I had been – like Dario and half the town have been claiming about my family all these years – I'd have let you go.'

There was now the hint of a smile, and she wasn't sure if he was being serious. Whether he was teasing or attempting to reassure. But she was in no mood for it. She pushed hard against him, broke away.

'Well, I don't care what half the town think,' she said from a few paces away, still catching her breath.

'*I* think you're mad. You frightened the *shit* out of me.'

'I'm sorry,' he said, starting after her. But she just hastened her pace, increasing the distance between them. 'I was trying to make a point.'

'Ah, *sorry*,' she said, mimicking him from earlier. 'Such an easy, throwaway expression.'

'So let me throw it a few more times. Sorry, sorry . . . *sorry*.' Marked pause. 'Do you forgive me?'

'No. Maybe in a year's time. Give me a call.'

Eight paces behind, she heard Mauricio chuckle, but it died quickly when he realised from her flat tone that she was deadly serious.

With her rapid pace and the heavy rain, she was almost as breathless now as when she first thought she was falling into the abyss.

Mauricio put on an extra spurt, catching up with her around the back of the castle. He put his hands on her shoulders again, but this time she was braced against the castle wall, no sheer drop behind. She thought he might try and kiss her again, but he just stared at her intently.

'Again, I'm really sorry. I'd never harm you, you've got to believe that.' He shook his head, desperate for understanding. 'But don't you see – that was the whole point of that little show I put on. Dario *would*. He'd smile at you one moment, pour on the charm – then push you over the edge the next. And not lose any sleep over it that night, or any other.'

'I know you've got your problems with Dario.' Isabel stared at him incredulously. 'But now you're being ridiculous.'

'Am I?' Mauricio raised a brow sharply. 'You think that what he did to my mother, pulling that trick so that she'd worked her life for nothing, his ancestors condemning my family to two hundred years of penury under a false cloak of madness – you think any of that was any better?'

She nodded numbly. He had a point, but she didn't want to agree and in any way excuse his actions. 'I don't know ... I don't know. It's terrible, but stealing isn't the same as murder, Mauricio. And right now, I don't feel like speaking to you about *anything*. I need to get my thoughts clear.'

She pulled away from him sharply and rested her back against the castle wall a few yards away, getting her breath back as she looked out at the majestic landscape of stark hills and ravines ahead, illuminated in another lightning flash.

Isabel didn't feel like just rolling over and forgiving him right now, it seemed too quick. *Maybe let him stew for a day or two.* She could understand his outrage and anger at what Dario had done to his family, the ongoing feud between them – but did she really want to get caught in the middle of that? Though a part of that conflict also intrigued her, spilt over onto her own quest to uncover her family's links to Alarcon.

She could feel Mauricio's eyes on her, he seemed to realise that he might have overstepped the mark and was trying to judge the best time to speak again; or perhaps he was wondering what to say next.

After a long moment, he edged closer. 'This story he's given you about this Eduardo Alarcon-Fabricante in Madrid? Do you believe it?'

'I . . . I'm not sure. I didn't really question it at the time.' Isabel's brow creased. 'But why would he do that?'

'Why would he rob my mother? He already has great wealth, why rob an old lady for a small fraction more?' He shrugged. 'Your father spent all that time convinced your name was linked to nobility here. Yet within twenty-four hours Dario comes up with a name and an explanation to discard it. Just strikes me as a little too convenient.'

Isabel let the thought settle, her laboured breathing also now calming down. 'But how would we find out if he's telling the truth or not?'

Mauricio cast his eyes down for a second, thinking. 'Perhaps probe him a bit more on the papers he's shown you. Ask for the originals and their place in archived registrations. Possibly even make a couple of calls to the archive halls in Madrid about Eduardo Alarcon-Fabricante.'

Isabel nodded slowly. 'But what if we still suspect he's lying, but find nothing conclusive in Madrid or the paperwork he shows us?'

'Then it might be time to visit Dario's archived files late at night when he's not there.'

Isabel felt immediately uncomfortable with the suggestion. Mauricio had just gone to dramatic lengths to convince her that Dario Alarcon was evil and ruthless, would rob an old lady, his mother, of her last pennies, would *smile in her own face one minute, then push her into an abyss the next*. And now he was suggesting rifling through Dario Alarcon's private files in the dead of night. She shook her head. 'No . . . *no*. However much I might be keen to prove my family's past links to this town, that's not a good idea!'

'Don't worry. It will be okay.' Mauricio shook her shoulders lightly, but it was a bracing, reassuring action rather than one to shake her from her apprehension. 'And I'll be doing it as much for myself. It's something I should have done long ago: I need to see if there was any paperwork from Luis Alarcon about my mother's house.'

11

Lapslie and Bradbury, now

An experienced local rock climber led the way, while another held the rope at the top of the rock face, having also secured a section of it through a gap in the stone wall bordering the castle rampart. The climber leading the way went all the way down to the lower rock outcrop, ten feet short of the river.

Then Jim Thompson and three forensic assistants started their way down. As the best, or rather *only*, forensic expert with climbing experience, Thompson was first down. Rouse had only approved one of his SOCO team from Chelmsford to accompany him, so Lapslie had organised the remaining two through Ruiz in Madrid. 'Two of your best forensic men, but they should also have good English.'

Jim Thompson stopped at the first rock outcrop fifteen feet down, where Lapslie had seen pink tinges the day before. He stood to one side to allow two others to make their way down without treading directly on the pink-tinged area, then he directed the last man, one of Ruiz's Madrid team, to make their way to the lower rock outcrop. 'Give me your first thoughts on what you might find down there.'

Before Thompson had got on his flight out, Emma Bradbury had done some research on local rock formations, in case the pink tinge was ingrained in the rock and a natural phenomenon for the area. It wasn't. The nearest such rocks were over forty miles away. Nothing like that was to be found among the rock structures around Alarcon.

Lapslie's only remaining concern was that, if indeed it was the remnants of blood stains, whether the rain and sun since had washed away and degraded them too much to leave any worthwhile samples. Lapslie observed Thompson scraping at two areas of rock and putting the scrapings in two separate plastic bags – one for each area of rock – before Thompson looked back up towards him.

'Should be interesting. Some of the flakes coming off are still quite soft, and there's no pink discoloration underneath.' Thompson studied the area more intently. 'Well, only minimal.'

'I wonder if we might find the same on the lower rock area.' Lapslie's gaze drifted past Thompson. He could see that Ruiz's forensic man had reached the lower area and was leaning over, inspecting. Then as he straightened up again, he appeared to lose his balance for a second, pulling at the rope to get it back.

Thompson appeared in his element hanging off a rock face while doing forensics, but the others looked uneasy, out of their comfort zone. He'd made sure with Ruiz that the men recommended didn't have a fear of heights; but that was still a long chalk from being entirely comfortable with them.

'How are you getting on down there?' Thompson said into his hands-free mouthpiece. They'd set up a six-way hands-free transmission. Lapslie could hear Thompson quite clearly from only fifteen feet down, but the eighty-foot drop to the lower rock outcrop was another matter.

'Think there are some pink marks here too, but I need to look again,' the forensic man lower down remarked. They watched from higher up as, his balance fully back, he leaned in closer to survey the area. After a moment: 'Yes, there are two or three patches here too.'

'Okay,' Thompson responded. 'If you can scrape and bag some surface samples up, as I'm doing, that would be great. Also, if patches are more than a foot apart, use separate bags for those.'

'Okay.'

After a few moments more of bagging rock scrapings and dust, Thompson leaned in closer, examining a couple of the crevices between the rocks. He then tweezered some particles into a separate bag, announcing, 'You might want to also bag some of the loose debris in the rock crevices. That might have absorbed more of any blood spilled, plus being slightly in the shade would hopefully be less degraded.'

'Will do,' the man below said into his mouthpiece, while Thompson's UK assistant close by simply started following his example with the two crevices on his side of the rock.

The second Spanish forensic man looked slightly lost for what to do for a moment. No room at the top for him to assist, and by the time he got to the bottom, his colleague would have likely finished taking samples.

Jim Thompson picked up on it, holding five plastic bags out towards him. 'Can you number these one, two, three and subsequently starting with the nearest to my thumb.' Thompson looked round briefly to get the position of the sun. 'So, we're running the sequence west to east, with those from my colleague running on from that.' Thompson followed his glance towards the lower rocks. 'Then those from your colleague, mark L-one, two, three, etc.'

A perfunctory nod after a moment; hopefully nothing vital lost in translation.

As Thompson went back to tweezering particles from a rock crevice into a fresh bag, Lapslie asked, 'How long before we might get some results?'

'If it is blood, maybe only a few hours, along with blood type. But DNA, if it hasn't completely degraded, will take longer.'

'Running through the timeline again,' Emma Bradbury said, glancing briefly at the notes she'd made on her laptop, 'Isabel was last seen here at the hotel at about nine-fifteen, nine-twenty on the eighteenth. And this viewing of her being apparently pushed from the castle ramparts was two nights beforehand?'

'Yes.' Lapslie nodded, then added, 'Luciana saw Isabel not long after that same night. So, she realised that she must have been mistaken.'

Bradbury nodded thoughtfully. 'And no possibility of Luciana confusing Isabel with a lookalike after she spoke to Benito the night of the storm, because Isabel was seen by others both in town the next day, as well as here at the hotel that night. Staff here have confirmed that it was her having dinner with Mauricio earlier that night, and they were seen going out together.'

'And the timing of that and Luciana's sighting tied in together?' Lapslie asked.

Bradbury briefly scrolled back in her notes. 'Yes, they did. Luciana clocked out of her work shift here just minutes before Isabel and Mauricio went out of the hotel together.'

They were sat at a table in the corner of the Parador bar. Rough stone walls gave it a cosy, rustic atmosphere, while a double-height vaulted ceiling with dark-wood beams accentuated the past medieval splendour of the castle, which was now tastefully converted into a four-star hotel. From leafing through a booklet by the bar, Lapslie noted that there were a hundred and four Parador Hotels throughout Spain, mostly converted old castles, manor houses and monasteries.

The vaulted ceiling continued through to the adjacent restaurant, visible through an archway to their side. Lapslie ran a visual line from there, through the bar towards the hotel entrance, picturing for a moment

Isabel and Mauricio finishing their dinner and heading out. He wondered what might have led to Mauricio pushing Isabel over the edge? Had they been arguing about something?

The restaurant staff they'd spoken to said *no*, everything seemed fine between them. And their amiable barman, Benito – who had very kindly acted as a translator with any Parador staff whose English wasn't as good as his – had confirmed that they appeared very cosy and friendly the next night when they spent about twenty minutes together at the bar before heading off.

'And I overheard them arranging to meet up again the next night – this time at the Café Marie in the main square.'

Lapslie picked up on that. 'What time did they arrange to meet?'

Benito shrugged. 'I didn't hear the exact time. But I got the impression it was going to be fairly late, because Mauricio said his work shift didn't finish until eight, and he had to shower and change. Isabel said that was okay, she'd eat first and then they'd meet up.'

'Did she dine in the restaurant?'

'No. I think she just grabbed a snack earlier in town, had it in her room before heading off. Passed me right here at the bar and waved to me.' Benito cast his eyes down. 'But she never got to meet Mauricio.'

Lapslie had nodded. That had been the account Mauricio had given to Inspector Ruiz when first questioned; he'd waited at Café Marie for a while, but she hadn't shown up. As Lapslie caught Benito's eye now, Benito smiled over towards them as he dried some wine glasses. That was something Lapslie had noticed with local enquiries; there were obviously allegiances running through the town, perhaps to be expected in such a tight-knit community. But it had never occurred to Benito that Mauricio might be lying about Isabel not meeting up with him that night; whereas to himself, Emma Bradbury and indeed Inspector Ruiz, Mauricio was a prime suspect. Because if he had met up with her, he'd have been the last person to see her.

Ruiz had at least checked the first part of Mauricio's account: Ignacio at Café Marie confirmed that he hadn't seen Isabel turn up there that night. But he also added that Mauricio didn't appear to wait long. 'No more than about six minutes before he headed off in the direction of the Parador.' And Benito had also confirmed that Isabel appeared to be in a bit of a hurry, checking her watch as she hastened past him.

Could it be that she was running eight to ten minutes late, so Mauricio had decided to head to the hotel, knowing she'd be coming that way? Lapslie considered. Or had he purposely wanted to meet up with her where nobody would see them, arriving early at Café Marie to engineer that?

Lapslie snapped back to the present moment to find Bradbury looking at him. 'Sorry, Bradbury, lost in my own thoughts. Certainly, Mauricio will be one of the first on our list to question.'

'After we have these test results from Jim Thompson.'

'Yes.' Lapslie checked his watch. 'Hopefully not too long now.'

Lapslie had remarked earlier that there was little point in pursuing any further questioning until those results were in, because whether or not it was blood, or what type it might be, could determine the entire nature of the investigation; whether it was only a missing person enquiry or a full-blown murder investigation. Along with also giving them an 'incident site' to inform their questioning.

So they'd decided to decamp to the Parador while they waited on Thompson's results. Lapslie had gone for a shower and clothes change, his second of the day, after watching Thompson and the other forensics on the rock face for over an hour in the intense heat. Then they'd had a light lunch in the hotel bar before talking to Benito and some hotel staff, and going back over some notes.

Ruiz's forensic men had brought a mobile lab unit. 'Sufficient for purposes to identify blood type,' Thompson had confirmed. 'Any possible DNA will have to wait until I'm back in London though.'

But when the call finally came through from Jim Thompson forty minutes later, it wasn't what they expected.

'Is it blood?' Lapslie pressed.

'Yes, it is.' Thompson sighed. 'But we've ended up with more than we anticipated.'

Lapslie's mind started racing. '*What*? You've got DNA as well?'

'No. That will still take a few days, if it's not too degraded.' A more measured intake of breath from Thompson. 'From the sample taken earlier, we've found *two* different blood types on the rock face.'

12

Isabel, then

'Mind your head on this next bit,' Mauricio said. 'It dips down a bit lower.'

'Okay,' Isabel responded, following a pace behind Mauricio in the narrow tunnel. The roof height had already dropped to under five feet, now they were down to just over four feet, bent half-over as they made their way through.

They'd made a few calls that morning to check files in Madrid on Eduardo Alarcon-Fabricante, but had found nothing conclusive to prove the link to Alarcon. They needed also to check from the Alarcon end.

After a moment in the narrow passage, Isabel could hear some muffled sounds above. 'What's that?'

'Some houses above. Probably the Romeros, or maybe the Delgados.'

Isabel was suddenly anxious; or more accurately,

suddenly *more* anxious than she already had been moving through the damp, dark tunnel – the only light from a small penlight Mauricio was holding. 'But what if they come down here to investigate?'

'They won't. They don't have any access to the tunnel from their houses, and probably don't even know it runs underneath.' Mauricio smiled tightly, 'As long as we don't make any noise to alert them.'

'Thanks. You're very reassuring.'

'Anyway, we won't be down here long. This is just a dummy run now.' Mauricio creased his brow. 'Is that the right expression in English – dummy run?'

'Yes, it is.' And quite appropriate, Isabel thought; because that's how she felt now, a *dummy* for ever agreeing to Mauricio's crazy idea. 'And remind me – why do we have to do this now, rather than just go straight in tonight?'

'Because I haven't used this tunnel for almost two years, and don't know if there might be obstructions now: someone could have found out about it and blocked it off, or a section of the roof could have caved in.'

'I see.' Isabel nodded numbly, a chill running through her at the thought of them being trapped down here.

Mauricio shrugged. 'Also, if I get held up and caught

while in Dario's office, you'll need to know the way back through the tunnels on your own.'

Isabel grimaced tautly. Mauricio had already explained that it wasn't just one passage going directly from his house to beneath Dario Alarcon's office. It was a labyrinth of passages spreading out under the castle and parts of the town, with many turn-offs and branches; and she'd have to recall the right ones to find her way back safely.

Constructed in medieval times, the tunnels were believed to have originally been for those seeking escape from the castle in the early Christian–Moors battles. Later, they had been used for smuggling contraband.

'Then during the Spanish Civil War, they were used again by those seeking refuge or escape.'

Isabel had raised a brow. 'But then surely Dario Alarcon would know about them?'

'Not necessarily. Don't forget, the communists, the working people, lost that war – so they'd have been the main people hiding away. If the landowning fascists and *capitalistas* in town knew exactly where the tunnels were, they'd have been useless as hiding places. The landowners might have known of one or two passages under the castle, but many others had been blocked off. The one leading to Dario's office actually stops two houses short.'

'So how will you get in?'

'I'll use the back alley for that last short stretch. The most important thing is that I'm not seen on the main street approaching his office.'

Isabel ducked down another couple of inches as the tunnel roof lowered yet again.

Her mobile buzzed in her pocket. She took it out, suddenly alarmed as she saw who was calling. 'Oh, my God. It's *Dario*.' She stared at the phone in her hand. 'Do you think he could know we're here, that we're up to something?'

'No, not possible.' Mauricio shook his head resolutely. 'I've told nobody of our plans.' After a second: 'Cut the call coming through. Text him that you can't talk now. Can he text you back with what it is?'

She nodded and spent a moment texting, the light from the screen giving her face a ghostly look in the dark tunnel. There was a brief anxious wait for a response, the two of them almost immobile, holding their breath despite Mauricio's reassurances a moment before. Finally:

I've got some more information about your family history. Can I see you again tonight?

Mauricio pulled a face as she turned the screen towards him. 'Maybe he does suspect something. But I don't see how.'

She texted back: *I can't tonight. Maybe tomorrow night?*

After a moment: *Tomorrow night I was planning to stay late at the office to catch up on paperwork. I'd rather not have to switch and work late tonight.*

She grimaced as she showed Mauricio the message. 'Either he does suspect something or he's impatient to see me.'

'Looks that way.' Mauricio nodded solemnly. But then a sudden brainwave lifted his expression. 'Look – meet up with him tonight! That way for sure we'll know he's not in his office. You'll also be able to keep him busy over a long dinner, so that I know he's not about to walk in at any minute and catch me by surprise.'

Mauricio's suggestion made sense, she conceded. 'But are you sure you're going to be okay on your own? And you don't mind me seeing Dario again for dinner?'

'I'll be okay on my own.' Mauricio smiled softly and stroked her cheek. 'And while you might be with him in person, I know that in spirit you'll be with me.'

*

'Are you sure Mauricio doesn't mind you having dinner with me again?'

'No. He doesn't *own* me, as the song goes.' Isabel saw Dario's brow knit for a second; apparently something else that hadn't travelled to Spain. She'd been in her first year at uni when the cover of the song had come out.

'Just that it seemed to cause a bit of a problem last time.'

Isabel shrugged. 'Mauricio was fine when I explained to him that it was to do with my search for my long-lost relatives and their link to Alarcon. He knows that's important to me.' She took the first sip of her wine. 'And he knows too that's the reason for our meeting again tonight.'

Dario nodded, but after a slight delay. He was looking at her intently, as if he didn't fully buy it; perhaps he thought that Mauricio's view of their relationship might not correlate with her own. He raised his own wine glass, a wry smile spreading across his face 'Just that you have been seen around in town quite a bit together.' He glanced briefly to one side, as if searching for the right term. 'A bit of an "item" as they say.'

Isabel smiled tightly. She realised that she might have to say more to put Dario off the scent. She had in fact become quite close to Mauricio over these past days and while far from lovers, they had certainly become more than just casual friends.

'Mauricio's great, and he's been a good guide to me these past few days in Alarcon.' Her smile turned down, became more deprecating. 'But let's not forget, he is just a bus driver. My father was a successful wine merchant. If he was still alive, he'd have a fit at the thought of me becoming serious about someone like Mauricio.'

As she watched Dario's smile grow in response, she knew it had been the right thing to say. *Play the class card.* As if someone like Mauricio wouldn't be someone her father would approve of, but he might be. In Dario's eyes, it put her immediately more on his side. But her experience with Terry had taught her not to judge people by background but rather on their substance. She silently apologised to Mauricio for the comment.– especially with him no doubt some way along the dark tunnel towards Dario Alarcon's office at that moment in his bid to help her.

'So, you're having the partridge in pickle this time?' Dario confirmed.

'Yes. I haven't had it since the first night here and, as you said, it is very good.'

Dario placed their orders with the waitress – he was having trout tonight – then as she retreated, reached into the small attaché case at his side and took out some papers. 'That extra information I mentioned earlier of Eduardo Alarcon. Quite interesting . . .' He passed across four sheets of paper.

She perused them slowly, keenly aware that each minute passed was another minute that Mauricio would be closer to having finished searching through Dario's files. Would he be in the office by now? Would he be just starting his search or almost done? 'I . . . I'm not sure what I'm meant to be looking for here.'

Dario leaned across, pointing. 'If you see here, Magdalena Alarcon, three years younger than Eduardo, left Alarcon five years later and went to Madrid. So the information I gave you before was wrong. Eduardo wasn't the last known ancestor of Fernando Alarcon to leave here and go to Madrid. His younger sister Magdalena was.'

'I see.' Isabel studied the documents again. Mauricio had told her earlier that he thought the most vital documents might have been scanned and put on Dario's computer. *The days of dusty old files stored in endless filing cabinets are long gone, even in a town like Alarcon.* Finding the relevant entries might be a problem, not to mention guessing Dario's password, but then Mauricio had managed to recruit one of Dario's past secretaries, Christina Escajeda, who had agreed to help him. She'd been unceremoniously fired eighteen months ago by Dario after sixteen years' faithful service in the notary office, so held a grudge. She knew the old passwords and the likely combinations Dario would use. 'So what might have made her leave then? Obviously, it wasn't work or trade, like Eduardo.'

Dario leafed through to the third page, tapping it. 'If you look here, you'll see that in that same house in Alarcon there's a Katerina Alarcon, who died that same year.' Dario leafed through the sheets, flicking to the fourth page. 'Her death certificate here.'

Isabel nodded thoughtfully. 'So she stayed on those extra years to take care of her mother.'

'Yes, it would appear so. She . . .' Dario broke off as their meals arrived and the waiter placed them down, then with a small bow, *buen provecho*, headed away. 'Magdalena probably stayed on that extra time because her mother was ill or frail, and she didn't want to leave her on her own.'

Isabel nodded again, took her first few mouthfuls of food. 'She looked back at the papers after a moment.

'I see here that Magdalena was twenty-eight when she left for Madrid.'

'Yes. Quite old at the time to be left unmarried. So perhaps there was the fear too of her being left a *solterona*.'

'A spinster,' Isabel translated.

'Yes, exactly.' Dario chewed at another mouthful of food, dabbed at his mouth with his napkin. 'Maybe her brother convinced Magdalena that there would be a wider selection of suitable single men in Madrid.'

'Eligible bachelors,' Isabel said, observing Dario's brow knit.

'What was that?'

'It doesn't matter.' But then she thought: the explanation would at least eat up more time. *The longer Dario spent over dinner with her, the better.* 'Eligible is another word for single. More to the point: single with a bit of money and good prospects.'

Dario smiled slyly. 'So, not a bus driver, for instance.'

Isabel felt uneasy as she smiled and nodded, as if she was further betraying Mauricio by even pretending to agree. But at least it meant that Dario had taken the earlier bait about her lack of interest in Mauricio: *he wasn't eligible.*

'Yes. Certainly not a bus driver,' Isabel said, playing it

up. 'Though doctors and lawyers would fit the bill. Or notaries.' As she saw Dario's sly smile shift to something more self-satisfying, she felt a twinge of discomfort. Hopefully she hadn't played it up too much, she didn't want him thinking that she was making a play for him.

They ate in silence for a second, Isabel feeling her face flush. She wasn't sure if it was because she felt she'd overplayed her hand in flirting with Dario, or because Mauricio was at that moment delving through Dario's private files while she misled him.

'Is it good?' Dario asked, indicating her plate with his fork. They were both two-thirds of the way through their meals.

'Yes, it is.' Isabel shrugged, 'Well, certainly as good as last time.'

Dario smiled complacently, then reached for his pocket. 'Excuse me.' His mobile was buzzing. As he took it out and looked at its screen, his face dropped. He scrunched his napkin at the side of his plate and half stood up. 'I'm sorry, something's come up. Bit of an emergency. I have to leave.'

'Why? What is it?'

'It appears someone has broken into my office.'

'Surely not?' She feigned incredulity, her heart

pounding hard. *Play for time*. 'But you haven't even finished your meal yet.'

'I know.' A tight, apologetic smile. 'But I've got to see to this. I'll make it up to you later.'

Isabel shook her head. 'Could you at least settle the bill? I'll look a bit of a lemon left here to pay it.'

'Of course.' Dario's face reddened at his apparent lack of grace. He snapped his fingers sharply at the waiter. '*La cuenta*,' as he took out his wallet.

'And while you're doing that, I'll just powder my nose.' As she caught Dario's quizzical look, she clarified, 'The washroom, *lavabo*.'

She was halfway to the toilet when she saw the waiter passing with the bill on a silver tray, her heart pounding harder with each step. As soon as she was inside, she took out her mobile and called Mauricio: *He knows there's been a break-in. He's on his way!* Twenty seconds later she got a response from Mauricio: *I need two more minutes. Hold him up!*

But as she came out of the washroom, Dario was already halfway out of the restaurant, the bill paid. 'I'll call you later,' he waved back, rushing out.

13

Lapslie and Bradbury, now

'This interview today will be conducted by Inspector Mark Lapslie, who has travelled from London with his colleague, Detective Bradbury, to make further enquiries about the disappearance of Isabel Alarcon.' Gabriel Ruiz waited for a brief nod from Mauricio Reynes, who was sitting at the other side of the oblong pine table. 'And the language used today will be English, as the only language common to all parties. Is that clear? Do you understand what is being said so far?'

Mauricio's brow knitted. 'Of course I do. Most of my conversations with Isabel were in English, even though her Spanish was fluent.'

'Well, I have to be sure. If there's anything you're not clear on as we proceed, ask me.' Ruiz smiled tightly and held his hand out to Mark Lapslie.

'Thank you,' Lapslie said, noting from Mauricio's

quizzical look that he thought that was unlikely; obviously, he considered his own English superior to Ruiz's.

Usually a stickler for detail, Lapslie hadn't bothered to correct Ruiz about them having travelled from Chelmsford rather than London. He didn't wish to delay things more than necessary. As it was, it had taken half the day to arrange the interview. Alarcon didn't have a proper police station, so they'd arranged the interview at the Guardia Civil station at San Clemente, a half-hour drive south. The alternatives were Cuenca, over twice that distance, or Valencia almost two hours away. But San Clemente, with a Guardia Civil complement of five, had a small interview room sufficient for their purpose. The only other delay then was getting an English-speaking *abogado*, lawyer. The only ones in Alarcon were Dario or his uncle, unsuitable given the circumstances. Mauricio had initially waved off the need for having one present, but Lapslie insisted on observing correct procedure. An hour later a mousey, bespectacled fifty-something named Enrique Navarre had been found and now sat alongside Mauricio. From the curious looks fired by Navarre in those opening minutes, Lapslie wondered just how good his English was.

Lapslie looked directly at Mauricio. 'I'll be continuing on from the interview you had with Inspector Ruiz the other day. Mostly filling in details, plus perhaps some fresh questions. My colleague, Emma Bradbury, will be recording the interview and also taking some notes.' Lapslie nodded towards Emma with her laptop open at his side. 'Do you understand?'

'Yes, I understand.'

Lapslie spent the first minutes clarifying how Mauricio first met Isabel, their early meetings and his acting as a sort of tour guide for her. 'And during that period, you became quite friendly?'

'Yes, we did.'

'But not friendly *all* of the time, it appears.' Lapslie came sharply to the night Mauricio was on the ramparts with Isabel. 'On the night of the storm, you were seen pushing Isabel Alarcon from the castle ramparts.'

Mauricio's eyes darted for a second, as if he was getting the question clear. He held out one hand. 'But that obviously wasn't the case, because she was seen later at the Parador and in town the next day. In fact, I saw her there myself.'

'Yes, you did. And the person who gave us this information accepts that too. But we wondered why it might have appeared that you had pushed Isabel from the rampart?'

'I don't know.' Mauricio shrugged. 'Maybe as I hugged her, she leaned back away from me.'

'So, you could say she was resisting your advances,' Lapslie pressed. 'There was some conflict between you.'

A gentle smile broke Mauricio's frown after a second. 'I don't think so. Because only a minute later, as I gave her another hug at the back of the castle, she gave me a kiss.'

'I see. So, a somewhat up and down relationship.'

'No, it wasn't like that.' Mauricio shook his head, his frown deepening.

'Wasn't it?' Lapslie raised a brow, staring the message home. 'So why was it that only two nights before, you were seen storming from the Parador restaurant when you saw Isabel having dinner with Dario Alarcon?'

'She said that she wasn't going to see him, and then . . .' Mauricio stopped himself suddenly, realising how he was coming across. He held a palm out. 'Look. We had a few small ups and downs, but they were nothing. Her main problem was with Dario Alarcon. And I was helping her with that.'

'In what way? What was the problem?' Lapslie noted Mauricio look briefly aside, as if carefully measuring his next comment; or perhaps concerned he'd already said too much.

'She was trying to trace some of her ancestors here in Alarcon. And I thought Dario might be misleading her – because he'd done the same with my mother, when there was a dispute over our family's house.'

Lapslie asked what happened with his mother, then in turn Isabel. He paused afterwards, thoughtful. 'Quite a difference between the two. With your mother it was quite a serious grievance, whereas with Isabel it appears mainly supposition based on your history with Dario.'

'You don't know Dario,' Mauricio protested, a bitter edge to his voice. 'If he could rob my mother, and others in Alarcon – you think he'd simply tell Isabel the truth about her family links?'

'Why not?' Lapslie shrugged. 'What would he have to gain by lying to her? The situation with your mother was very different.'

'Maybe not so different. Because it appears with Isabel that . . .' Mauricio's voice trailed off, as if suddenly realising that again he was heading into uncharted territory or saying too much. He shook his head. 'But you're probably right. It was all just supposition. Wishful thinking.'

'Wishful about what?' Lapslie pressed, sensing Mauricio was on the edge of saying something important.

Those eyes darting again, then a light dismissive laugh.

'Ridiculous, really. But Isabel's father was convinced their family was linked to the main ruling families here, the nobility.'

'I see.' Lapslie was pensive for a second. 'And as "ridiculous" as that claim might have seemed – you think Dario took it seriously.'

'Yes. Don't you see?' Mauricio leaned forward, his eyes full of intent. 'Because if it was a serious claim, it could change much of the landholdings in Alarcon.'

'But you don't think it's a serious claim?'

'I'm not sure.'

Lapslie nodded thoughtfully. 'Don't you think it's a more realistic scenario that you've now invented this supposed conflict between Dario Alarcon and Isabel, when in fact the real conflict is between you and Dario – as you've admitted, going some way back. And you've now put Isabel in the middle of that conflict. Then when it all went wrong between you and Isabel, you invented this story to put the blame on Dario – your old adversary, and so the ideal scapegoat.'

Mauricio started shaking his head halfway through, and now closed his eyes for a second, as if summoning strength. 'No . . . no. You've got it all wrong. It was Dario who had the problem with Isabel, not me.'

Lapslie rolled on. 'And I think what happened is that you met Isabel again that last night, and you went with her to the edge of the rampart. And this time, unlike the dress-rehearsal of two nights previous, you pushed her for real.'

Mauricio's head-shaking became more vehement. 'No . . . *no*. I didn't do that!' His voice spluttered. 'I went to meet her, but she didn't show up.'

'But you didn't wait long at Café Marie, did you?' Lapslie said sharply. 'Then you headed off in the direction of the Parador. We checked with hotel staff – Isabel left the Parador only a minute before you left Café Marie. You'd have bumped into her on the way.'

'No, no . . . I didn't see her. You should be talking to Dario about her disappearance, not me.'

'Oh, we will. When he's back from Madrid tomorrow. But why on earth would he choose exactly the spot where you and Isabel were two nights beforehand to kill her? And why choose to push her, as you were seen doing forty-eight hours before? Quite the coincidence.'

Mauricio rubbed at his forehead, his voice a mumble: 'You'll have to ask him when you see him.'

'Curious that you've not at any time asked why we're sure Isabel was thrown over the edge at that very same location.' Lapslie looked at Mauricio intently for his reaction as he delivered the news: 'We found traces of blood on the rocks directly below, and it matches Isabel's blood type.' Lapslie didn't want to give away that two blood types had been found, and they still had a few days to wait for any possible DNA match.

Mauricio cradled his head in his hands. 'Oh, my God. *Dios mio.*'

Feigned shock, because he already knew, or dire concern now he feared Isabel had been harmed? Lapslie wondered. The taste that had reached him for much of the interview had been lime with a smoky edge, as if Mauricio was being evasive rather than directly lying. *What big secret was Mauricio hiding? Or series of secrets.*

Mauricio looked up slowly. 'Like I said. You have to look to Dario for what has happened to Isabel, rather than me. I would never have harmed Isabel.'

'And as *I* in turn said, we will.' Lapslie took a fresh breath; a tone of finality. 'But the problem there is that Dario left for Madrid at 5 p.m. that evening, four hours before Isabel disappeared. So, he couldn't have pushed her over the edge.'

14

Isabel, then

'I just need a couple more minutes.'

Faint rustling, movement, clatter and mingled voices from the restaurant. Then Isabel's voice again: 'I tried my best to hold him up. But he's on his way *now*. You have to get out of there!'

'Okay. Don't worry.' Mauricio hung up, bringing his attention back to the computer screen in front of him. He'd already got most of the old details on his mother's house and the Madrid connection with Isabel's ancestors when her call came. But there were some vital missing links and some notes about her father's visit eight years ago which had intrigued him, and he was still busily exploring those.

How long for Dario to get here in his Ferrari? Twenty seconds across the car park and starting up, no more than another ninety seconds or so to arrive in front – and he'd be driving flat-out. Mauricio smiled to himself. From the Ferrari's distinctive throaty roar, he practically knew its position in town at any point in time. He'd hear its approach, and there was always that last-second roar and rattle as Dario cut the ignition.

He'd already transferred eight files to his USB drive and was halfway through transferring another two when he heard the distant high-pitched whine of the Ferrari. He quickly checked his watch. He didn't have time to check and scroll through more. He'd just have to pick the most likely ones from their file names and transfer those.

He picked another four and transferred those: twenty-four seconds transfer time, that whine getting closer, sharper.

He chose another two: *fourteen seconds*. Heard the Ferrari making a sharp turn, revs rising again. *Just a block away now*. Sweat beads popped on his forehead as he noticed another two seemingly key folders: two files in one, three in the other. *Would he have time for them*?

Mauricio went for it. Dario was probably still twenty seconds away, and he still had to park and get out.

But those last two folders seemed to be taking longer, the files larger, and he heard that last roar and rattle while it was still downloading. '*Venga de prisa . . . de prisa . . .*'

He looked around frantically as he heard the key in the door . . .

Descarga completa . . .

He yanked out the flash drive, shut-down, and hustled towards the back as he heard the entry security bleeps by the front door and Dario's footsteps approaching.

Larry Gilbert had followed the girl with interest the past forty-eight hours, trying to discern some sort of pattern in her movements. She seemed to nearly always return to the Parador early evening before going out again, the gap between the two far longer if she was having dinner there.

Tonight, it looked like she was having dinner there again. But from the red Ferrari in the car park, it looked like she was alternating between the bus driver and the Mayor's son. *Dangerous game.*

As was what he'd witnessed the night before with the bus driver; *play acting at pushing her over the edge.* He'd had to blink twice to realise that she was still there a second later – before shoving the bus driver away in anger and storming off around the curve of the castle.

He'd headed back to his car. Nothing he could do while she was with the bus driver. Though that little display had given Larry the seed of an idea.

He was parked in pretty much the same position in the car park tonight. One row back from the front: a good clear view of the hotel entrance, but wouldn't easily be.seen, especially as he'd slump down when he saw anyone approaching or exiting. And if he was seen, he'd no doubt be pegged as a cab driver dropping off or picking up.

After twenty minutes waiting, he became bored, restless, so put on the radio. But that soon became tiresome as well; and as the song playing changed from Julio Iglesias's *Besame Mucho* to *Magdalena*, he switched it off.

What was it about this part of Spain? Stuck in a time-warp, not just the architecture, but the local radio stations as well.

Largo jolted as he saw Dario Alarcon rush out of the Parador and jump into his Ferrari. He slumped down in his seat on impulse. A throaty roar drowned out everything as the Ferrari started up.

He saw the girl come to the entrance as the Ferrari sped off – but then she turned back inside, saying something into her mobile phone.

It didn't look like she'd be leaving anytime soon; in any case, whatever made Dario leave in such a rush looked far more intriguing in that moment. He started up and followed.

15

Beneyto, then

Inspector Javier Beneyto and his colleague, Antonio Vidal, were the only ones in the squad of eight men to carry handguns. The rest were all GEOs – *Grupo Especial de Operaciones*, the Spanish equivalent of a SWAT team – armed with fully automatic MP-5s.

Beneyto favoured a handgun because you could turn and manipulate quicker. That split-second to swing around an automatic rifle could make all the difference; and, besides, once he'd fired his single shot, far heavier fire, if required, would follow a split-second later.

Dawn raid on the Marbella villa of drug dealer Alan Vaughn. Beneyto and his drugs enforcement team had been monitoring the activities of a ring of drug dealers in the area – many, like Alan Vaughn, gangsters who'd left England in the 1980s for the Spanish *Costas*, then later turned to drug dealing to fund their lifestyles. But Vaughn was so far the only one they'd got sufficient evidence on to warrant a raid.

The element of surprise was lost as they approached the villa and two Dobermans started barking viciously, one of them jumping up high with his front paws against the inside of the gate.

They'd known in advance that Vaughn had dogs, so two of his team were prepared for 'dog handling'. Both dogs were quickly floored with adjusted-voltage tasers, then dart-drugged. No bullets – as it was they often got complaints from animal rights activists. *'Okay. A man killed in the raid, but what about the two dogs that were unconscious for twenty minutes?'*

But now with the dogs having barked, sound was no longer the issue, speed was. The gate was burst open, a deafening alarm ringing out, and within seconds the team were storming the front of the villa and ramming open the front door.

Beneyto caught a flicker of movement from a front patio door, a gun being raised. He fired, and saw the gun quickly dropping as two MP-5 red dots swung onto the man's body.

A shoulder wound, Beneyto discovered as he entered

the villa behind four GEO men, their rifles raised and rapidly swivelling to every corner.

'What other people in the house?' Beneyto asked the man, mid-thirties, probably a guard or henchman.

'Uh, just me and Alan. Oh, and a cousin who is visiting.'

'No other guards?'

'No.'

Beneyto turned as another voice came from the side.

'What's the meaning of all this?'

A man in his early sixties in a dark blue terrycloth robe approached, bald except for a dark ring of hair, stocky with a heavy paunch. Beneyto recognised Alan Vaughn straight away.

'It means you're under arrest,' Beneyto said calmly, his tone matter-of-fact. His English was quite good; a prime requirement for drugs enforcement officers, who often had to liaise with foreign police forces.

'What for?' Vaughn held his hands out helplessly.

Javier Beneyto didn't answer that, he simply turned and instructed his men in Spanish to cuff Vaughn and take him out.

Meanwhile he'd talk briefly to this 'cousin'. If he was just that, an uninvolved family member, he'd be let go; if not, he'd also be taken in for questioning.

Beneyto lit up a cigarette, drawing heavily as he watched Vaughn and his henchman led to the black police van.

Apart from the henchman's shoulder wound, it had gone well, but he knew at heart that Vaughn was only a minor player. Beneyto just hoped he might be able to get something from him to nail the local drug kingpins in their sights: Danny Blake and Vic Denham.

16

Lapslie and Bradbury, now

'I'll set off from Café Marie here in twenty seconds,' Lapslie said into his mobile. 'You set off two minutes after that, but I'll tell you when over the phone in any case – so obviously keep the line open meanwhile.'

'Okay,' Emma Bradbury said from her end, standing in the entrance of the Parador. 'I'll wait for your signal.'

'Then let us see where we meet up.' Lapslie held a hand half-up – part acknowledgment, part holding gesture – towards café owner Ignacio standing a few yards to his side on the front terrace, cigar stub in one corner of his mouth, intrigued by the goings-on – some excitement in Ignacio's day.

It had just become fully dark ten minutes ago, so the dinner rush hadn't yet started. Ignacio had some time spare to observe with mild amusement the antics of these *extranjero* police. Lapslie had purposely waited until it was dark so that visibility was more or less the same as it would have been that night when Mauricio and Isabel planned to meet. The timing was gauged from their questioning of Ignacio and Parador staff as to when Mauricio and Isabel, respectively, had set off that night.

'I'm starting my walk now,' Lapslie announced as he finished counting the remaining seconds. '. . . Just approaching the far end of the town square,' he said after forty yards, his breath already catching with his rapid pace. He'd instructed Emma to walk at an even more hurried pace, as they'd been told by the hotel staff that Isabel had left in a rush, already obviously aware that she was late for her meeting with Mauricio.

Looking ahead, Lapslie saw that the view beyond the end of the town square was quite narrow, and it was almost impenetrably dark beyond the row of houses that spread eighty yards at the far end beyond the square; the last of the town petering out.

Lapslie had just passed the last of those houses as he said into his mobile, 'Okay. You set off now.'

The dark stretch of cobbled road extended for another two hundred yards before the lights of the castle and its car park picked up, illuminating at most a fifty-yard stretch around it.

Still, it took Lapslie a moment to pick out Emma Bradbury heading away from the Parador entrance towards
him. A few seconds later she was obscured again behind
a section of the rampart approach walling and some
cars in the car park, reappearing again seven seconds
later. Lapslie noticed she was more indistinct as she
moved away from the castle lights. Then within another
ten seconds she was swallowed up in the same level of
darkness and shadows as he was.

'I can't see you any more now,' Lapslie said breathlessly into his phone. 'Can you see me?'

'No. I haven't been able to see you since I set out. The
last glimpse I got of you was waiting in the entrance here
for your signal, just as you were leaving the town square.'
Bradbury added after a second: 'Or, at least, I think it
was you. Quite a distance to make out people clearly.'

'Yes. So, it would have been pretty much the same
scenario that night for Isabel and Mauricio.' Lapslie wondered now whether Mauricio had been able to identify
Isabel clearly as she'd moved away from the Parador, or
whether he'd just assumed it was her because he knew
she'd be leaving at that moment.

Lapslie didn't get a clear view of Bradbury again until
she was about thirty yards away. As she approached,

he checked the time on his mobile: 4 mins 32 seconds since he'd set off, 2 mins 32 for Bradbury. Normally an eight- to nine-minute walk – it made sense with both of them walking rapidly, Lapslie considered. He looked each way.

'So, this is where they'd have met that night, give or take ten yards either way.' He held a hand out. 'Any first thoughts on what might have happened?'

'Well, he could have done practically anything to her here, and he wouldn't have been seen.'

Lapslie followed Bradbury's gaze to the houses behind him trailing off from the town square. They were side-on, so unless someone had been hanging out of a window, they wouldn't have seen anything; aside from the pitch darkness swallowing up everything fifty yards beyond the last house.

'Only problem is, anything he does to Isabel here,' Lapslie said with a fresh breath, 'a coshing, throttling or a knock-out punch – he's still got to carry her all the way back in the direction you've just come to get to the point on the rampart where her blood has been found. That's a good two hundred yards.'

Bradbury nodded, surveying the castle rampart behind her for a moment. 'He's a strong lad, burly. All that bus driving and looks like he works out too. He could have easily done it with a fireman's lift.'

'I didn't mean just in that way. I meant the fact that he'd have risked being seen once he was within the lights of the castle. Anyone coming out at that point, or perhaps looking from their room.'

'I suppose. People approaching or coming outside is definitely a factor.' Bradbury grimaced. 'But have you seen what passes for room windows? They're hardly more than slits, just enough to fire an arrow through. And the walls are so thick, there's hardly any sideways vision. So it's doubtful they'd have been seen from any of the rooms unless they were in a direct line.'

'I daresay.' Lapslie nodded towards the castle. 'But let's head that way and see what they would have passed, and who might have seen them.'

The last eighty yards towards the castle, the incline was steeper, and Lapslie felt his breath catching again, especially after the rapid pacing of only moments ago. He peered keenly towards the hotel entrance as they passed it.

'Quite visible at this point. Anyone coming out the hotel would have seen them.'

'Yes,' Bradbury agreed. 'But the entrance courtyard

doglegs back sharply towards the main foyer – so they wouldn't have been seen from the foyer itself.'

Lapslie nodded again, his gaze shifting to the hotel windows. 'I see what you mean about them being narrow slits. But from this one here there would have been a clear view of them as they passed.'

Bradbury looked up towards the window Lapslie indicated. 'Yes, there would.' She shrugged. 'But we're talking maybe only a four- to five-second slot before they passed the angle of view. What are the chances of someone looking out of that window at precisely that juncture?'

Lapslie looked ahead as they approached the side of the rampart. 'The other question remaining is, if he didn't knock her out and fireman-lift her, how and why did they arrive at this point that night?'

'It certainly wouldn't have been during an argument, sir. If things were tense between them, Isabel would likely be keen to keep away from the edge – especially given what that cleaner thought she'd witnessed two nights beforehand.'

'So, he'd have brought her here on some pretence,' Lapslie mused aloud. 'Things quite settled between them before it all went wrong.' Lapslie looked down at the river below, only just visible with the reflected light from the castle, then the shadowy shapes of the cliffs and rolling hills beyond. 'It is quite a dramatic viewpoint, so perhaps he brought her here to show her something specific.'

'Except there was no electrical storm that night, just some heavy rain later. And the moon wasn't much brighter than it is tonight, and partly obscured by cloud. I checked.' Bradbury held a hand towards the vista. 'So not much more than now would have been visible.'

Lapslie took a fresh breath as he surveyed the scene. One thing he always liked about Bradbury that made her such a valuable assistant: her attention to detail. Perhaps why they meshed so well. She'd concentrate on the conventional details which would usually bore him, then he'd pick up on the oddities that everyone else had missed. Or sometimes the smells and tastes assaulting him would point him to those. All that reached him now on the night air was the smell of meat and fish grilling from the nearby Parador restaurant, quite pleasant, but there was a faint ammonia overlay. *Something vital was being held back from them. What was it?*

Lapslie looked down at the rocks where that morning Jim Thompson and the forensics had been. While one of the blood groups found on the higher rock, O-positive, matched Isabel's, it was quite common, so didn't tell them much, unless or until they got DNA. The other group, Lutheran B-negative, was far rarer, but most tellingly that had been the only blood type found on the lower rock. No O-positive had been found.

When he'd earlier run through a possible scenario with Thompson, it appeared that both parties had obviously hit the higher rock, 'Then the Lutheran B-negative party tumbled down and struck the lower rock also before falling into the river.' When pressed about the O-positive party, Thompson surmised that they could have survived the fall onto the higher rock. 'The only thing then would be if they hit it in such a way that they bounced clear of the lower rocks and fell straight into the river.'

'So, we have a possible match on one of the blood groups to Isabel,' Lapslie said now to Bradbury. 'But the other remains a mystery.'

Bradbury nodded pensively. 'Along with why that person would be with Isabel at that particular point that night? Or with Mauricio, if he was still around?'

17

Isabel, then

'Are you sure?' Mauricio pressed the archives clerk on the other end of the line. *'Seguro?'*

'Yes, absolutely. There's no possible doubt. I have the file open right in front of me. I can send it to you now as an attachment, if you wish. Along with the others we discussed.'

'Yes, thank you. To the email I gave you earlier, if you could.' Mauricio had given him Isabel's email address. An enquiry about Alarcon family history from a current Alarcon family member interested in her family's gene-alogy seemed more natural, would likely raise fewer eyebrows.

'Of course. I'll send through now. Is there anything else I can help with?'

'No, that's fine. You've been most helpful. *Hasta luego.*'

Isabel had been standing expectantly by Mauricio's

side as he made the call. He'd been on the phone to the Madrid family archive section for almost twenty minutes, but after the first ten she knew he'd hit on something: an anomaly between the information he was getting now and that given to her the other day by Dario Alarcon. Another few minutes' wait for the file to come through to see the full details; Isabel chewed anxiously at the back of her knuckles.

'Okay, here it is,' she said after a moment. Four file attachments. She clicked on the one headed Eduardo Alarcon. Mauricio came over, hovering by her side. But as it opened, even that was too long for them to both read at the same time on-screen. 'I'll print a couple of copies – one each.'

As the printer whirred, Mauricio grabbed one copy and handed the other to Isabel, both of them falling silent for a moment as they read in unison.

'He's right,' Isabel exclaimed halfway through reading. 'It's right here: Magdalena left Madrid after only two years there with her brother, Eduardo, returning to Alarcon.'

Mauricio nodded. 'And if you read on, you'll see in fact that the family home was never sold on when her mother Katerina died – because that's the address in Alarcon which Magdalena returns to. It was simply rented out to a local tanner, Jose Alvina.'

'Yes, I see,' Isabel said, reading the same segment. She looked up, wrapping the papers with the back of one hand. 'But why would Dario lie to us – mislead us into thinking that Magdalena Alarcon had sold up and left Alarcon for good? Never to return.'

Mauricio smiled wanly. 'I think we went through this before, when I asked myself the same question: why would he bother to rob an old lady like my mother?' He shrugged helplessly. 'For gain, or if he had something to hide?'

'Yes, but . . . *what*?' Isabel looked equally helpless as she searched the air for answers.

Christina walked back in then with the fresh coffees she'd made. Since being fired from Dario Alarcon's office eighteen months ago, she'd set up a small private secretary business at home. And having helped Mauricio with Dario's passwords, she'd offered to let them use her house to dig down for any details on the files; after all, it wasn't the sort of sensitive information they could pursue at Café Marie or the Parador, and Christina also had a printer and fax machine.

'I think part of the answer might be here,' Mauricio

said, halfway through their coffees, having printed out two more files to scour through. 'Joaquim Alarcon. Eduardo and Magdalena's ancestor from four generations back on their father's side. Alberto, Katerina's husband.'

'And remind me again just who Joaquim was?' Isabel asked.

'Joaquim was the little boy who returned with Isabella, your namesake, all those years back after a two-year absence. He was the son of the woman she came back with.'

'So, the son of a friend of Isabella's. Why would that be significant?' Isabel held a palm out. 'And how did he end up with the name Alarcon?'

'As you've seen, many who left the town for larger cities ended up with the name. Jose or Miguel de Alarcon. Then later the *de*, the *of*, was dropped. But in Joaquim's case he had the name practically from the start while still in town. Well, from when he was in his early thirties, when his apparent mother died.'

'*Apparent*?' Isabel's brow knitted. 'I don't understand.'

Mauricio smiled slyly. 'How do you think the rumours about Isabella getting pregnant came about?' He looked briefly at Christina to one side, sipping her coffee and nodding her support. Obviously, she'd already heard these stories, Isabel reflected. Local folklore, spun time and time again over the centuries among only two hundred people. 'The *apparent* mother's name was Esmerelda Ferrer, eight or nine years older than young Isabella. She was announced to the town as Isabella's chaperone and Maid of Honour – so explaining why they were always together. But the townspeople observed how Isabella would dote on little Joaquim, seemed more caring and loving of him than Esmerelda. As if she was the *real* mother and Esmerelda was just a nanny . . . and so the rumours started.'

Isabel nodded slowly. 'Okay, *rumours*. But that doesn't explain how he ended up with the Alarcon family name.'

Christina interjected. 'When Esmerelda died, Isabella adopted Joaquim – so of course then he took the family name.'

'Exactly,' Mauricio concurred. 'And when Isabella eventually got married about six years later she only had two daughters.' He gestured. 'So, if the rumours are true, Joaquim would have been the only male heir to the Alarcon principality.'

'But, again, just rumours.' Isabel shook her head, slightly lost with following the lineage. 'So why would Dario and his father go to such lengths to cover it up?'

'Because at times those rumours went deeper than that,' Christina said. 'Started to take on more substance.'

'Very much so.' Mauricio nodded solemnly. 'So, if true – and if you are indeed descended from the line of Eduardo, Alberto and finally Joaquim Alarcon – you'd be heir to the Alarcon principality.' Mauricio waved one arm theatrically. 'You'd be heir to all of this rather than Dario or his father and uncle.'

18

Lapslie and Bradbury, now

'I think we need a couple more days here, sir,' Lapslie said to Chief Inspector Rouse who was at the other end of the phone in Chelmsford.

'Have you found any connection to Vic Denham's possible involvement yet?' Rouse enquired.

'Not yet, sir.'

'*Not yet*,' Rouse repeated pointedly. 'What's the hold-up? You've already been there three days.'

'Yes, I appreciate that, sir.' Lapslie lifted his eyes heavenward to Emma Bradbury as she sat a couple of yards away. It was the reaction they'd expected with the lack of progress on Vic Denham so far, Rouse giving them a hard time. 'But liaising with officers from Madrid over a hundred miles away, who can't turn up in Alarcon at the drop of a hat, obviously creates some delays. Then also we've had to wait for blood-test results from

Thompson and his team – with any possible DNA results still to come.'

'When are those expected?'

'A couple of days more – if they haven't been too weathered and degraded by the sun, that is.' There was a moment's silence at the other end. 'Besides, we still have to wait until tomorrow for a crucial interview.'

Rouse sighed. 'And is that interview possibly Vic Denham-related?'

'No, sir. It's Dario Alarcon, the main notary here and he's also the son of the Mayor. The third wheel in a possible love triangle with Isabel Alarcon – but he's away in Madrid on business right now, due to return tomorrow. I think I mentioned that situation in our last conversation, sir. It's also in the subsequent report I linked in my email.'

'Yes, you did.' Rouse sighed deeply. 'But I thought you might have moved on from pursuing that by now. Because – as I said clearly to you then – if the likely cause appears to be this love triangle, then it's more something for the local Spanish police to pursue.'

'Yes, sir. I hear you loud and clear on that front. But we've had the issue of this Dario Alarcon being away and so we haven't been able to ascertain whether he is connected to Isabel's disappearance.' Lapslie looked towards Bradbury. Picking up on him getting put on the ropes by Rouse, she'd typed on her laptop in big letters MYSTERY MAN, then turned the screen towards him. 'We have in fact been looking at other factors in the meantime – but, obviously, we had to pursue this love triangle first. Because, if it is that, we can head out of here and leave things to Inspector Ruiz and his team. So that has to be eliminated first before we can fully focus on the other main plank of our enquiry.'

'Which *is*?' *Barely concealed impatience.*

'A man seen outside the Parador, who seemed to be taking a special interest in Isabel Alarcon.'

'When was this?'

'Just two nights before she disappeared. But he was also seen in town the day of her disappearance.'

'And since?'

'No. There's been no sign of him in Alarcon since Isabel's disappearance.'

'I see.' Rouse fell silent, thoughtful for a moment. 'And you think this might be our Vic Denham connection?'

'It's a possibility, sir. He's certainly not a local. The town here is at most two hundred strong – everyone knows everyone. And the maid who first saw him, plus the two people who reported further sightings since – they're a hundred percent sure he's from out of town.' Lapslie took a fresh breath. 'Also, the maid described him as very tall. And the man that we discussed in my last call, who broke into Terry Haines's old villa in Marbella, was described by Haines as particularly *large*.'

Silence for a moment from Rouse, then a faint huffing. 'Is that all we've got? Very tall . . . *large*. Seems a bit vague, and far too tenuous to hang a link on to Vic Denham.'

'Yes, sir. But it's *something*. And I'm sure we will start fleshing out that link as we ask more questions around town about this mystery man.'

There was a faint bitter-almond taste in Lapslie's mouth. *Withholding information.* Except this time, he himself was the guilty party. What he'd neglected to mention was that Alarcon was very much a transient tourist town, its numbers swelled by foreign tourists throughout the week, as well as Spanish nationals from Madrid, Valencia and Barcelona at weekends. So, while their mystery man's height and appearance might earmark him as 'not a local', an *extranjero*, there were any number of six-foot-plus Dutch, Swedish and German tourists who would descend on the town, then disappear days later.

But he didn't want to dilute the potential importance of their 'mystery man' sighting and the door it kept open in terms of a Vic Denham link. In part because it kept them in Alarcon, and Lapslie was starting to enjoy his stay in the town.

'Yes, well, we can but hope that thread progresses,' Rouse said at length. 'Let me know how you get on.'

'Yes, sir. I will.' But he heard the line go dead mid-sentence.

Lapslie looked out at the valley ahead from the pathway. Like the castle rampart, the path had a bordering two-foot-high stone wall; the only protection from an almost sheer hundred-foot drop a yard beyond.

Not too different to the point where Mauricio had appeared to push Isabel, and where they feared two people had gone over the edge for real two nights later – one of them possibly Isabel. Though this spot was two hundred yards beyond that, practically the furthest point on the pathway that led from the back of the castle rampart.

The river below was just a faint murmur in the distance, and beyond that nothing but silence. The castle and the promontory behind cut off the sounds of the hotel, the main town and roads beyond. And ahead the view was glorious: rolling hills and plains stretching towards the horizon.

Lapslie inhaled, as if he was breathing in the peacefulness. Filling his lungs with it. One of his favourite hobbies was sailing, primarily to gain that same peace and solitude, to be away from all the hustle, bustle and noise which would lead to an unsettling medley of smells and tastes assaulting him.

This was the closest he'd found to the solitude that came with sailing in a long while; the distant babble of the river almost matching the lapping of water against his boat's hull, and when he closed his eyes, the breeze hitting him in his exposed position wasn't so different to a sea breeze.

Since he'd discovered this spot two days ago, it had become one of his favourites. It allowed him to relax, to let his thoughts run freely and wind down from the cacophony of smells and tastes from throughout the day. That was the main reason Alarcon had started to grow on him: *its solitude*.

If it wasn't for discovering this private spot, he might have been inclined to give in more readily to Rouse's impatient urging, to wrap it all up quickly and leave it to the Spanish police.

Bradbury's voice from behind disturbed him. 'Sir. We should see the rest of those hotels now.'

Lapslie looked around. She'd stayed about forty yards back. Close enough to be heard, without impinging on his personal space. *She knew him so well now; knew all his foibles and traits.*

She'd grabbed a coffee in the Parador bar while he went out to the point for half an hour to get his thoughts clear.

'Five minutes, I'll be with you,' he called back. 'I'll see you in the Parador bar.'

Silence again as the last of her footsteps receded. *Solitude.* Lapslie breathed it in again as he surveyed the panorama spread before him.

'Quite tall, six-foot-two or so, and fairly broad.' Lapslie held one hand up, and then both outwards to illustrate. 'And light-brown or dark-blond hair.'

'Sounds a bit like Olaf Magnusson,' the girl behind the reception desk at the Sol-Vista hotel commented.

Carla? Or was that the name of the last girl they'd seen? Three hotels visited – four or five more to go – some of the names and descriptions had blurred together, Lapslie reflected.

'*Dark*-blond?' Carla questioned, and Lapslie was unsure

154

for a moment whether she was just confirming, or didn't fully understand the expression.

All of the hotels had one or two people who spoke good English – but there was a limit to the dexterity of that English with some. They'd had to take it in easy stages at times. As Lapslie had finished his earlier phone conversation with Rouse, Bradbury had commented, 'Having built up the possibilities of a Vic Denham-link with our "mystery man", I daresay we should find out if any substance can be put to that.' Two men so far who roughly matched the description of a 'tall, stocky, blond-haired man', and now this one.

'Because I think that Olaf Magnusson was just normal blond,' Carla said.

'*Normal* blond,' Bradbury picked up. 'What would that be? Boris Johnson blond . . . Bjorn Borg? Justin Bieber . . . Ryan Gosling? Leonardo DiCaprio?'

'DiCaprio . . . *si*,' Carla said.

Lapslie noticed that Carla appeared slightly lost at first, possibly unsure of the names suggested – *not her generation* – so Bradbury included some younger names.

Carla's brow knitted. 'But how DiCaprio looked in his early films. Maybe even a shade lighter. He's gone darker with his hair in some recent films.'

Lapslie nodded. From Luciana's description, their man seemed a shade darker than that. 'No other men of that size with blond or light-brown hair staying at that time you can think of?'

'No. Mr Magnusson was the only one.'

'And Mr Magnusson's age?'

'Early to mid-forties.'

Five to ten years adrift, Lapslie considered. Luciana thought the man she saw was mid-thirties.

Bradbury asked, 'And when did Mr Magnusson leave the hotel?'

Carla checked on her computer for a moment. 'Mid-morning on the twenty-first. Left just after eleven with his wife and son.'

Lapslie nodded again. Two days beyond when Isabel disappeared. Doubtful too that someone would come to pursue a target or execute a hit with a family in tow. 'And where was Mr Magnusson and his family from?'

Another quick glance towards her computer screen. 'From Gothenburg, Sweden.'

'Thank you. You've been most helpful.'

The scenario run through at the remaining four hotels was similar, though the last two were little more than lodging homes, only half a dozen rooms each.

The number of men who roughly fitted the description was now five, but only two of those had left the same night of Isabel's disappearance: one from Munich, the other from Ghent. But Lapslie tuned in keenly when, at the last but one hotel visited, the Miramar, a man fitting their description hailed from Malaga, just down the road from Vic Denham's stomping ground.

'And he had light-brown or blond hair?' Lapslie confirmed.

'Yes, light brown,' the desk clerk, Amparo, a woman in her late forties, answered. She lifted one hand to her own hair. 'But it had some blond streaks in it too.'

Lapslie nodded. Not the sort of thing that would be picked up on a dark night by Luciana, but would be noticed close-up across a hotel desk. 'And when did this Tobias Mercer leave the hotel?'

'Late on the nineteenth or the next morning.'

Lapslie noticed that Amparo hadn't checked the hotel register. Perhaps with such a small hotel, she felt she could recall all the comings and goings.

'*Which* is it? The nineteenth or the twentieth?'

Amparo wiggled one hand. 'Well. He checked out the night of the nineteenth and settled his bill by credit card over the phone. But he said he couldn't pick up his things until the next day and could they be put in a storeroom meanwhile for him to pick up then?'

Something unsettled Lapslie about this information. 'And did Mr Mercer pick up his things the next day?'

'Yes, he did.'

'You saw him personally?'

'No, I didn't . . .' Amparo's eyes shifted briefly to one side. 'But that's only because I wasn't on duty then. My daughter Sara was. Sara!' she called out, and seconds later an attractive girl with dark-brown hair in her mid-twenties opened the door to a small office on one side. Amparo asked her, 'When Mr Mercer came to pick up his things on the twentieth, did you actually see him?'

Sara looked a bit vague, quizzical at first, and her mother prompted, 'You know, the big man from Malaga with blond streaks in his hair. I wasn't here that morning, you were on duty.'

'Yes, yes . . . I remember now,' Sara said. 'We had his suitcase in the office here, and he came by in the morning to pick it up.'

'You personally saw him?' Lapslie pressed.

'Yes, I did,' Sara answered, more confidently now; she appeared on firmer ground.

19

Isabel, then

At times the rumours went deeper than that . . . Isabel listened intently as Mauricio and Christina filled in the gaps in the history of Joaquim Alarcon during the years after the death of Isabella, his adoptive mother.

'Not long after Isabella died, the rumours started to have more substance,' Mauricio explained. 'Joaquim started saying what everyone had already suspected – that Isabella had been his real mother all along and Esmerelda had been just a nanny. It caused a stir with Isabella's two daughters, of course – his stepsisters, if Joaquim's claims are to be believed.'

'What about their father?' Isabel asked. 'Isabella's husband?'

Christina offered, 'Guillermo? He had died a good ten years before that.'

'Yes. He was eight years older than young Isabella, in

any case,' Mauricio piped up. He grimaced. 'The tales passed down say Joaquim didn't dare say anything until after Guillermo's death: Guillermo was quite stern, unforgiving. But it appears his two daughters might have taken a leaf out of his book. The story goes that they packed him off to Madrid for a while, so that the town didn't hear any more about Joaquim's claims. Out of sight, out of mind – I think the saying goes.'

Isabel smiled, nodding.

Christina commented, 'They made out that they were doing Joaquim a favour – an apprenticeship with a Madrid artist that Joaquim admired. They knew that Joaquim had a strong interest in art.'

'And meanwhile,' Mauricio said, 'the two stepsisters buried any possible trace or proof relating to Joaquim's claim of being Isabella's real son.'

'Shame they didn't have DNA in those days.' Isabel smiled crookedly. 'Seems this family has got a history of burying possible descendants. Any claims to the *thiefdom* of Alarcon.' Her smile widened. 'Sorry, *fiefdom*. Freudian slip.'

Mauricio and Christina looked at her, puzzled. Some expressions didn't travel well, she reminded herself. And she couldn't think of a way of translating it accurately, either, so just shrugged. 'Sorry. English humour.'

'But no joke for Joaquim's descendants,' Mauricio said with a sly smile, as if to say, *we Spaniards know how to spin a joke too*. Then his expression dropped. '. . . And now your father and yourself.'

'No joke for you either,' Isabel added. 'If you look at the way Dario made sure your mother was disinherited.'

Mauricio nodded slowly, but then something appeared to lift his disconsolate mood. 'But this little visit to Dario's office now might have helped with that also. As I was clearing "history and activity", a couple of extra folders and files caught my eye – so I grabbed those too on the memory stick. Just seconds before Dario's Ferrari pulled up outside.'

'That's good, Mauricio,' Isabel said encouragingly. 'But, like I said, you shouldn't have left things so close.'

'That's okay. I'm a big boy now.' Mauricio shrugged it off macho-style. 'And it was worth it: look at the end result.'

Isabel smiled in appreciation. The least she could do, faced with Mauricio's *Look what I risked for you* expression. Relating the story earlier, he'd very much played on the excitement and risk: getting Isabel's call from the hotel and knowing that Dario was on his way – 'I could hear the roar of Dario's Ferrari from halfway across town, getting closer street by street – but I was determined to get every possible file. So I left it until he was practically outside.' And Isabel had first admonished him at that point, 'You shouldn't have left it so close.'

But this time, as Mauricio ran through the events, Christina appeared lost in thought. 'Did you say you noticed those two extra files while you were already clearing "history"?'

'Yes, why?'

'Did you go back in and clear history again *after* downloading those last two files?'

Mauricio lapsed into thought for a moment. His worried look, face starting to flush, gave the answer.

'Because if you didn't clear history again after those last two file transfers,' Christina said, 'Dario will know that you were in his office.'

20

Beneyto, then

Javier Beneyto waited outside the Judge's chambers at the Malaga courtroom, his colleague Antonio Vidal at his side; Judge Miguel Alvarez, due to preside over a case in Courtroom 4 at 11 a.m. His clerk had come out briefly and asked, 'What is this concerning?'

'Some wire tap requests that need urgent approval.' Beneyto handed over a slim folder.

The clerk raised an eyebrow. 'More than one?'

'Yes.' Beneyto didn't intend to go into detail of why they were needed with just a Court clerk.

The clerk went back into the chambers and reappeared two minutes later. 'His honour might be able to spare you some time before his hearing.'

As almost another four minutes passed with no activity, the minutes dragging like hours, Beneyto glanced anxiously at his watch: 10.46 a.m. At this rate, there wouldn't be sufficient time to discuss everything with the Judge and get the approval he hoped for. And already he was craving a cigarette.

Beneyto tapped his fingers on one thigh, his watch reading forty-seven minutes past before the door finally swung open and the clerk announced, 'You can go in now.'

As Beneyto entered, Judge Alvarez held one hand up. 'Just you, Inspector Beneyto. Your colleague should wait outside. Some of what we discuss now might be sensitive.'

Beneyto nodded back at Vidal, then at Judge Alvarez as he took a seat on the other side of a walnut desk and the door closed behind him.

Judge Alvarez looked down at the folder open on his desk. 'So, your reason for requesting wire taps in these three cases is suspected drug trafficking?'

'Yes, sir.' Beneyto was pleased to see that the Judge had already started reading the file; that should save some time explaining. 'We've already made an arrest of one of their colleagues but feel that wire taps would be required in these cases to gain full evidence for prosecution.'

'What do you have so far on these men?'

'Mostly third-party claims. But since a number of

these claims are from fellow criminals, their reliability might be brought into question at trial.'

'I see.' Judge Alvarez nodded, leafed back in the file. 'And some past history of convictions, I see, mainly for armed robbery in England, and one failed conviction on this Daniel Blake for drug trafficking in this very courtroom four years ago.'

Beneyto nodded solemnly. 'Yes, sir. That's why the request for a wire tap – we don't want a repeat of that. We need to make sure the evidence this time is conclusive and watertight.'

Judge Alvarez spent a moment more reading. He eased out a weighted breath as he looked up. 'Now I can easily see the rationale for granting wire taps in the cases of Daniel Blake and Victor Denham – both have a number of past convictions. And while most of these have been for armed robbery, as we're both aware, many of these former robbers have turned to drug-trafficking for income. One by-product of the digital money age.' A pained smile, then Alvarez gestured at the third file. 'But in the case of this Larry Gilbert, I see no convictions at all. His record is completely clean.'

'Yes, sir.' Beneyto nodded in lame submission. 'He's been very careful.'

'Is he a suspected drug trafficker as well?'

'No, sir. He's a hitman. A hired killer, known locally as "Largo".'

Judge Alvarez blinked slowly, failing to make the connection. 'That may be. But this is obviously all just from rumours and speculation. And with no past convictions, what earthly grounds would support my granting a wire tap in his case?'

Beneyto leaned forward, fearing he was rapidly losing this part of his request. 'The thing is, Larry Gilbert is the key to the other two, possibly others as well. In the past decade, with their increasing gang and drug turf wars, Gilbert has been hired by a number of Marbella gangs.'

Alvarez held both hands out on his desk. 'But no proof as yet?'

'No.' Beneyto gestured. 'But Gilbert could be essential in nailing the others. If we can't get them on drug trafficking, we might at least get them on ordering hit-contracts.'

'I see.' Alvarez lapsed into thought for a moment. 'I must say, you make a strong case for Gilbert. The other two I have no problem with . . .'

Javier Beneyto simply nodded numbly as he awaited Judge Alvarez's final deliberation: whether he'd get a full house or would just have to settle for two out of three.

21

Lapslie and Bradbury, now

'I think you're making too much of it, Inspector,' Dario Alarcon commented. 'Yes, there was some bad feeling between myself and Mauricio Reynes, but nothing that serious. Certainly not enough to harm or kill someone over. And particularly not Isabel. I hardly knew her, I only just met her. But what I did find out about her in the brief time we met, I liked.'

'Yes, we know,' Lapslie said. 'Liked her enough in fact to invite her to dinner on two occasions in that short period. And that added fuel to the rivalry between you and Mauricio.'

Dario shrugged. 'You'd have to ask Mauricio about that, not me.'

'We've already spoken to Mauricio,' Lapslie said flatly. 'And so now we're talking to you. And from what Mauricio has told us, you were uncomfortable about some history Isabel was digging into surrounding her family name.'

Lapslie noticed that his voice seemed to echo in the large room. They were in the dining hall used for Alarcon council meetings, pictures of the past provincial Marqueses looking down at them from the oil portraits lining the walls. Dario's uncle, Jose, was sitting to one side as his legal representative, and made brief notes, but so far had said little. Dario's father, Gabriel, had also been with them for the first few minutes of intro-ductions, then left them to it. *'I'll be in my office, if you need me.'*

Dario shook his head. 'I was trying to help her in that regard, not hinder. That's why I had those dinners with her – to give her extra information, help her in her quest.'

'Mauricio said that you were feeding her misleading information, trying to deter her from digging deeper.'

Dario smiled disdainfully. 'Well, of course he's going to say that given the rivalry you mention between us.'

Bradbury interjected. 'Are you saying that Mauricio's claim isn't true?'

'Yes, I am. You catch on quickly.'

Lapslie kept his stare level on Dario Alarcon for a

moment, a taste of acrid lemon touching the back of his throat for a moment. *Avoidance or open deception?* Certainly, quite arrogant for his young age, and a somewhat chauvinistic class-conscious player; aiming his put-downs at the only woman in the room.

Lapslie took a fresh breath. 'So, let's return to that rivalry for a moment. Apparently, this goes back quite some way to a problem over Mauricio's mother's property.'

'Yes, it does. Mauricio's mother was making a claim outside of what was on the property register. My action in defending that registry notation was perfectly correct and legal.'

'I'm sure it was.' Lapslie smiled pleasantly. 'But you're hopefully an intelligent man' – Lapslie couldn't resist an oblique put-down of his own – 'So I'm sure you can easily see how that might cause problems in Mauricio's eyes with regards to Isabel, given that old rivalry between you.'

'In what way?'

Honestly unsure or being coy, feigning ignorance? Lapslie wondered. 'Mauricio clearly liked Isabel too – they were often seen in town together.'

'I suspect you'll find there was probably less affection

between them than you think. Especially from Isabel's point of view.'

'What makes you say that?'

'Well, when I probed one night over dinner, asking how she felt about Mauricio, she was quite disdainful, commenting that he was "only a bus driver".' Dario shrugged. 'So maybe that caused some problems and friction between them. Mauricio seeing their relation-ship one way, Isabel having another view of it.'

If true, it was certainly something Mauricio hadn't shared with them: Isabel being derisive of their possible relationship.

Lapslie eased into a smile after a moment. 'To para-phrase your earlier comment: of course, you're going to claim that, given the rivalry between you.'

'Just that it happens to be true, Inspector,' Dario said sharply, Lapslie gaining some satisfaction at seeing him rattled for once. *The first chink in his smug, arrogant armour since the interview started.*

'And did that make you feel good?' Bradbury enquired. 'Hearing Isabel talk about Mauricio that way?'

'I'm sorry . . . I'm not sure I follow you.'

'Given your standing in the town.' Bradbury gestured towards the Alarcon-dynasty portraits lining the walls. 'You're clearly a bit more than just a bus driver. So perhaps in a roundabout way she might have been praising you.'

'I suppose she might have been,' Dario conceded, carefully treading a thin line towards accepting that praise and adding fuel to the rivalry between himself and Mauricio. 'She was just stating the facts, so I never really gave it much thought.'

Lapslie nodded. Bradbury had done well drawing him out on that front, but then he'd as quickly settled back into his sense of entitlement and how he saw the order of the world.

'So, you maintain that there were no problems with Isabel digging into her family history,' Lapslie pressed. 'As Mauricio has claimed?'

'No, none at all. I happily passed on all the details about her ancestors in Alarcon. And that was the end of the matter.'

'He's lying,' Mauricio said, shaking his head. 'Isabel would never say something like that. She wasn't a social snob like Dario.' His initial anger verged into a crooked leer after a moment. '*Ridiculous*. It's the sort of thing *he* would think or say, so he's just passing it off as Isabel.'

'You don't think she said it?' Lapslie asked; a doubting tone.

'No, I don't. But I think it's the sort of thing Dario might try on.' The leer widened. 'He's stupid enough to think everyone thinks the same as him.'

They were back in the interview room at the Guardia Civil station in San Clemente with Mauricio's mousy, bespectacled lawyer, Enrique Navarre, observing proceedings. Bradbury was videoing the interview on her laptop both for the record and for Ruiz's benefit, while Navarre made notes the conventional way by hand.

Lapslie smiled dryly at the comment, then Bradbury said, 'Or maybe, following the same drift, Isabel said it purely because she knew that might be what Dario wanted to hear. She was keen to flatter him, because she wanted something from him.'

'Maybe.' Mauricio shrugged. 'But I wasn't there, so I have little hope of knowing. And I'm not sure Isabel was a player like that, either.' But then Mauricio reminded himself that this was the night he was inside the tunnel in question and so Isabel would have been keen to keep Dario occupied, *possibly flattering his pride, if that's what it took.* But he couldn't let on about any of that.

'. . . Particularly something like this information about

her family history,' Lapslie picked up, 'which you claim was at the root of problems between them. If Isabel thought Dario was holding back on that front, then she'd have been keen to butter him up.'

'Yes . . . I suppose.' Mauricio was uncertain what to concede to. Did they know something? *Perhaps they knew that was the night he'd sneaked into Dario's office?* If Dario had complained about a break-in at his office, he might have even commented that he thought that Isabel and he were behind it. Even if Dario hadn't mentioned any names, the police now might be filling in the gaps themselves.

'But we understand that Dario left that dinner-date in a rush that night,' Lapslie said.

'Yes . . . apparently.' Mauricio tried to maintain a flat, non-committal tone.

'Do you know why that was?'

Mauricio felt suddenly hot. *They must know!* He hoped the flushing didn't show in his face, hoped he didn't sound flustered. 'I . . . I'm not sure. Didn't Dario tell you?'

'Yes, he did. But we wanted to hear your account.'

Again that steady stare straight through him. He ran one hand through his hair. He decided to be economical with the truth rather than openly lie. *After all, he wasn't there at the time!* 'Isabel said simply that he was dragged away in a rush – some text he got on his phone. But she didn't know what.'

'Yes, it was a text Dario received on his phone . . .'

A heavy pause, and Mauricio expected the worst, anticipating the bombshell about the break-in, the heat intense on his face and neck, faintly tingling . . . and so at first the comment about Dario's father didn't fully compute. '*What* was that?' he asked sharply; perhaps *too* sharply.

Lapslie repeated, 'I said it was Gabriel Alarcon texting to remind his son that he had some work to finish urgently that night.'

Mauricio was in a daze after the interview.

He nodded as the waiter brought his *carajillo* – strong black coffee with brandy chaser – and put it on the table. It was late morning, his second coffee of the day, and normally a *carajillo* would be his first coffee of the day, to kick-start the senses, to prepare him for the activity of the day. But after the interview, he felt he needed something stronger, so straight afterwards he'd ambled to the nearest café in San Clemente.

Navarre had nodded his accord, 'Let me know when

you might need me again,' and headed in the opposite direction, towards his car. Mauricio still wasn't sure how useful Navarre was, especially with his obviously limited English; he'd said little throughout the interview.

But the main problems Mauricio now faced were things he couldn't even share with his lawyer, particularly the break-in to Dario Alarcon's office. *How could a lawyer defend something he didn't even know about?* And why hadn't Dario Alarcon mentioned the break-in – instead, openly lying, saying that it was a message from his father about some urgent work? Mentioning the break-in would have highlighted the problems between them, plus also painted himself in a bad light: *if he can involve himself in one criminal activity, then why not another?*

But as he took the first few sips of his *carajillo*, it suddenly struck him why Dario hadn't mentioned the break-in. By that very same virtue of highlighting the problems between them, a reported break-in – particularly one he suspected Isabel was behind – would have then given Dario a strong and apparent motive for getting rid of Isabel.

Mauricio took another sip of his *carajillo*, grimacing as it burned down his throat and exploded its warmth in his stomach. But was Dario avoiding putting the break-in on the table with the police purely because of how he feared it might appear to them, or due to the fact that he was in fact guilty over Isabel, so wanted to avoid any paths which might point to that?

And if Dario *was* guilty, how did the large blond *extranjero* fit into that, who Mauricio knew the police had been actively asking about around town?

22

Isabel, then

The terrible realisation that Dario would know that his office had been broken into and some files downloaded hung over the group of three for a moment.

Then Christina asked, 'So what exactly was in those last two files downloaded? Was it just relating to your mother's past property problems with Dario?'

'Yes, mostly,' Mauricio answered after a moment's thought.

'*Mostly*?' Christina became more insistent, her voice edgy. 'So what else was downloaded in that last minute?'

Mauricio sighed. 'Thinking about my mother made my mind also go back to Isabel's father – his earlier probing and problems. And I noticed two extra files in a folder with his name I'd missed before – so I downloaded those too.'

'How many extra files in total?'

'Only five, no more.' Then with Christina's eyes still on him, starting to shake her head: 'It only took forty seconds – I was still out of there in time.'

'And are you sure you didn't do another file history clean?'

'No, I . . . I don't think I did.'

Christina closed her eyes for a second, took a fresh breath. 'Okay . . . okay. It's done now. Dario will know not only that someone was in his office, but also that it relates to both yourself and Isabel.'

Isabel nodded sombrely. 'Might that now cause a problem?'

'Could do.' Christina shrugged. 'I daresay Dario wouldn't be too worried about getting found out over his property dispute with Mauricio and his mother: *one* property lost would mean little to him. But contesting his inheritance of the majority of Alarcon's properties would be another matter.' She looked at Isabel keenly. 'I would suggest you avoid him for a few days.'

Mauricio nodded. 'He will probably tell the police as soon as he returns from Madrid.'

'Probably. But it's done now.' Christina turned back to her computer, continued scrolling down the files from the flash drive. 'Let's see what else is in this treasure trove of files you got.'

23

Beneyto, then

'And you've located the girl?'

'Yes. She's staying at the local Parador, like you said she would be.'

'Have you actually seen her yet?'

'A couple of times. And one of those she was with a young guy a few years older than her. So, I'll have to choose my times carefully.'

A long silence from the other end, as if the caller had some thoughts and concerns about the mention of her being with a man; but concerns that in the end he decided not to voice.

'Let me know how it goes.'

'I will. You'll be the first to know when it's done.' Brief chuckle from Larry Gilbert. 'In fact, you'll be the only one to ever know about it.'

Javier Beneyto looked up at the other two men across the table as the recording came to an end.

Judge Alvarez had granted a wire tap on all three targets, Danny Blake, Vic Denham and Larry Gilbert, 'Largo'. Beneyto's assistant, Antonio Vidal, had spent the past forty-eight hours with another colleague, Jose Mesquida, monitoring calls on all three. Tiring, monotonous work, the listening vigil had to be 24/7, so they'd taken it in twelve-hour shifts.

'So, that's now only the second call made?' Beneyto confirmed.

Vidal proffered a palm. 'It's only the second call of any substance. There have been a few inconsequential, day-to-day calls from Gilbert in the meantime.'

'And the caller? Could that be Denham's voice?'

'Not sure.' Vidal said. 'Seems a bit deep. But difficult to tell, because I think they're using some masking device to disguise their voice. So, it could be him.'

'And the number they're calling from – that's not Denham's?'

'No. It's from a pay-as-you-go phone we don't have listed. We've picked up the call on Larry Gilbert's phone.'

Beneyto sank into thought for a second. 'Where's the caller phoning from?'

'Cartagena this time, just up the coast from Malaga.'

Beneyto nodded. The first call made had been from

Denia, slightly further up the coast. 'And where's Larry Gilbert taking the call?'

Vidal raised a brow. 'That's the thing. Not his normal stamping ground. He's in a place called Alarcon, mentioned in their first call. A small inland village a couple of hundred miles from Marbella.'

'Where *exactly* is that?'

Jose Mesquida, who had a map up on his laptop commented, 'About halfway between Valencia and Madrid.'

'You said small,' Beneyto addressed Vidal. 'How small is it?'

Again, Mesquida, who had the town stats up alongside his map, interceded. 'Population of only just over two hundred. But apparently tourism is a big thing, so that more than doubles or triples at holiday time and weekends.'

Beneyto sighed. 'No remaining doubt that Gilbert's planning a hit of some kind on this girl mentioned between them. Do you think we should notify someone, issue a warning?'

'Who?' Vidal held a hand out. 'The town's so small, they don't even have a police station. Only a local warden. And we don't have a name for this girl.'

'Yes, you're right.' A heavier sigh from Beneyto after a

second. 'Simply a "girl". Even among that small number it could be anyone.' Then he was suddenly struck with an afterthought. 'The local *Parador* is mentioned. How many guests does that have?'

Mesquida looked up on his laptop. 'They have capacity for thirty-two guests. So, I suppose under normal circumstances half of them could be women.'

Beneyto nodded keenly. 'Sixteen is certainly a more workable number.'

Vidal looked concerned, interjecting after a moment's thought, 'Thing is, if we start fishing around and issuing warnings, Gilbert is going to catch-on that we've got his mobile phone tapped.'

'Yes, you're perfectly right,' Beneyto said, looking down after a second, dejected. He wished now he'd never considered the possibility of saving this girl, whoever she was. Now he was faced with balancing that out against the many other lives lost to the drug gangs they were targeting; the added weight on his shoulders of letting her die to save his operation.

24

Lapslie and Bradbury, now

'Okay, let's see him,' Lapslie said.

A brief burst of Spanish and a nod from Bernardo Ruiz, and one of the four men at his side – Lapslie presumed forensics, he recognised one of them from the Alarcon Castle rock face search – lifted the blue plastic sheet from the body.

Certainly a large man, Lapslie observed, but there appeared to be some body-bloating too. Two-thirds of his face was encrusted with a white, scaly film, only the remaining third recognisable as skin tissue.

'Could be our man, I suppose,' Lapslie remarked.

Jim Thompson, standing to one side, nodded. 'From the description you gave me, I thought so too. Already measured his height, one-nine-two centimetres, just over six-foot-three. And took a blood sample not long before you got here.'

'When will you have the results by?' Lapslie asked.

'If our Spanish partners here have come down with a mobile unit – only an hour or two. Add on another hour or so if we have to go to Denia or Alicante.'

Ruiz spoke again in Spanish with the men at his side, then turned back towards Lapslie and Thompson. '*Si*, yes. They have come with a mobile lab.' He pointed to some dunes three hundred yards along the beach. 'They're parked just over there. Not a big unit, but hopefully it will be sufficient.'

Lapslie nodded. He was unbearably hot. At least in Alarcon he could dive for shade intermittently behind the buildings there, particularly with its narrow streets. Here, it was completely open: a wide stretch of beach, then sand dunes behind. He'd started to feel hot on the drive down, their hire car's air conditioning barely coping, the scenery becoming increasingly barren and desertlike as they headed south from Valencia towards Denia.

Bradbury commented, 'They filmed the old Clint Eastwood spaghetti Westerns not far from here.'

'I can see why,' Lapslie said as the rocky, dusty landscape rolled by punctuated by cacti and whitewashed pueblos.

They finally stopped at a town called Oliva, then followed the signs north to Burguera Beach, stopping by some sand dunes. 'We'll have to walk the rest,' Bradbury informed him. 'This is the closest we can get.'

As he'd opened the car door, it had felt like walking into an oven. By the time they'd trudged over the sand dunes and three hundred yards of beach, Lapslie felt as if he was melting. Jim Thompson had flown into Alicante with his assistant, so had a shorter journey to get here. Lapslie tried to take some comfort in what little breeze there was as he peered out to sea.

'And this is where the body was found?' he enquired.

Ruiz pointed. 'Well, about five miles out, and maybe two miles up the coast from here. It was found by a fishing trawler, then brought in here as simply the nearest safe spot.' Ruiz waggled one hand. 'Some shallow rocks just north of here, and sandbars south. Even a small police launch might have run aground there.'

Lapslie surveyed the seascape again. 'And how do you think the body might have got just off the coast here all the way from Alarcon?'

Ruiz addressed another of the Spanish men, middle-aged with greying sideburns, who nodded and answered in English, 'Yes. I think I'll be okay without assistance with my English. Thank you.' He looked directly at Lapslie, took a step forward. 'Luis Guillen, Oceanographic Institute, señor. Maybe it help if I show you a map.' He folded out the map clutched in his right hand, pointing with one finger. 'See here the River Júcar, spelt Xuquer in Spanish – but sounds with a J in English.'

'Yes, I see it,' Lapslie said.

'See here it comes out on the coast fifty to sixty kilometres north of here.' Guillen traced the finger inland. 'But if we follow the Júcar's path, we see that its origin is just north of Alarcon.' Guillen prodded the finger on the map again.

Bradbury commented. 'So is that the same River Júcar that runs by the castle in Alarcon?'

'Yes, very much so,' Guillen said. He continued tracing a finger along the map. 'Joined later by some minor tributaries. But I understand also there was a heavy storm the night you think your man might have fallen into the river. The run-off from the Júcar combined with those tributaries into the sea at its end would have been quite rapid.'

'And the remaining fifty–sixty kilometres of sea?' Lapslie enquired.

Ruiz commented, 'That's apparently consistent with

sea currents and eddies along this stretch of coast, and the time elapsed.' Obviously, this bit of key information he'd gained from Guillen in advance.

'So, now we await that initial blood test.' Lapslie felt himself wilting with the heat. He turned to Bradbury. 'Hopefully we can find a good air-conditioned bar or restaurant nearby while we wait on that.'

It took them longer to find a shady refuge than they'd hoped. The first couple of bars or restaurants in nearby Oliva Emma Bradbury had poked her head in first, then held one hand up towards Lapslie just behind. A clear *'Not suitable'* signal. The restaurant had been jam-packed, the noise level with voices and background music echoing off the tiled floor at mega-decibel levels.

She knew from past bitter experience that Lapslie would find it unbearable, would develop a headache and feel nauseous within minutes with the different smells and tastes assaulting him from the noise. The second bar-restaurant wasn't much better, a TV blaring out a live football match with various patrons shouting protests at missed opportunities or referee decisions.

She found herself often like an usher, checking noise levels in public places before giving Lapslie the nod.

Although a decided ailment with numerous drawbacks, synaesthesia also had some benefits. The comments and tone of voice of suspects would give rise to distinctive tastes and smells in Lapslie's throat and sinuses, which in many cases would indicate whether they were lying or covering up information. *Proof* was another matter, but at least that initial indicator would often put Lapslie on the right path whereas other detectives might get sidetracked or misled.

Bradbury was sure that without that 'edge', the Cheltenham force's hierarchy would have got rid of Mark Lapslie years ago. Not least because his ailment, his synaesthesia, would often make him abrasive and short-tempered with colleagues and assistants; he didn't suffer fools easily and his people-handling skills were virtually nil. She'd often find herself making excuses for him or interjecting to calm the waters in fraught confrontations. In a way, it made for a strange bond between them. She understood him better than anyone else, all his faults and foibles, and so that made her indispensable: the assistant he could never get rid of, although at times he'd been so insufferable that she'd felt like walking. But then she'd put herself in his shoes; how all those strange tastes and smells assaulting him must grate on his nerves. Personally, it would drive her mad, have her on the edge of screaming in no time. On days when she had a migraine, she'd be insufferable too, edgy, snappy and bitchy with workmates; and Lapslie's ailment was ten times worse than that and he had to live with it around the clock.

She wondered how he could possibly cope. And like someone going to the aid of a cripple they'd watched suddenly stumble and fall to the ground, she'd quickly forgive him and be at his side offering the mental support to get him back on his feet.

Bradbury swung the door open to the third restaurant. Half-full, a tiled floor as well, but she spotted a spare table in the corner with tapestry rugs on the wall which partly absorbed the echoing voices.

'This one looks good,' she said.

Lapslie was enjoying his gazpacho. Not usually a fan of cold soup, in this climate he could see why the cold cucumber soup with its onion and pepper bite made sense. Within ten minutes, combined with the air conditioning in the restaurant, he felt his body-heat settle back down. Equilibrium restored. The past couple of hours, he'd hardly been able to think straight with the intense heat.

'How's yours?' Bradbury enquired. They were both having the same main course of grilled hake.

'Good, but a little dry.' Last time he'd had hake in Spain, it had been in a top seafood restaurant and baked in rock salt, so he was probably somewhat spoilt on that front.

Jim Thompson's call came through when he was halfway through his *Crema Catalana*, the Spanish version of crème brûlée.

'Looks like we might have a match.'

'*What?*' Lapslie was astounded. 'Lutheran B-negative?'

'The same. I ran it through twice, just in case.'

'What are the odds on that?'

'Lutheran B-negative is found in only one in a thousand people. But combine that with the fact that this is the only body to have been washed out to sea in the past week, and its direct eddy-current flow from the mouth of the River Júcar – then you have multiple-odds factors. Probably pushes it up in the hundred-thousand to one region or more.'

'So not quite DNA-stat odds then?' The main odds quoted that Lapslie knew would stand up with the CPS or in Court.

'No, but getting close.'

'Might it be worth getting the girl who saw this "large man" the other night in for a visual ID of the body?' Lapslie asked. 'To try and clinch it?'

'Possibly.' Thompson sighed faintly his end. 'But his face is a mess right now, and I'm not sure what their facial reconstruction units are like down here. I'll come back to you on that one.'

'Thanks, Jim. I think I owe you another bottle of Heine on this one.' Lapslie chuckled lightly. 'Let me know.'

Bradbury was looking at him keenly as he hung up. 'Looks like it might have been a game-changer after all.'

'Yes, it certainly does.'

When the call had initially come through from Ruiz that a body had been found – just two hours after their last interview with Mauricio Reynes, and with their focus still very much on a likely love-triangle battle between Dario and Mauricio over Isabel – Lapslie had commented that if the body's blood sample matched that found on the rocks by Alarcon Castle, it *'Could be a major game-changer.'*

Both of them were aware that the O-sample match wouldn't be significant, because it could match numerous people – but a Lutheran B-negative match was another matter.

'Starting to look more unlikely that it's conflict-related between Dario and Mauricio,' Bradbury commented, 'Whether over Isabel as a love-interest or this fraught ancestral-search Mauricio has raised.'

'Yes, seems that way,' Lapslie said, his thoughts still slightly lost.

'And a Vic Denham hitman – the possible link that brought us down here in the first place – starts to look more likely. Especially with Terry Haines having also described a "large man" in that attempted assault on his Marbella villa,' Bradbury added.

'Yes, it does.' Lapslie sat up, breaking himself out of his contemplative lethargy. Perhaps the heat was still affecting him. 'Still a fair few shades to fill in though on that front: the how, where and when of it tying into Denham. And also why he appears to have gone over the edge with his victim.' Lapslie took out his mobile phone. 'But it's probably enough to buy us a few more days with Rouse.' He smiled tautly as it started ringing.

25

Isabel, then

Mauricio looked over from reading on the computer screen. 'I think part of the answer of why Dario wanted to cover up Magdalena returning to Alarcon is here.' He clicked to print the file.

Isabel and Christina looked at him expectantly.

'. . . It appears she was tried in Court two years later for "spreading dangerous and subversive" tales.'

As the pages came out of the printer, he passed them to Isabel and Christina; he'd printed two sets, one for each. He left them in silence for a moment to read. Christina was first to hit the main body of the file.

'. . . She was finally found insane, committed to an asylum near Madrid.'

Mauricio held a palm out. 'So Dario completely skips the period that Magdalena was back in Alarcon, wipes it from the record.'

Isabel's brow knitted. 'Could he have been covering up her insanity – perhaps wanting to avoid the embarrassment of it?'

Mauricio smiled ironically. 'That doesn't sound like the Dario I know. Also, we see it's the town elders – his direct ancestors – who ordered that committal. No, I think it's more to cover up these tales she was spreading.'

Christina nodded eagerly as she reached a key point in the file. 'Yes, very much looks that way. Because it says here that not only are these tales spread by her "unacceptable and have no substance" – they are also "damaging to the rightful heirs of Alarcon, by their very nature anarchic".'

'It looks like she started digging up and talking about the old Isabella–Joaquim connection rumours,' Mauricio said. 'So, they needed to keep her quiet.'

Isabel nodded slowly. 'Do you think they kept her in the insane asylum long?'

Mauricio looked back at the file. 'There's no mention of it here, nor in fact any direct mention of her talking about Joaquim Alarcon.' Mauricio smiled grimly. 'But knowing Dario Alarcon and his family, I daresay they threw away the key.'

The portent of that comment – the lengths the Alarcon family might go to in order to bury any possible alternative heirs – hung over them for a moment, then, breaking the mood, Isabel asked if anyone else wanted another coffee. 'I'm grabbing one myself.'

Mauricio said yes but Christina shook her head. 'I already had a cup before you arrived, thanks.'

They'd started going through the files early, just after 8 a.m., because Mauricio had a bus-driving shift starting at midday, finishing at eight, just an hour before he was due to meet Isabel again that night. They'd put on a bit of a display at the hotel bar about meeting up again that night, giving the impression that they wouldn't be seeing each other in between; the last thing they wanted to hint at was that the three of them were now putting in an intensive four hours going through Dario Alarcon's lifted files.

Mauricio appeared thoughtful when five minutes later she walked back in with the two cups. He leaned closer to the screen as he took his first sip.

'Appears we're not the only ones to have picked up on the missing link with Magdalena.' He looked towards Isabel. 'Looks like your father was enquiring about that years back when he was here.'

'Which files are those?' Christina asked.

'Seb-Al 12. Eight letters in total back and forth between Gabriel Alarcon and Isabel's father, Sebastian.'

'When was that?' Isabel asked.

Mauricio was absorbed for a moment again reading. 'Ah, September, 2009.'

Isabel felt a twinge of apprehension. 'That's just two months before my father died. From those letters, was there any resolution reached – or did they just stonewall my father? Feed him the same nonsense regarding Magdalena that Dario has fed us?'

Mauricio and Christina were lost for a moment in reading through the letters. Christina was the first to speak.

'Not a complete denial, stonewalling as you call it – but in letter seven, the last but one sent, Gabriel Alarcon comments, "We don't know why the records in Madrid should differ to ours here in Alarcon. Possibly some files misplaced or misrecorded either there or here. After all, it is some time ago. But if you wish to pursue the matter further, we do know of a British historian and researcher who has spent much time studying Alarcon's history, so he may be able to help. We can refer you to him, if you wish?"'

'And is that referral eventually made?' Isabel asked. 'Did they pass on the name and address of this historian in England?'

'Yes, they did,' Mauricio said after a quick glance at his watch. He had to leave in half an hour to catch his shift. 'It's in the last letter Gabriel Alarcon sent to your father. An Arthur Maitland and an address in a place called Challock, Kent.'

Isabel nodded. *Challock, Kent*? Something struck her as familiar about that, but she couldn't immediately fathom what. At least they hadn't completely blocked her father. They'd offered him a possible lead to find out more about their family's ancestors.

26

Lapslie and Bradbury, now

'Yes, I know him,' Terry Haines said after a keen study of the photo handed him by Lapslie. 'Or, rather, I know that *face*. I know him as Larry Gilbert, not this something-Mercer you mentioned.'

'Tobias Mercer.'

'Yeah, Tobias . . . Toby, either one.' Terry Haines shook his head. 'He was known to me and everyone in the Marbella neck of the woods as Larry Gilbert . . . *Largo* for short.'

Lapslie raised a brow. Sounded like a criminal fraternity nickname. 'Someone of notoriety?'

'You could say.' Terry shrugged. 'Not the sort of guy to get the wrong side of.'

Lapslie nodded. They'd got an enhanced blow-up from the passport photo-page left with the Hotel Miramar for Tobias Mercer, and sent a scanned copy through to Jim Thompson who at that moment was in Madrid at one of the best forensic-facial reconstruction units. 'They're only halfway through the process,' Thompson commented, 'but I think there's already enough in place to confirm, yes, that's him.'

Then they'd shown the photo to Luciana, the cleaner from the Parador, and asked her if that was the 'large man' she'd seen that night watching Isabel. It took a second for her to match the image in her mind, but then she was quite firm in her confirmation, repeating twice, '*Seguro*,' when Lapslie had pressed whether she was sure. Now this added to the link from Terry Haines.

'Is he somehow connected with Isabel's disappearance?' Barbara Haines asked. She'd sat quietly for the most part, but sat forward more keenly as she saw her husband's reaction to the photo.

'Could be,' Lapslie said. 'The truth is, we're not totally sure yet. We've had a sighting of him in Alarcon, and a few loose ends which make no sense – until we can tie them together, that is.' He took a fresh breath, looked back at Terry Haines. 'So perhaps we can start with where, when and how you know this Larry Gilbert, *Largo*?'

Terry Haines's eyes drifted for a second, as if there was a barrier he was still crossing by talking about fellow criminals, *grassing*, to the police. Before resolving that this involved the disappearance and possible murder of his goddaughter; *this was different.*

'Larry was part of the old school of villains who came to Marbella in the late seventies. Or, rather, his dad Freddie Gilbert was, who hightailed it out here on the back of a big bank robbery for which it looked like he was prime suspect and about to be collared.'

'What, *the* Freddie Gilbert?' Bradbury asked. Even though it had been before her time, the name Freddie Gilbert had gone down in London criminal folklore, along with the Krays and the Richardsons. Probably brought home to her personally all the more because she'd heard her partner Dom waxing lyrical about Freddie Gilbert on many an occasion.

'The same,' Terry said flatly; no need to dress up or glorify, and trying to diminish the name and its con-nected 'rep' would probably be equally futile. 'Larry was the product of a cute Spanish waitress Freddie shacked up with not long after his wife left him, clearing out half of one of his secret Marbella bank accounts at the same time.' Terry smiled. 'I recall him lamenting to me at the time, "There's no fucking honesty left in the world".'

Lapslie faintly mirrored his smile. 'Perhaps he was being ironic.'

'Freddie didn't do irony that well. But, trouble is, you never knew with him. Certainly, the comment tickled me.'

'You were close at the time?'

'Yeah, we were.' Terry sighed. 'We drifted apart a bit later, didn't exactly see eye to eye.'

Lapslie raised a sharp brow. 'Enough for his son, Larry, to join forces with Vic Denham in targeting your daughter?'

'No, no . . . nothing on that level.' Terry shook his head resolutely. 'Freddie too had drifted into drug dealing, which he knew I didn't agree with – but we certainly weren't daggers-drawn like it was between me and Vic. But his son, Larry, was a different matter.'

'In what way?'

'Not with me directly.' Terry held a hand out, wiggling it. 'More with his father. He fell out with his father and went his own way in his early twenties. But as the old saying goes – the apple doesn't fall far from the tree. Within no time, he was dealing himself, then became an enforcer for some drug gangs. He was found particularly proficient at taking people out, and two years later he'd gone freelance as a gun for hire.'

'... Of the sort that Vic Denham might have hired?'

'Yes. Highly possible. Vic wouldn't have been keen on using his own crew because of the direct link back. Using Larry Gilbert leaves that question open.'

Lapslie sank into thought for a second. 'At our last meeting, you mentioned that the man who made the attempted assault on your old villa in Marbella was "large". Could that have possibly been Larry Gilbert?'

'Yes, I suppose it could have been.' Terry glanced briefly to one side. *Unsure, or suddenly on less comfortable ground in directly ratting?* 'But, like I said before, I didn't get a good look at him.'

Bradbury made a brief note, then asked, 'And might Larry have known about your past friendship and association with his father?'

'I doubt it. It was so long ago, he was only just born then.' Terry shrugged. 'Even if he did, it would have made little difference. He hated his father.'

'Looks like another notch on your belt to support the Vic Denham theory for your next call to Rouse,' Bradbury said as they pulled away from the gatehouse to the Cruz de la Gracia estate.

'Yes, certainly does,' Lapslie agreed. 'But still a fair few loose ends to tie up, things that don't quite make sense.'

As they'd finished their meeting with Terry and Barbara Haines, Lapslie had explained about the two blood groups being found, and one of those almost certainly belonging to Larry Gilbert aka Tobias Mercer, 'Along with his body now also being found washed out to sea.'

'And the other blood group?' Barbara Haines had enquired.

'No likely match to that, because it's so common,' Lapslie answered. 'And it's apparently too degraded for us to get DNA.'

'And any other body found?' Terry asked.

'No, none as yet. Larry Gilbert was the only one we can be sure went fully over the edge – not only because of his body being found off the coast, but his blood group was also quite rare and was the only group found on the lower rocks in Alarcon, close to the river.'

'Good on Isabel!' Terry Haines had half-punched the air. 'She gave the bastard some stick – gave as good as she got.' Then he became more subdued, morose again, after the look his wife shot him. The cloak of Isabel's possible death quickly hung over them again.

'We'll let you know, of course, the moment we know more.'

Bradbury looked up at the road sign ahead, then took the next turn off onto the A-3 out of Valencia. She took a fresh breath.

'I suppose one of those loose ends that doesn't quite make sense is how someone as small as Isabel managed to push a heavyweight lug like Larry Gilbert over that precipice.'

'Yes. And also why Larry Gilbert was seen picking up his own luggage from the Miramar Hotel the morning *after* he apparently died.'

27

Isabel, then

Isabel was frantic.

Four hours after the intense morning session with Mauricio and Christina, it had suddenly hit her why *Challock* had struck a chord.

I can't take your call right now. Leave a message and I'll phone you back. Hasta luego.

Isabel ended the call, didn't leave a message. Second time in half an hour she'd tried and got the same recorded message from Mauricio's phone. The only message she'd left then had been: 'There's something I suddenly recalled after our meeting this morning. Something important. Call me back.'

She hadn't wanted to elaborate beyond that – the details of what she had to share were too sensitive to leave on an open message – and she'd left that first message in English to reduce the chances of a listener knowing what it was about if they did hear it.

Isabel tapped her fingers on the bed, her phone to one side. She'd planned to go down to the hotel bar for tea and a snack, but this wasn't the sort of conversation she wanted to have with anyone listening in.

Another round of finger drumming, and she decided to order something from room service.

Twelve minutes later, a knock came on her door, and just as the waiter put down her tray with tea and a club sandwich, her mobile started ringing.

'Yes, thank you . . . I'd better get this.' She ushered the waiter out, answering her phone as he was still a pace away from the door, concerned that she might not catch it in time. 'Mauricio, *thank goodness* . . .' Brief pause as she waited for the door to shut. 'I couldn't talk straight away, but it's okay now.'

'I haven't got long, either,' Mauricio said. 'I'm still in the middle of a work shift. A three-minute stop here in Tarancón for passengers, then I head off again. What's the urgency?'

'I suddenly recalled why Challock, where this Arthur Maitland lives, rings a bell.' No response the other end, so she prompted, 'You know, that historian and researcher recommended to my father by Gabriel Alarcon.'

'Yes, I remember. Somewhere in Kent.'

'Well, Challock is just off of the A252 in Kent. And it was only four miles from Challock, on the road to Canterbury, that my father was killed in his car accident.'

Slow exhalation Mauricio's end. 'What? You think it's somehow connected?'

'Yes, could be. I mean, my father died only two months after this correspondence with Gabriel Alarcon, and only a few miles away from a man they recommended to him.'

'You think your father was on his way to see this Arthur Maitland when it happened?'

'Could well be. After all, they'd have known my father was planning to see him. All that would have been needed then was a brief follow-up from Gabriel Alarcon: We made a recommendation to a Sebastian Alarcon to see you regarding the history of Alarcon. Hope you don't mind. Then a response from Arthur Maitland: Yes, as it happens Sebastian Alarcon is planning to come and see me at two next Thursday afternoon.'

'So, Gabriel Alarcon would have known precisely where your father was at a given time that day?'

'Exactly.'

Mauricio's breath seemed to catch momentarily at his end, as if this next thought was a step too far. 'You're thinking that maybe your father's death wasn't an accident after all?'

'Yes, I am. If that had been suggested to me a few days ago, I wouldn't have believed it. But now seeing all this skulduggery with Dario and Gabriel and their ancestors – committing Magdalena to an insane asylum, robbing your mother – I wouldn't put it past them.'

Mauricio in turn sighed in acceptance. 'Thing is, how will we ever know or find out?'

'I know.' Isabel lapsed into thought. The police had it down firmly as an accident, and it was so many years ago now. 'But I think I know someone who might be able to help with this. An old friend of mine, Melanie Taylor.'

'Is she with the police?'

'No.' Isabel chuckled lightly at the thought. 'But she's the type that this sort of sleuthing would appeal to – it's right up her alley.'

'*Sleuthing*?'

'Yeah, you know: investigative work, digging down to find the truth.' Isabel was again reminded that Mauricio's English had its limits. Suddenly, she could hear increased noise his end.

'Got to go,' Mauricio said. 'Last passengers are getting on now. Tell me more about it tonight when we meet up.'

'Yeah, okay. Nine o'clock, Café Marie.'

28

Lapslie and Bradbury, now

'This is nice,' Charlotte said, looking around the restaurant after her first few mouthfuls.

'So, the pheasant's good?' Lapslie asked.

Charlotte wiggled one hand. 'Pretty good. I meant the whole package: the centuries-old castle, the rough stone walls and old beams.' She took a quick survey around, raised her glass of red wine at him. 'And the company. Especially given the fact that I haven't seen you for over two weeks now.'

Lapslie nodded, grimacing as he sat opposite his partner of the past few years, Charlotte. They hadn't got around to living together, and their hectic schedules – hers as a hospital physician and his unforgiving police roster – often squeezed out the little quality time they could theoretically spend together. He'd planned to see her this weekend, but it looked like he might still have a busy Monday and Tuesday wrapping up loose ends in Alarcon – so rather than fly back and out again, he'd offered to send Charlotte a ticket to come out. *You'll enjoy it. It's a complete change of atmosphere. Like Windsor Castle on the edge of a mini Grand Canyon.'*

And his hunch had paid off. After a quick tour of the town, on the edge of the castle rampart with its dramatic view over the river gorge and hills beyond, not far from where they suspected Isabel Alarcon and Larry Gilbert had gone over the edge, although he didn't mention that detail – *didn't want to start on a dampener* – Charlotte had given him a hug. *'You're right, it's beautiful, in a stark, dramatic sort of way. Thanks for asking me.'*

'I thought you might like the pheasant,' Lapslie said. 'Because apparently they're reared locally. One of the chef's recommendations.'

'So, he might have been the pheasant plucker as well?'

'Yes, he does seem a nice chap, now you come to mention it.'

Charlotte laughed. Then, after they discussed plans for the next day – a quick trip to Madrid and the Prado and back to Alarcon in time for dinner – she asked, 'How much longer will you be here?'

'Two or three days more, that should wrap it up.' He

went on to explain that he'd have probably had things already wrapped by now, 'But a key witness is away right now.'

When he'd gone back to the Miramar to ask Sara how Tobias Mercer, aka Larry Gilbert, had picked up his own luggage that morning when it appeared he'd died the night before, her mother, Amparo, informed him that Sara was away on a four-day hoteliers training course, back late Monday. He'd wondered whether Sara was on a real course or whether it was just an invention to avoid being questioned again. The problem with the town was that it was so small, Chinese whispers spread quickly. Or it might be that suspicion had arisen from it being the only thing he'd asked Sara about, Larry Gilbert personally picking up his luggage. Everything else had been discussed with her mother.

'So that's the only thing now holding you up?' Charlotte enquired.

Lapslie shrugged. 'Well, that and a couple of other loose ends – including the fact that we haven't found one of the bodies yet.'

Charlotte's brow creased. 'I thought it was just a singular disappearance or murder enquiry.'

'Yes, it started out as such. But now it appears as if

we might have ended up with *two* victims. It looks like the hitman sent to get her went over the edge at the same time. It was his body we found washed up off the coast the other day.'

'Good for her! She put up a fight.'

'Pretty much what her godfather said.'

'And where did this happen? Where did they go over?'

'Not far from where we were looking out at the view from the castle ramparts earlier.'

Charlotte smiled. 'I always knew you were a hopeless romantic.'

Talking about the ramparts reminded Lapslie. 'Before we head off tomorrow, remind me to show you my favourite spot in town. Might remind you of when we go off sailing.'

'So, can we expect to get hit with a force ten gale?'

Lapslie returned Charlotte's smile wryly. On one of their first times out sailing, they'd got caught in a heavy storm. 'Hopefully not. I was thinking more of the peace and solitude.'

Charlotte nodded. 'And where's Emma this weekend?'

'Flown back to England to be with her partner, Dom. If she spent too long away, he might start thinking she's got another man.' Lapslie could have added '*again*' to that sentence, given Emma's past run-ins with Dom on that front; but that was one confidence he hadn't shared with anyone, including Charlotte.

Charlotte took another sip of wine as she finished her pheasant, pensive for a moment. 'Are you still hopeful of finding this Isabel's body?'

'Maybe not so much now with the time that's passed. It could have been swept even further out to sea or dragged under.'

Charlotte held a hand out. 'Also, could be that she's still alive?'

'Doubtful. She'd have surfaced or been in touch with someone by now. And we've got her blood group right by the blood of this hitman whose body we've found, who is far larger and stronger than her.'

'And the other loose ends you mentioned?'

'The main one will be linking that hitman to Vic Denham. Denham will likely have covered his tracks well – which is no doubt why he hired an independent hitman. And the normal route back of the hitman himself spilling the beans on a plea-deal now can't happen.' Lapslie sighed. 'So that too might end up like the body that hasn't been found – a loose end that won't get answered. A mystery.'

29

Isabel, then

'How much longer did you say you'd be staying there?'

'Two or three days more, then I'll head off to Madrid.'

'So, when do you think you'll be back home then?'

'Ten days, no more. I should be no more than seven or eight days in Madrid.'

'And you'll call us when you get to Madrid?'

'Yes, I will.' Isabel glanced at her watch on the bedside table. She was going to be late meeting Mauricio. She'd just come out of the shower and was halfway through drying her hair when her mobile rang: her godmother, Barbara, asking how she was getting on. Barbara was lovely, salt of the earth, very caring – but she did have this uncanny knack of calling at the worst possible time and rambling on.

'I didn't think there was much to see in Alarcon,' Barbara said.

'No, there's not. It is a very small town. But there's a lot of family history to catch up on, and I've been lucky enough to find a good local guide – Mauricio.'

'Is he nice?'

Had her tone given away that she felt some affection for Mauricio? *Or was it just something that mothers and stepmoms instinctively picked up on?*

'Not bad ... not bad.'

'What does he do?'

One of those generational things, Isabel thought. Someone her own age group wouldn't have bothered to ask, they'd have stayed in 'hunk' territory: physique, colour of eyes, etc. Perhaps with Terry forging his way out of the East End through robbing banks, money was important; they didn't want to see her back there courtesy of a new partner. 'Well, he's manager in a tour company,' she lied, keen to avoid the *'are you sure he's right for you?'* conversation that might follow the revelation that he was a bus driver.

'Probably why he's such a good guide,' Barbara said.

'Yes, probably.' Isabel couldn't resist a smile.

'Oh, Terry's just back in. Golf with mates, and as usual he's spent too long at the nineteenth hole. I'll put him on in a sec.'

'No, no . . . it's okay. I'm meeting Mauricio for dinner, and I'm already late as it is.'

'Okay. I'll give Terry the message – you can chat to him another time. Won't hold you up any longer.'

'Speak again tomorrow . . . must fly!'

'Yes. And you have a nice dinner with this Mauricio. Give him our regards.'

'Speak again tomorrow . . . must fly!'

'Yes. And you have a nice dinner with this Mauricio. Give him our regards.'

Larry Gilbert switched off the signal tracker as the call ended. He looked keenly towards the hotel entrance from his car, parked second-row back in the car park.

At least he could be sure now she was still in the hotel, and from the sound of it she'd be leaving any minute. He looked around. It had been dark for well over an hour, and there was only faint moonlight. Nobody nearby in the car park, as far as he could see. The ideal conditions – as long as nobody else was heading out of the hotel at the same time as her, or this Mauricio wasn't planning to meet her at the hotel. That would then entail taking *both* of them out at the same time, which hadn't been part of the plan – or he'd have to simply bide his time until later. *As he had been doing the past two days.*

Headlamps approaching from behind! His nerves were on edge as the light swung over his car, and then the approaching car pulled in on the far side of the car park. He watched as a middle-aged couple got out and walked towards the hotel, Larry praying that Isábel didn't appear at this moment.

A quick release of breath as the couple went from view in the entrance, then almost instantly he was impatient again, starting to drum his fingers on the steering wheel. Almost five minutes since her phone call. *Thought she said she was already late!*

But as she did finally appear, he was caught unawares. She emerged swiftly, at a half-run – he was suddenly unsure he'd be able to cut her off as he'd planned.

Out of his car, no time even to press the remote lock, he rapidly built up to a run too. The girl spotted him as he was halfway across the dark car park, but at first she appeared to think he was running for the hotel entrance.

It was only at the last moment, as she realised the angle of his run was slightly off – combined no doubt with his eyes fixing intently on her – that she faltered slightly in her run, her breath half-catching.

Larry would be upon her any second, and the rest was mapped out clearly in his mind: he'd hit her body with a mid-section rugby tackle, taking the rest of her breath away as he stooped and then fireman-lifted her over one shoulder.

She was less than half his weight, the lift would be easy, his step hardly faltering before he was back to a half-run headed towards the side-rampart and the sheer drop to the gorge below. He'd feel her writhing and her hands flailing at his back, her scream garbled and weak with her breath still robbed from the heavy winding as he'd struck her – but none of it would serve any purpose. He'd have her gripped too tight as they approached the edge.

His expression dropped as she turned sharply and started running away. But then quickly lifted again as he realised she was running towards where he'd hoped to carry her anyway – towards the rampart edge and the gorge below. Less distance to carry her! And he had the benefit of momentum as she'd only started to run. He'd catch up with her within the next few long strides.

30

Lapslie and Bradbury, now

'So, you're saying now that you're not a hundred percent sure it was this Tobias Mercer picking up his luggage that morning?' Lapslie said.

Sara looked at her mother for a moment uncertainly, and Lapslie wasn't sure if it was because her English was weaker and she was waiting for her mother, Amparo, to clarify, or simply that she was nervous of saying the wrong thing in front her mother.

'I suppose it couldn't have been,' Sara said finally, 'with what you've told me now.'

'But you said before that it was him.'

'Yes, be . . . because I thought at first it was him.' Sara became more hesitant, shrugged. 'But maybe it was a friend of his.'

'Didn't you ask for any identification?'

'No, I didn't.' Sara chewed at her lip, another nervous

glance towards her mother. 'Because I thought initially it was him.'

Lapslie sighed, glanced towards Bradbury at his side in the small office making notes on her laptop. 'So, did you get a good look at him? Could you give a description?'

'No, that's the problem.' She looked down for a second. 'He came in so quickly, said he'd come to pick up the luggage left the night before. I was on the phone to someone else at the time, so I just opened the office door and pointed him towards it.'

Lapslie nodded. 'But you got enough of a look at him to think it might be either him or a friend. So, a big man was he?'

'Yes, quite big.'

Lapslie's brow knitted. 'But you weren't able to differentiate whether it was this Tobias Mercer or a friend?'

Sara looked at her mum, said something briefly in Spanish, though Lapslie picked out the word 'differentiate'.

'*Diferenciar,*' Amparo translated.

'No, I'm afraid not.' Amparo shook her head. 'Mr Mercer used to deal mostly with my mother. That was the other problem. I saw him only briefly once or twice.'

'So why did you say that you were sure it was him

first time we asked?' Lapslie said. 'Why didn't you just say you weren't sure?'

Sara glanced briefly towards her mother again before looking back directly at Lapslie. 'Because I was afraid of getting into trouble for letting his luggage go to someone I shouldn't have.'

'What do you think?' Bradbury asked as they walked from the Hotel Miramar and into the nearby Place Marie.

'I certainly think she's covering up something, but *what*?' Lapslie glanced towards the archway at the end and the castle, visible in the distance, as if for inspiration. 'It probably is a friend or associate picking up his luggage – who else would bother to pick it up? Standard cover-up op. They know the hit's gone wrong, so an associate swings by to pick up his things and bury all traces.'

Bradbury nodded. 'Question then is: how did that associate pick up so quickly on it going wrong?'

'Maybe there was some regular phone-in arrangement between them.' Lapslie sighed. 'Though we'll still be left with the question of just *who* that associate is.'

'Yes, and we probably won't get far pursuing that route. With them already knowing that things had gone wrong, they'd have been super careful to bury all possible traces.'

Lapslie grimaced. 'Probably why they made sure to pick up the luggage when Amparo was out. They guessed, and rightly so, that the daughter wouldn't be so officious or observant.' Lapslie was suddenly struck with another thought. 'But sometimes playing odds like that can wear thin. I daresay Larry aka Tobias would have hired a car to get here. Having used false identity papers and passport, he wouldn't have used his own car.'

'He could have stolen one.'

'Too risky. If it got traced before he's done the hit, the game would have been up. No, with him having false papers, he'd have used those for the hire car also – and that car would have to have been dropped off, probably by the same person who picked up his luggage.'

'Unless his car's still here,' Bradbury ventured.

'Unlikely. Why go to the trouble of picking up the luggage, then leave the other loose end of the car hanging?' Lapslie looked tellingly at Emma. 'And his car hire company might have a better description of who dropped the car off.'

31

Isabel, then

Isabel was desperate, her breath catching in her throat. She was a good runner, but the man was tall and heavy-set, his stride far longer. And he was in full flight, whereas she'd only just started her run. *He'd be upon her any second!* She put on an extra spurt . . .

. . . And suddenly she was running along Southend pier with her best friend, Melanie. They'd met at Southend High in their first year there, and within a few months had become firm friends, the two of them inseparable.

They'd go everywhere in town together after school, the shops, beach, the pier, the fair – rollercoasters, dodgem cars, candy floss or ice cream – or sometimes would just idly watch the fishermen along the pier.

They normally walked the mile-distance towards its end, had only caught the small tourist train a couple of times. But one day as the train had trundled past them, Melanie had suggested they race it.

'Come on, it'll be fun', she urged, sensing Isabel's initial reluctance.

'Okay,' Isabel said finally. 'But we should start our run at the beginning as the train sets out, otherwise it won't count for much. Won't be a proper race.'

'Okay.'

They'd been barely twelve years old when they'd done their first run against the train, and they were hopelessly short. The train beat them to the end by a good eighty yards.

But each time they improved a bit, closed that gap to sixty yards, forty, twenty . . . and by the time they were thirteen, they were matching it, coming in breathlessly either a few yards short or ahead of it.

Six months later, they were beating the train by ten or twenty yards, and by the time they were fourteen, they were fifty or sixty yards clear, coasting easily that last stretch, smiling and waving to the passengers on the train . . .

But Isabel wondered now if that flashback was to remind herself that she was good at running, or a version of *life-flashing-before-your-eyes* as the man bore down on her.

If only she'd got a couple more yards head start, had been able to build up some momentum.

He hit her mid-section solidly, took her breath away, scooping her up as if she was weightless. Then lifted her high, hardly pausing as he continued his run.

Isabel tried to shout and scream, but she found it hard to draw breath, let alone call out with any strength. The man was clutching her so hard, obviously afraid that she might wriggle loose, but the main effect was to squeeze the last breath from her . . . her own voice sounding strangely weak and distant, disembodied, and barely audible even to herself above the heavy buzzing in her ears with the sudden blood rush to her head.

Her view spun and swayed: the cobbled path, the stone-wall side of the Parador, the low rampart wall and the gorge beyond. *Oh God, she'd even run part of the way towards where he was headed, she'd made his journey easier!*

She flailed and punched at the man's back, writhing and kicking now too. But he seemed impervious, like a rock, the rampart wall approaching closer in her jolting vision, the view over the gorge widening, seeming to fill her vision, drawing her in and down . . .

She managed to draw breath to scream louder then,

but the wind rising up from the gorge and the rush of the river below seemed to drown it out.

And as they came up to the edge and the man lifted her from his shoulder like a rag doll – so that all that filled her vision was the drop into the gorge below – she found herself doing the opposite: trying to claw and clutch onto him for dear life rather than writhe and flail free.

She clutched one hand onto his hair, the other on his shirt. But as she felt him tense to throw her, she feared it wouldn't be enough. *Not nearly enough.*

Mauricio looked at his watch: *eight minutes late already.* He'd tried Isabel's number just before leaving for the square and Café Marie, but it had gone into message. Either she was on the phone to someone else or in the last minutes of getting ready.

He wondered whether to try again, but as he looked towards the floodlit castle two hundred yards away, there was little point. Walking fast, he'd be there in a couple of minutes, and if she'd already left he'd meet her halfway.

He signalled to Ignacio that he'd left the money for his coffee on the table, and headed off.

At first, the castle and hotel were just a solid blaze of light beyond the darker stretch at the end of town, and he couldn't pick out any shapes clearly amongst it.

When he did finally pick something out, he wasn't sure at first – it didn't fit in with the image pre-set in his mind of Isabel walking from the hotel towards him. But his step did pick up a notch from his already rapid pace, so that now he was almost at a run – eager to get the image of what he thought he'd seen clearer and make some sense of it.

And as those final component parts fell into place, all pretence was lost, he was running towards that strange tableau – a large man with Isabel slumped over one shoulder – at a flat-out sprint.

As he watched in horror, the man lifting Isabel from his shoulder as he approached the edge, Mauricio's first fear was that he wouldn't get there in time to stop Isabel being thrown over. But coming as quickly after, as he closed in on them, was the worry that his momentum would throw them *both* over the edge.

The man only became aware of his approach then, shooting a startled half-glance Mauricio's way as he tensed to throw Isabel over – and Mauricio hit them both solidly, at the same instant grabbing hard onto Isabel to stop her from tumbling over.

The large man flew back with the impact, the low rampart wall providing little barrier – the man tall and top heavy – and, as he realised in horror that he was toppling over the edge, the situation was reversed: he was desperately clutching on to Isabel to stop from falling.

Mauricio felt a terrible wrench to his right arm and shoulder, and then suddenly he was lying prostrate over the rampart wall, desperately hanging onto Isabel the other side of it, her weight in turn multiplied threefold by the large man holding on to her left leg; the only thing stopping him from sailing into the abyss below.

Mauricio knew that he couldn't hold on to her much longer. The combined weight was too tremendous, every muscle and sinew of his body straining and aching for release after only seconds.

'Kick him free with your right foot!' Mauricio screamed. 'I can't hold you any longer!'

Isabel looked down. The man's desperate face by her left calf, clinging on for dear life, but no sense of plea; more like contempt. But if she kicked him free, it was certain death for him; a second's pause, but then as she felt Mauricio's grip slip a few inches on her arm, she realised there was no choice . . . *no choice!*

She kicked out once, *twice*, saw his nose split, his face bloodied . . . and on the third kick, his grip finally released.

But the jolting motion of her kicking out at him also seemed to jerk free Mauricio's last grip of her, and she felt herself sailing into the dark abyss a second after the large man.

32

Lapslie and Bradbury, now

Emma Bradbury ran along the pathway stretching out from the back of the castle ramparts, waving to get Lapslie's attention. His favourite spot now, he'd go out there practically every morning and sometimes at sunset as well. He finally saw her, turned and walked towards her.

'What is it?'

'I've just had Inspector Ruiz on the phone. Something important has come up. He tried getting you, but when you didn't answer, he tried my number.' She was still slightly breathless from the short run, pausing for fresh breath. 'While Ruiz was checking on the Spanish national system for anything on Larry Gilbert or Denham, particularly anything connecting the two, the name of a special drugs unit in Marbella came up. Ruiz got in touch with them, and they said they were in fact about to contact him when they discovered his department was investigating Larry Gilbert's death.'

'Oh, right. And is there any connection to Vic Denham?'

'Very much so, sir. This unit has apparently been monitoring calls between drug gang leaders in Marbella, including Denham. And Gilbert was also included in that monitoring.'

'So, they feel they might have something incriminating on those recordings?'

'It appears so.'

They'd been walking steadily back towards the Parador, Lapslie intense, thoughtful. Obviously thinking this might be the Gilbert–Denham breakthrough they'd been hoping for.

'What does Ruiz suggest to progress this?' Lapslie asked. 'Does he want me to phone him back?'

'You could do, but he'll probably already be in his car. He thought the best thing was a meeting with this Malaga detective, Javier Beneyto. Ruiz is heading from Madrid and Beneyto the other way from Malaga. They're planning to be here in an hour and a half.'

They managed to grab a small conference room at the Parador for the meeting. Inspector Javier Beneyto had come with his colleague, Antonio Vidal, and after introductions all round and coffee and tea brought in by a waiter, Beneyto gestured towards Vidal.

'Perhaps best if we start everything with the first suspect call we received on Larry Gilbert's phone.'

Vidal smiled at the small gathering and clicked an icon on his laptop.

'You've got it clear where she is? Place called Alarcon, halfway to Madrid.'

'Yeah, all clear. But why somewhere so remote?'

'That's where she is right now. Plus it gives us the opportunity not to mess on our own doorstep.'

'I see. And how long's she there for?'

'Five or six days.'

'I should have it all wrapped within two or three days. I'll let you know.'

'Okay. I'll make the first transfer now, as arranged. The rest when the job's completed.'

'Fine. Speak later.'

Lapslie was thoughtful for a second after the recording ended. 'Certainly sounds like someone keen to mask connections to either Marbella or Valencia. But that doesn't sound like Denham's voice.'

'No. It's too deep,' Beneyto concurred.

Vidal elaborated. 'We suspect that it could be Denham – or anyone else for that matter – using a voice-masker which lowers it a tone. Or he's using a go-between.'

'I'm guessing the caller used a pay-as-you-go phone,' Lapslie said. 'If Denham had used a phone registered to his name, we wouldn't be bothering with this speculation now.'

'Yes,' Beneyto answered. 'Paid for in cash just a few days before.'

'And where was the call made from?'

'Denia. Up the coast from Marbella. But Larry Gilbert was using his own phone.'

'And did that trace to Alarcon?'

'Yes, it did.'

Lapslie shook his head after a second. 'With the call-masking and a pay-as-you-go phone, doesn't put us any closer to directly linking Denham to Gilbert and nailing him. As you've said, it could be anyone on that call.'

'Yes, it could,' Beneyto conceded.

In the moment's awkward silence that followed, Lapslie decided to take a step back, fill in some shades. 'So, what made your department think there might be a connection between Denham and Larry Gilbert?'

Beneyto grimaced. 'Not just Denham, but a number

of other drug kingpins in Marbella. We recently raided and arrested one of them, Alan Vaughn, two months ago – but so far we haven't been able to get enough on the other two in our sights: Danny Blake and Vic Denham. And when applying for court orders to monitor their phones, it struck me that it might bear fruit if we also monitored Larry Gilbert's phone.'

Lapslie arched a brow. 'I didn't know Gilbert was involved directly in any drug-trafficking.'

'No, he wasn't. But he's been used as a drugs enforcer by a number of others, including Blake and Gilbert. And we also heard rumours that Gilbert had the habit of recording many hit instructions to save as later insurance policies if he was at any time caught. A plea-bargain tool.'

Lapslie nodded thoughtfully. 'And so when you heard about Gilbert's death, you contacted Inspector Ruiz handling the case.'

Ruiz tightly smiled his accord. 'Well, actually, I tried to contact his team first – but it was restricted access. I didn't know what their interest in the case might be. And then shortly after, Inspector Beneyto called me to explain.'

Vidal interjected, 'In fact, our first sign that something

was amiss was when there were no longer any calls taking place. It wasn't until a few days later that we learned that Larry Gilbert was dead.'

Beneyto looked from Vidal back to Lapslie. 'That time gap aside, we had to be cautious in making contact. To ensure secrecy would be maintained and our ongoing investigation against Blake and Denham wouldn't be jeopardised.'

Lapslie steepled his hands together. 'So, we're a step closer with a loose link between the two, but still nothing solid.'

'Yes, I suppose you could say.' Beneyto took a fresh breath. 'There was in fact a second call recorded – this time from Cartagena, slightly closer to Marbella – but still nothing solid, no firm names betrayed on that call either. Although it does become clear from that conversation that a planned hit was quite imminent.'

Beneyto nodded at Vidal, who clicked the second icon.

Lapslie's face clouded halfway through the brief recording, and as it came to an end he looked sharply at Beneyto.

'This recording makes it quite clear that Gilbert was about to make a hit on a girl in Alarcon. Why weren't the police warned earlier?'

Beneyto held a hand out helplessly. 'But they refer just to a "girl", no names mentioned.'

Lapslie shook his head. 'Alarcon is not at all a big town. And the Parador is mentioned directly. It wouldn't have taken much to narrow it down.'

Beneyto nodded solemnly after a second. 'Don't think I didn't take that into consideration. But apart from the difficulties of narrowing it down, if we'd started fishing around in Alarcon, we'd have endangered our entire operation.'

Lapslie in turn nodded, but his tone was acid. 'As per usual. Operations and "protocol" over lives.' Both Beneyto and Ruiz appeared quizzical, and Lapslie realised that part of that had got lost in translation. 'You do appreciate that Isabel Alarcon has been missing now almost two weeks. Probably killed by Larry Gilbert – who you have here, clearly recorded, planning everything.' Lapslie hooked a thumb towards Vidal's laptop.

Ruiz held a calming hand up. 'Look. This is getting us nowhere, trying to lay blame. And might I remind you that Inspector Beneyto has come forward to offer his help. He could have just stayed silent, kept out of it.' Ruiz looked directly at Lapslie, took a fresh breath.

'So let's see what might be gained from this looking forward, not backward.'

'I'm sorry. I was probably being too hasty,' Lapslie said after a second, catching a *'not for the first time'* half-smile on Emma Bradbury's face. Or perhaps she was just pleasantly surprised to hear him apologise for something. He held a conciliatory hand out. 'So, how might we turn this to the good? Get some positive link to Gilbert that might help nail Denham?'

'One step ahead of you,' Beneyto said with a half-smile; obviously more comfortable now, being on positive ground. 'I've already applied for a court order for a search on Gilbert's apartment in Marbella. I hope to hear back from Judge Alvarez tomorrow.'

33

Melanie and Christina, now

'So, have you managed to find this Arthur Maitland?' Christina asked, on the phone to Isabel's friend Melanie Taylor in England.

'Well, put it this way: I've narrowed it down. He's moved from where he was in Challock last time, and while it's not that common a name, there are actually seven of them in the UK. I've discounted two of them, now I'm working on the other five.'

'Not so surprising that he's moved, I suppose. After all, it was a few years ago now that he was at that address.'

'Six or seven, actually,' Melanie Taylor said. Her sleuthing abilities coming through? Or was she just being pedantic about the exact timing of the last known contact with Arthur Maitland? That had been the first thing agreed that she would pursue on her *sleuthing* checklist: might this Arthur Maitland have some valuable extra information on the family history of the Alarcons?

'Do you think you'll be able to nail him down from those five remaining?' Christina asked.

'I think so. Age narrows it down a bit, and I might get lucky and hit on a last-known-address link.'

'Let's hope so. Good luck with that.'

'After that, I daresay the next step would be making contact with Maitland,' Melanie said. 'Find out what he knows – *if anything.*'

'No. Hold on for the time being. Mauricio just phoned. He's had another meeting with this British Inspector, and it appears they suspect Isabel was a victim of some gangland feud.'

Heavy pause. 'I . . . I don't understand.'

Christina realised that some of this had come up only in the last twenty-four hours, after Melanie had started her tracking of Arthur Maitland. 'This large man has been identified by the police as a hired hitman connected to criminal groups in Marbella. *No* connection to any local families.'

'Oh, I see.'

'So, if and when you've tracked Maitland down, hold off on making final contact with him, until I've spoken to Mauricio again.'

34

Lapslie and Bradbury, now

'Looks like he has delusions of being a Roman emperor,' Emma Bradbury commented as they passed the succession of Roman statues lining the approach to the palatial villa. An automatic iron gate rolled shut behind them.

There were more Roman statues surrounding the pool and terrace area as they looked out from the lounge, but now Vic Denham was with them, so Emma just smiled tightly, with a knowing look directed towards Lapslie.

Now in his mid-seventies, Denham was an almost cartoonish Mr Pickwick shape, a large rotund body on spindly legs; it was difficult to imagine him now kicking anyone to death, as his past reputation suggested he often had done.

Denham gave their warrant cards one last look before handing them back. 'That old dog Rouse still there?'

'Yes, very much so,' Lapslie said. 'He's Chief Inspector now.'

'Give him my regards, will you?' Denham leaned forward with a sly smile. 'That means, "tell him to go fuck himself" in my neck of the woods, by the way.'

'That's okay,' Lapslie said coolly. 'He already asked that I pass you his regards.' Lapslie noticed Bradbury suppressing a smile at the double-meaning, and he noticed too the middle-aged man, by his laptop at the dining table a few yards away, frown at Denham's remark. Denham had introduced him as his lawyer, Miguel Seguero. 'He's here in case you overstep the mark. So hopefully he won't need to pipe up too much.'

Denham looked directly at Lapslie. 'Lapslie? I've heard the name, but I don't recall you. You were probably still in shorts when I was around.'

'Still am in some respects. In fact, brought a pair with me.' He smiled tightly. 'It is rather hot out here.'

Denham drew a tired breath, as if, realising he wasn't going to get far taunting Lapslie, the meeting suddenly held less interest for him. 'So, what is it I can help you with?'

Lapslie passed across a photo of Larry Gilbert from his file. 'I wondered if you know this man?'

Denham studied the photo for a second, passed it to Seguero. 'Yeah, it's Larry Gilbert, nickname *Largo*. He's well-known in the local community here: son of an old pal of mine, Freddie Gilbert.'

'Did you know that Larry worked as a gun for hire, a hitman?'

'I've heard rumours,' Denham said cagily. 'Never used him myself, mind you.' Then, as he caught the look from Seguero. 'Nor *any* hitmen, for that matter.'

Lapslie nodded slowly. 'So, you didn't hire Larry Gilbert for a recent job?'

'No, I didn't,' Denham said flatly. 'Why on earth should I?'

Lapslie stared at Denham steadily with a '*You tell me*' expression. Then after a second, he said, 'Do you recall the threat you made to Terry Haines and his family?'

'In what way? I'm not with you.'

'Terry Haines claims that you thought he was involved in your son's death. And that in turn you made a threat against his family.'

'Yeah, sure. I suspected at the time that Terry was involved – but what could be proved?' He gave a helpless shrug. 'We say these things in moments of heat. But as far as I'm concerned, it's water under the bridge. All forgotten.'

Lapslie looked down for a second before looking back steadily at Denham. 'Also, a couple of months after that threat, Terry Haines mentioned an attempted assault on his old villa in Marbella. Part of the reason he moved to Valencia. And he described the man as "large".' Lapslie took a fresh, strained breath. 'Are you saying that you had nothing to do with that attempted assault?'

Denham sniggered disarmingly, though with a second's pause. 'Of course not.' Then another thought appeared to strike him. 'Did Terry say directly it was Larry Gilbert?'

'Not exactly. But with the rough description, and with the later disappearance and possible murder of Isabel, his goddaughter – certainly everything is pointing that way.' Lapslie fixed his gaze again on Denham. 'Are you claiming that you're not involved in that either?'

Another helpless shrug. 'I didn't even know she was missing.'

'It's been in the news: Isabel Alarcon went missing ten days ago.'

'Oh, right. Seem to remember something now ... *Alarcon*. That's what threw me. With the name, I didn't make the connection to Terry. You're saying that's his goddaughter?'

'Yes, I am.' Flat tone, Lapslie wondering if Denham was being honest, or was playing him. 'And you're sure you want to stick to your guns about having nothing to do with her abduction and possible murder?'

'Yes, I do. Absolutely.' Equally flat tone, and an incredulous expression fired at his lawyer. 'Can you believe this guy and his accusations?' He looked back at Lapslie. 'Besides, what on earth has her disappearance to do with Larry Gilbert?'

More playing cute? Lapslie's steady stare at Denham didn't waver. 'We have firm reason to believe that Larry Gilbert was involved in Isabel's murder.'

'Oh, I see.' Denham looked lost for a moment, his gaze drifting towards the pool and terrace area beyond the glass doors, as if for inspiration. Then another shrug, this time more doubtful. 'And you think I might have been behind it? I didn't even like Larry. I was more mates with his dad, Freddie. If I was going to use anyone –' Quick sideways glance as his lawyer coughed '– Not saying that I ever have, or will. But Larry's the last person I'd use.'

'Yes. We worked out in advance that you'd have used someone independent, to keep it as far away from your involvement as possible. But are you also claiming that you had nothing to do with this phone call?' Lapslie nodded towards Bradbury, who clicked an icon on her laptop. The first of the two recordings from Beneyto's team began.

Lapslie watched Denham's expression closely as the recording played. Classic poker face, then a brief shrug as it finished.

'I don't know what that's meant to mean as far as I'm concerned. And that's certainly not my voice there.'

'On the face of it, doesn't *sound* like you,' Lapslie said, in turn shrugging. 'But sound experts consulted think that voice-masking has been used. So it could indeed be you. Or you could've used a go-between.'

Denham didn't respond, simply shook his head and fired an incredulous '*can you believe these guys*' leer towards his lawyer.

'And on this next recording, it becomes even clearer that a hit is about to be made by Gilbert in Alarcon.' Lapslie nodded and Bradbury clicked the second icon.

They'd agreed with Beneyto that they'd test Denham out straight away with the recordings; 'A guilty or haunted look, even for a split-second, can be quite tell-tale,' Lapslie had suggested. But Denham maintained the same poker face, if anything now slightly quizzical as the recording ended.

'I don't know why you're wasting your time playing me those,' Denham said. 'As I've told you before, I'd never use someone like Gilbert. Didn't like the man.'

'That's not what the word on the street is,' Lapslie said flatly. 'Word has it that despite your personal opinion of Gilbert, you've used him before several times. He's efficient and the ideal independent to keep everything at arm's length from you.'

'Word has it, eh?' Denham smiled crookedly. 'Listening to some back at the old Essex manor, they think you're quite a good police officer. Whereas others think you're just a lame duck with some weird illness that Rouse has kept on purely because he's got a soft spot for lame ducks.' Denham's smile broadened. 'Probably developed during his days with Tim Sayle.'

Lapslie just stared back evenly; he didn't rise to the taunt. 'Our sources are obviously a tad more reliable than yours.'

Denham looked uncomfortable after a moment under Lapslie's steady stare, waved one arm; a discarding gesture. 'Besides, that voice on the second recording obviously isn't me either.'

Lapslie smiled at Denham ingratiatingly. 'Having gone to the trouble of using an independent contractor to bury any possible traces of your involvement, you'll have obviously taken precautions: as said, either used voice-masking or a go-between. So, now we'll have our technicians strip away the masking and make voice comparisons with your known associates.'

'Good luck with that.'

Denham shrugged, and Lapslie wasn't sure whether he was unnerved or simply going for a knee-jerk bluff-call. Or perhaps he was suddenly remembering past conversations he'd had with Larry Gilbert where he hadn't used voice-masking or a go-between. Beneyto had got his court order granted earlier that morning and planned to search Gilbert's apartment just a few miles down the coast in only an hour or two. If it turned out to be the gold mine they hoped, they'd be making a swift return to see Vic Denham.

In the uneasy silence that had settled, Denham's lawyer commented, 'Are we finished now here, gentlemen?'

Lapslie nodded ponderously and Bradbury closed her laptop. 'I do believe we are.'

35

Mauricio and Christina, now

Mauricio felt the pressure of the questioning building steadily.

'We'd like to return again to that night you were meant to meet up with Isabel, but never in fact met her,' Inspector Lapslie commented.

They were back in the Guardia Civil station at San Clemente, Lapslie's female assistant and his own lawyer, Enrique Navarre, taking notes, with Inspector Ruiz simply observing.

'Now while we accept that you never actually met Isabel that night,' Lapslie continued, 'are you sure that you at no time saw her?'

'Yes, I'm sure. I never saw her.'

Lapslie sank into thought for a second. 'Now the only problem I have with that is that from the time you said you left Café Marie and the time Isabel was observed leaving the Parador, you'd have met up half-way.'

Mauricio shook his head resolutely, starting to feel hot. 'No, I never met up with her. I didn't see her at any time.'

'Didn't even *see* her?' Lapslie was peering sharply at him. 'Now even if we were to accept that you didn't actually meet her, seeing her becomes another matter.' Lapslie gestured towards his assistant. 'You see, myself and my colleague Emma Bradbury did a reconstruction of that night, and given the respective times – the time that you left Café Marie and Isabel the hotel – you'd have met up just two hundred yards past the last houses in town. Quite dark there, but you'd have had a clear view of the hotel lit up in the distance.'

'Not enough to make anyone out clearly.' Mauricio knew his town geography well, knew the visibility from any given point, so he wasn't about to fall for that one. 'I didn't see Isabel.'

But Inspector Lapslie appeared undeterred. 'But as you moved closer, you would have seen her clearer.'

'I . . . er . . . I saw some figures at one point, thought one of them might have been her,' he covered quickly. 'But as I got closer, they weren't there anymore. Perhaps gone back inside the hotel. So that was the first place I checked.'

Mauricio observed Lapslie absorb this information. Hopefully thinking that he was inside the hotel looking for Isabel while the large man was grappling with her in the darkness of the rampart further up, or considering that both of them might have been over the edge by that point.

'So, are you saying that you never saw Isabel with a large blond-haired man by the hotel entrance or side-rampart that night?'

'A large man?' Mauricio decided to play coy.

But from Lapslie's wry return smile, this tactic appeared to fall on stony ground. 'Yes, I'm sure that even if you didn't see this "large man" that night, you'd have heard we've been asking about him around town. After all, Alarcon is quite a small community.'

Mauricio had heard directly from Sara at the Miramar about them enquiring about 'Tobias Mercer', but the less he said about that, the better. He shrugged. 'I had heard some rumours, nothing more.' Then it suddenly hit him how he could turn things around. '*Why?* Do you think this "large man" was with Isabel that night?'

'Yes, we do,' Lapslie said. Flat tone on the back of a sigh.

Mauricio's eyes shifted uncomfortably, feigning surprise. Although one part of the puzzle was already known to him, the other was still out of reach. He looked at Lapslie directly. 'So, you think this man was directly involved in Isabel's disappearance and murder?'

This time Lapslie glanced briefly at Ruiz and Bradbury before answering, 'Yes, that is our suspicion.'

Eyes closed for a second, shaking his head. 'I don't understand . . .' Then, hitting realisation, knowing that the only way to draw this Lapslie out would be a direct accusation: 'So, Dario got someone else to do his dirty work for him. That's why he made sure he was away in Madrid when it happened.'

'No, no . . . we don't think that's what's happened here,' Lapslie said. 'We think it's more to do with some old family dispute amongst the gangland community, involving Isabel's godfather in Valencia. But, obviously, we can't say too much until that link is fully verified.' Lapslie held a hand out, smiled tightly. 'Just that I thought you should know you're barking up the wrong tree with Dario.'

So, this Lapslie was saying that it was all a gangland hit, nothing to do with Dario Alarcon. But still one part made no sense to Mauricio. 'I don't believe it. What about all the other problems between Isabel and Dario?'

'*What?* This ancestral-digging link?' Lapslie sighed. 'If there was a problem there, it obviously wasn't enough for Dario to take such drastic action.' Lapslie looked briefly towards his colleagues again, as if he needed to fully explain his last comments. 'And, look, I'm only telling you all of this now because I wouldn't want you doing anything rash with Dario. There appears to be enough bad blood between you as it is.'

Mauricio shook his head again after a moment, suddenly struck with another way of shaking things up. 'You mention all these rumours about the large man. But what about Dario complaining around town about his office being broken into, and thinking that Isabel was responsible?'

Another look from Lapslie towards his colleagues, Ruiz shaking his head. 'I'm sorry. We've heard nothing about that,' Lapslie said.

So, his suspicions were right: *Dario Alarcon hadn't mentioned anything since to the police about the break-in.* Pained smile. 'If Dario hasn't mentioned anything to you about that, Inspector, then I think you need to ask yourself why.'

36

Beneyto, now

Javier Beneyto drew hard on a cigarette as he looked out at the view from Larry Gilbert's apartment terrace while his team were busy with their search.

A Los Monteros penthouse with panoramic sea views in front, Nikki beach to the east and Puerto Banus just visible to west. The terrace was almost as large as the interior of the three-bedroom apartment. Palm trees at each far corner and a large jacuzzi in the middle to get the best of the view. Being a drugs enforcer obviously paid well, Beneyto thought.

'Nothing in the safe, either,' Vidal's voice drifted from behind.

Beneyto nodded back at Vidal, checking his watch. Thirty-five minutes they'd been here, twenty-five of which had been oxyacetylening Gilbert's wall safe.

He'd gone with Vidal and three others of his team,

a locksmith – though they'd got the apartment-block porter to open the main lock – and two local *bomberos* armed with oxyacetylene equipment.

Beneyto stubbed out his cigarette and went back inside the apartment. 'What in fact was in the safe that needed safeguarding?'

'Just some insurance documents, property deeds, and a pile of gold chains and sovereigns.'

'How big a pile?'

'I'm no gold expert.' Vidal shrugged. 'But I'd say a good forty thousand euros' worth.'

Beneyto whistled softly. 'And have we checked every cupboard back and drawer bottom for false compartments?'

'We've done most of them.' Vidal cast a glance towards one of their men knocking a wall in the lounge for any hollow sounds. 'Just checking through the rest now.'

They ambled into the master bedroom, where every vanity drawer was now out and stacked on the floor, and most of the wardrobe drawers. Their team-man pulled out the last wardrobe drawer, looked underneath with the aid of a torch, then grimaced back at them.

'*Nada*. Nothing here either. Only the back and side wardrobe panels now to check.'

He was halfway through his knocking when a voice sailed above it from the kitchen.

'*Venga!* Here . . . over *here*! I think we've found something.'

Beneyto and Vidal rushed into the kitchen. Most of the cupboard doors were open, but he pointed to where the base plinth had been pulled out.

'Found this tucked under the last but one cupboard.' He raised a black cloth bag, then from inside fished out an automatic pistol and two mobile phones.

Beneyto smiled softly. 'Looks like we have struck gold. Hopefully, that will prove to be worth more than the chains or sovereigns.'

37

Lapslie and Bradbury, now

Lapslie looked out over the view. There were some hills the other side of the ravine, the river snaking through it to his right. But between the hills, the panorama spread for miles: flat plains, some green, some dry and dusty, punctuated by smaller rolling hills. He felt a warm breeze drifting up from the gorge, and he closed his eyes as he felt it play across his body – imagining for a moment that he was out sailing.

He'd asked Charlotte to do the same as they'd stood in this same spot the morning before she left, asked her to inhale and feel herself sink into the warm embrace of that breeze and the silence beyond.

'Can you feel it? Do you see what I mean?'

'Yes,' she'd agreed after a moment. 'It does almost feel like being out sailing . . . once you get into it.'

Now, he was trying to use the silence and the breeze

to clear his thoughts, blow the cobwebs of this case from his mind. Clarity . . . *clarity!*

He felt himself swaying with the breeze after a moment, his legs feeling unsteady, as if the gorge was trying to draw him in and down . . . *the image superimposing of Isabel falling into the gorge only a hundred yards from where he now stood.* His eyes snapped open, visual assurance that even if he did topple from where he stood, he'd fall onto the edge of the rampart wall, not beyond it.

That meant that the large man and Isabel would have had to be right up against the edge of the rampart wall to topple over. Or perhaps Larry Gilbert, with his extra height, would have been more top-heavy, would have gone over the edge easier. But Isabel was far smaller. So did that mean that Gilbert was carrying her, or had he pushed her ahead of himself?

Carrying seemed the more likely option, Lapslie considered. Would have made him even more top-heavy and unsteady, if he'd pushed Isabel ahead, unlikely that he'd have then lost his balance and gone over as well. Unless Isabel had fallen only as far as the first set of rocks, and so he'd clambered over to push her all the way down . . . and that's when he'd lost his own balance.

Sound of footsteps approaching. Lapslie looked to one side towards them: Emma Bradbury.

'Sorry to disturb you, sir,' she said as she got closer. 'But I just finished speaking with Inspector Ruiz. Thought you'd want to know: neither he or his assistant have heard anything about a possible break-in at Dario Alarcon's office.'

'So, not only nothing directly from Dario Alarcon, but nothing from anyone in town either?'

'No, not according to Ruiz.'

'Thought it worth checking, at least.' Lapslie surveyed the view again for a moment. 'All that Spanish chatter going on in the background at interviews, you can never be too sure.'

'It *is* their native language, sir.'

'Yes, well . . . I suppose I can't begrudge them that.' Lapslie returned Emma's smile equally as dryly, making it clear he was joshing. 'But makes you wonder why Mauricio said there was talk around town about that.'

'Maybe just part of his ongoing conflict with Dario. Trying to point the blame his way.'

'Maybe. But if there was a break-in and only Mauricio is aware of it, the question then is *why*? And also why Dario didn't mention it?' Lapslie took a fresh breath. 'I must admit – Dario's excuse for rushing out halfway through dinner that night with Isabel didn't ring true to me.'

Bradbury was thoughtful for a second. 'But with Isabel there with Dario, why would he think she was involved in the break-in – as Mauricio has claimed?'

'True.' The view ahead didn't seem to be yielding any ready answers. He looked back at Bradbury. ''So perhaps we should put our focus back on Larry Gilbert, particularly with Beneyto's search now. Any luck with tracking down the car he might have hired? The same "friend" who picked up his luggage at the Miramar might also have returned that.'

'Yes. Initially, things were looking good. You were right in guessing that he wouldn't have risked stealing a car.'

'Thought as much,' Lapslie said, but Bradbury's mention of 'initially' tempered his enthusiasm.

'. . . And the car he hired, a Seat Leon, was hired under the same name as his registration at the Miramar, Tobias Mercer, so was easily traced.' Bradbury sighed. 'But then the possibility of sighting this "friend" started to cool off. The hire bill was settled by phone on Mercer's card, but then the caller, the hire company couldn't tell whether it was Mercer or not – presumably *not*, since that call was made the day after he'd died – said he'd left the car at an industrial estate a mile from Valencia airport.'

Lapslie closed his eyes for a second. 'Obviously being cautious not to get picked up by airport CCTV, so doubt we'll get much there either.'

'Probably not. But it certainly starts to look as if this "friend" is another professional. Someone who knows what they're doing.'

'Certainly does.' But Lapslie was suddenly struck with an afterthought. 'The hire company have obviously got the location of this industrial estate?'

'Yes – because they had to pick up the car from there.' She observed Lapslie pensive for a moment as he scanned the panorama ahead. 'What are you thinking, sir?'

Lapslie exhaled, the view in that moment suddenly seeming more open. 'While they might have gone to the trouble of avoiding airport CCTV, many warehouses also have them. We might pick something up on those.'

'So, nothing in Gilbert's safe?' Lapslie confirmed.

'No, nothing. Well, apart from over forty thousand euros' worth of gold chains and sovereigns,' Beneyto amended. 'But nothing of interest to us. The main find came from under the plinth in Gilbert's kitchen – a gun and two mobiles.' Beneyto took a fresh breath. 'But while that yielded some useful names in general crime terms, nothing on the main men in our sights – Blake and Denham.'

'You said *useful* names. Might any of those trace back to Denham?'

'I doubt it. One's a Russian mob boss who deals in both drugs and people-trafficking – but he's hardly ever here on the Costa del Sol. Most of his time is spent between the South of France and London. So, we have to decide whether to wait till he shows again here, or pass his name on to Interpol. Another is a mid-level drug dealer of little interest to us, and a third voice we've yet to identify.' Beneyto sighed. 'But we've already run it through for any matches with Blake or Denham associates. Nothing.'

Lapslie sank into thought for a second. Beneyto's call had come not long after they'd got back inside the hotel, Bradbury already on her laptop checking the possibility of CCTVs at the Valencia industrial estate. So now they were back to square one with a provable Gilbert–Denham link, unless something came up through this 'friend' who'd dumped Gilbert's car the day after his death. Lapslie was suddenly struck with an afterthought.

'Certainly proves one thing.'

'What's that?'

'That the rumours about Gilbert recording his hit instructions are true. So, if Denham and Blake have used Gilbert for past hits – as rumour also has it – Gilbert would have probably also held onto those mobiles with their voices recorded for insurance.'

'Yes, I see what you're saying,' Beneyto said after a moment. 'But they're certainly not in his apartment, we've stripped every inch. And Gilbert's lawyer says he wasn't holding anything for him apart from his will.'

'No, I get that. And you've done your best.' Lapslie sighed. 'But those insurance policies are out there some-where.'

38

Isabel and Melanie, then

Melanie Taylor had been Isabel's closest friend at school, particularly in the last few years before her father died and she'd moved to Spain to stay with Terry and Barbara. They'd been inseparable in their schooldays together, going on mad-cap runs along Southend Pier to try to outrun the train, or to the beach, funfair and local shops.

Even after Isabel's move to Spain, they kept in contact – less frequent than they'd have liked as phone calls were expensive – but some summer holidays Melanie would come out to see her in Spain or she'd go to England to stay with Melanie's family in Southend. Those stays had a bittersweet edge to them, because sometimes Isabel would pass her old family home just half a mile away, and she would be overcome with memories of when her father had been alive.

Then Skype had been invented, and so they had

more regular visual contact. But for some reason, when they were in their late teens – perhaps through all the changes and pressures with boyfriends and exams – that contact had faded out. Six months or more would go by without them having any contact with each other.

Isabel's first year at Cambridge, she'd only spoken to Melanie once. She was far closer to Melanie then than she had been in Spain; Cambridge to Southend was no more than a two-hour journey, but all the newness – new location, new studies, new friends – had seemed to fill her available mind-space, creating a gap, albeit an unintentional one. She'd hardly given Melanie a thought in that first year.

Then Melanie had phoned out of the blue. 'We should see each other, catch up. It's been a while now, what have you been up to . . .?'

And after a breathless fill-in of the ten months since they'd last been in touch, they'd got around to when and where? 'Do you want me to come down to see you in Southend some time?'

'No. I was thinking of somewhere more local to you. That's why I'm phoning now.' Melanie had found a Groupon offer for a 'Murder-Mystery' weekend at an old manor house near Forncett in Norfolk. 'Less than an hour's run from you, and they have a great price for two bookings.'

'Oh, I don't know. Murder-mystery . . . what would that entail?'

'A lot of clue-tracking and "sleuthing". Come on, you know how much we used to enjoy playing those old Cluedo games. You'll love it.'

'Yes, but we were only twelve or thirteen then.' But now she thought about it, she'd never bothered to ask why – when it was too rainy to go on their runs along the pier or around the shops – Melanie would often get the Cluedo board out at her house. Why not Monopoly or Trivial Pursuit? Obviously, Cluedo had been very much a favourite of Melanie's.

'And if you're not totally into it,' Melanie urged, 'There's always the atmosphere of that fine old manor house, usually a bit creepy – lots of suits of armour on minstrels' galleries and all that – and some great food.'

'So will I find Peter Sellers or Herbert Lom in one of those suits of armour?' They both laughed almost in unison, a reminder of old times, and Isabel added, 'Okay. You've got me tempted. And even if I find all of this "sleuthing" crap, we've got a lot to catch up on. To start with, why I'm your first call for a weekend away rather than a boyfriend?'

'Don't start . . .'

And over that weekend they'd filled in the gaps on the respective ups and downs of their love-lives. Isabel had also found out why Cluedo had been such a past favourite of Melanie's, and why she'd been attracted to this 'Murder-Mystery' weekend now. Her father had been an investigative journalist.

'Oh, I didn't know,' Isabel had responded. 'I thought he was a "foreign correspondent".'

'Yes, that's how he ended up. Jetting off to the latest war zone or famine relief area, microphone in hand. Much of it for TV by then. But he started off as an investigative journalist for a local newspaper, then the nationals.' Melanie shrugged lamely. 'So maybe this is my attempt to follow in his footsteps.'

'And why not?' Isabel had picked up on Melanie's defeatist tone. 'But why stop at just this? Maybe you should go for it for real. What are you studying now?'

'Journalism and social sciences – but just locally at Southend University.'

'There you go . . .'

Defeatist Melanie quickly resurfaced. 'But I'm not

sure if I'll stick with it. I don't know in the end if it's the thing for me. Maybe Cluedo and murder-mystery weekends like this will be the closest I'll get.'

'You shouldn't put yourself down so . . .' But something about Melanie's lost countenance – thoughtful, almost maudlin at times in their conversation and a lot of reminiscing – stopped Isabel from pushing the issue further.

And as the weekend had progressed, Isabel wondered more why Melanie was so doubting of her own abilities: often she was first in games to find the right path on clues given, first to nail the suspect – even up against far more seasoned players, who'd been going regularly to similar Murder-Mystery weekends. Isabel hadn't done badly either, for a novice; but was nothing in comparison to Melanie, with her dazzling sleuthing abilities. Melanie had been a natural.

She'd pushed Melanie again about following more seriously in her father's investigative-journalist footsteps, 'Or if not perhaps a career with the police.' But again that lost, defeated response. For whatever reason, Melanie didn't think she'd be good enough. Isabel had eventually backed off.

But now hit with the dilemma of trying to track down

this researcher in England, Arthur Maitland, Melanie was the first person she thought of. Someone outside of the system who could do a bit of digging without raising alarm bells. Melanie would probably love some sleuthing like this: a modern-day detective game, linked to a centuries-old family secret. It might be the final thing to convince Melanie to try it in real life, to pursue investigative journalism or joining the police with more conviction.

Isabel glanced at her watch: two hours before she was due to see Mauricio at Café Marie. She'd try Melanie in the meantime.

The four or five months after the Murder-Mystery weekend, she'd had more regular contact with Melanie, but then they'd drifted apart a bit again. She'd tried her number five months back, but Melanie had been out at the time; then Isabel's own hectic schedule with finals had got in the way since. Melanie's number started ringing. Hopefully she'd be there this time . . .

39

Lapslie and Bradbury, now

The handy thing about Dario Alarcon's Ferrari was that you could pick out its distinctive roar from most parts of the town. Café Marie was also quite central, so Lapslie chose the café's outside terrace as his spot that morning for a coffee and catch-up on the English news from the paper he'd bought at the Parador; they had all the regular foreign papers from England and Germany brought in every morning.

Emma Bradbury was meanwhile with Ruiz at the industrial estate in Valencia, to see if they could find out more about Tobias Mercer's hire car drop-off.

Lapslie reasoned that he would hear Dario Alarcon's Ferrari approaching from this position, and it would be no more than a block or two to amble and chat to him. Lapslie wanted this talk to be casual and impromptu; he didn't want it to be at a pre-set time in a formal setting, where Dario would be more likely to prepare his answers.

Lapslie's earlier phone conversation with Rouse had been awkward.

'So, you're saying that these insurance policies of Gilbert's have led to various other gangsters in Marbella, including a Russian mafia kingpin,' Rouse blustered. 'But still nothing to link him to Denham?'

'No, sir. But we're pretty sure those other mobiles with recordings are out there somewhere.'

'And is this Beneyto fellow still looking for them?'

Lapslie paused for a second. 'He's trying to work out where else Gilbert might have them stashed away.'

'I'll take that as a "no", at least for the time being.' Rouse sighed. 'Might I remind you that Denham was the main reason I approved this little sortie to Spain – not to help the Spanish police nail every other criminal in Marbella.'

'I understand that, sir. But our assistance in those other collars does stand in our department's favour, nonetheless. Along with demonstrating stronger working accord with foreign police forces.'

'I suppose there is that.'

A begrudging tone, even though Lapslie knew that

'feather in their caps' was of no light significance; the record of good working relationships between British and foreign police had often been lamentable.

'Also, we might find out more about Gilbert and a possible Vic Denham link from whoever dropped off Gilbert's hire car *after* he was already dead,' Lapslie added. 'Obviously, an accomplice of some sort. Bradbury is right now visiting the industrial estate where it was left to study their CCTV cameras.'

'I scc.' *Temperature raised to lukewarm begrudging.* 'Let me know how that goes.'

Lapslie brought his attention back to his newspaper and the latest on Brexit and Cabinet fall-outs. He was halfway through his second cup of coffee when Dario's Ferrari pulled up outside the Town Hall opposite. Lapslie didn't look up or over, merely folded his paper on the table and ambled across just as Dario was getting out of his car.

'Nice car,' Lapslie said. 'I hear some of the Italian police now have these to catch speeders on the motorways. Be a while before we see them in England, though – if ever. Any with the Spanish police that you know of?'

Dario looked nonplussed for a second, caught off guard by the line of conversation. 'Ah, I don't think so.'

Lapslie surveyed the car again for a second before looking back at Dario. 'Glad I bumped into you, though. You probably heard that we caught a suspect in Isabel's disappearance or murder: a hired hitman from Marbella, Larry Gilbert, but staying in town under the name of Tobias Mercer.'

'Yes, I heard.'

'Both his blood group and what we suspect is Isabel's were found on rocks over the rampart edge by the Parador.' Lapslie pointed towards the end of the square and the castle beyond. 'And we found Gilbert's body washed out to sea just the other day.'

'Oh, I see.' This was a detail Dario obviously hadn't heard before. 'And what was the connection between this man and Isabel?'

'Some gangland connection with her godfather, we believe.' Lapslie didn't want to say anything beyond that. He grimaced. 'But you know that Mauricio is still convinced you're behind it, because of this ancestral link?'

'I know Mauricio and I have had our problems in the past – but as I told you before, that's ridiculous. Which now this gangland connection has proven.' Dario sighed. 'But, nevertheless, I'm sorry to hear all of this. Isabel was a nice girl. I was hoping to hear she'd turned up alive and well somewhere.'

'Me too.' Lapslie nodded slowly, thoughtful. 'But there was in fact something about that last dinner you had with Isabel I wanted to ask you about. You had to break off halfway, went off in a rush. Remind me again, what was the reason for that?'

'Er, like I said before, it was my father reminding me about some work I was meant to finish urgently that night.'

'By text message, if I recall?'

'Yes, that's right. He sent me a text, and I realised I'd forgotten all about it.'

'So, that was enough to make you leave in such a rush?'

'Yes, as I told you before, Inspector.' An impatient tone now in his voice.

Another slow nod. Lapslie decided to use Mauricio's ruse; probably the only way of testing the story. 'Just that we've heard from some people in town that you had a break-in at your office that same night – which would then more adequately explain you rushing away.'

Dario's face flushed heavily. 'I'm not sure why or where you might have heard that, Inspector.'

Lapslie stared hard at Dario. '*You* tell *me.*'

A head shake, a light dismissive guffaw. 'Look. There was a problem with the office alarm – that's why I had to rush off. But it wasn't an actual break-in.' Dario shrugged helplessly. 'My father was last to lock up, and usually we put the cat in a back office – its food, water and basket is there – so that it doesn't set off the motion alarm. My father forgot to put the cat there and close the connecting door.'

'And why didn't you tell us this before?'

Dario smiled primly. 'I thought it might reflect badly on my father. There's enough talk around town as it is about him being too old to handle the town's affairs, and that he should have retired long ago.'

'I see.' Lapslie held an even stare on Dario. *The truth, or was Dario making it up as he went along?* A faint camomile and creosote tang at the back of his throat told him the latter. But he could hardly share with Dario that his taste buds indicated he was lying. 'Well, in future, please stick to an accurate account. Small town like this, the truth has a habit of coming out.'

Lapslie could feel Dario's eyes still on him as he walked back across the road to his terrace table.

40

Lapslie and Bradbury, now

'Señor Romero says that there's nobody in this warehouse now,' Bernardo Ruiz translated the burst of Spanish from the smaller man at his side. 'Hasn't been for some while.'

The small man nodded eagerly, as if he knew the translation was accurate. Emma Bradbury suspected that he had as little idea as she did. She in turn now nodded, looking back towards the dilapidated warehouse, at least six months' dust now encrusted on its oblong windows ten feet up; too high for them to peer in. Her eyes drifted to the two cams four feet above the windows.

'And how about the security cams?'

Another exchange of Spanish between Ruiz and Romero, then: 'He says that he doubts those are working now. In any case, any links to computers would have gone. The electricity was cut off some while ago.'

Bradbury grimaced, taking her mobile from her pocket and comparing the images from the hire car company of them picking up the Seat Leon. Definitely this spot. It looked like their drop-off man knew what they were doing here too. Picking a warehouse where the security cams were obviously out of action.

She looked back the way they'd come: a fifty-foot-square car park with two other warehouses flanking, then a short drive leading to one of the main arterial roads on the industrial estate.

'What about these other two warehouses?' Bradbury pointed.

'The first warehouse belongs to Señor Romero,' Ruiz clarified, then after another exchange in Spanish, 'The second, the guy's not here right now. Only comes in two or three times a week to pick up and drop off materials. Some sort of scaffolding company.'

Bradbury nodded. 'Let's see at least what Mr Romero might have on his cam records.'

Pepe Romero seemed to understand enough to start leading the way before Ruiz had finished translating.

It was insufferably hot inside Pepe Romero's small office. He had air conditioning but, with the sun beating down on a tin-flanked side and then rising to his office perched above the workshop floor, it was struggling.

A lot of time was spent winding backwards and forwards to get to the right time frame. Then finally, among the chain of trucks and vans and other cars, finally they saw the Seat Leon approaching.

'That's it ... *that's it!*' Bradbury leaned forward, pointing.

Romero dutifully slowed the frame sequence. But, disappointingly, when the Seat pulled up, it was out of frame. They couldn't see it, nor see the person getting out of the car.

Still, Bradbury held her breath. As they walked back the way they'd driven, hopefully they'd be in view. But, again, it was as if the driver was aware of the warehouse cams. He gave a far wider berth on his way back – he was out of view for most of the time, apart from the last few yards where he had to angle back in to make the narrower approach road.

'Stop it there ... *right there!*' Bradbury instructed.

Romero stopped before Ruiz called *s'arrete!* One word she realised was international from the many STOP signs she'd witnessed in Spain.

She leaned forward, looking closer at the figure

on-screen: eighty percent back view, only a trace of profile: little discernible.

Emma Bradbury was just finishing up with Ruiz when Lapslie's call came through.

'Ruiz still with you?'

'Yes. We've probably got no more than ten minutes here, then we're wrapped.' She sighed. 'Nothing in the end, I'm afraid. But there's one last warehouse at the end where the cam might yield something. Only problem is, the owner's not here right now – might not turn up for another couple of days.'

'I see.' Lapslie's tone mirrored her frustration. 'If that's what we're faced with, nothing else we can do.' Fresh breath; fresh hope. 'But it was actually something else I was calling about now. Can you put me on to Ruiz?'

'Ah, yes . . . of course.' Bradbury nodded with a smile and passed her phone to Ruiz.

The idea had first struck Lapslie when he'd thought about Beneyto's team monitoring Larry Gilbert and Vic Denham's calls. To tie the remaining loose ends of this puzzle together, they needed to follow the calls of the other main players still possibly involved. He asked Ruiz how long it would take to get court orders to monitor phone calls on the four or five people possibly connected with Isabel Alarcon's disappearance and murder.

'Well, we can get those quite quickly here, sometimes twenty-four hours – depending on the seriousness of the case. We don't have the same red-tape that you have in England.'

Lapslie smiled to himself. Code for: *we don't observe the same protocols*; he'd observed as much about Spanish life. If it suited them, they simply went their own way, damn EU rules and any other external influences. 'And I suppose a suspected murder case like this would warrant "sufficient seriousness"?'

'Yes, it would.'

Lapslie rattled off the list of people whose phones he felt should be monitored: 'Mauricio Reynes, Terry Haines and Dario Alarcon.'

'Why Terry Haines?' Ruiz questioned. 'Surely he wouldn't be involved in his own goddaughter's disappearance and murder?'

'No, he wouldn't. But if by chance she's still alive – then a ransom demand could come in. Or Denham or one of his stooges might be stupid enough to leave a gloating message: "we warned you to watch your back where family were concerned", that sort of thing.'

Ruiz called Lapslie back later that night. 'All in place already. I struck lucky and got a judge's approval late afternoon. From then, things moved swiftly.'

'Thanks, Bernardo. You're a star.' Lapslie exhaled tiredly, the rigors of the day catching up with him. 'Will be interesting to see what comes in over the next few days.'

41

Christina and Melanie, now

Melanie tapped her fingers on the side table as the number rang. She'd managed to narrow down the five possible Arthur Maitlands to just two, one in Chesterfield, the other in Lydden, closer to the Kent coast – but then there was no other way of making sure apart from phoning them directly. She'd already phoned both numbers once: The Chesterfield number had been on an answerphone – she hadn't left a message, and in fact had dialled 141 to withhold call registration each time – and the Lydden number had simply rung without answer. She was trying the Lydden number again, but this time someone picked up.

'Hello.'

A man's voice, slightly gravelly. *Could be from age or a long-term smoker.* 'Is that Arthur Maitland?' A pause from the other end. 'You used to live near Challock, Kent?'

'Who *is* this?' Non-committal.

'My name's Melanie Taylor.' Common enough name that a search would bring up numerous Melanie Taylors, many more than there were Arthur Maitlands. 'I have a research project coming up and I was given your name, but I don't know if I've got the right Arthur Maitland. So is that Arthur Maitland, the researcher?'

Longer pause this time. 'Yes, it is.' A fall of breath. Easier, accepting. 'And what is this research I might be able to help you with?'

'It's to do with something in Spain.' Hopefully vague enough, Melanie reminding herself of Christina's advice to hold off until she had more input from Mauricio. 'I'm waiting for more specifics from my contacts in Spain on what they want precisely, and then I can get back to you.'

'Which contacts are those?'

Melanie could sense him pressing. She didn't fall for it. 'I have to wait until I've spoken to them again – I hope you understand. For now, I just wanted to make sure you were the right Arthur Maitland.'

'Yes, I'm the right Arthur Maitland. Or *was*, last time I checked.' A light chuckle. 'Look forward to hearing from you again when you're ready.'

*

'I only managed to speak to Mauricio briefly – he's still on a driving shift right now,' Christina said. 'But he says he thinks the police are still leaning towards a Marbella or Valencia connection with this hitman, Larry Gilbert, rather than anything to do with affairs here in Alarcon.'

'Okay. I was ringing mainly to let you know that I've located this Arthur Maitland. He's now at an address in Lydden, closer to the Kent coast.' Melanie didn't let on that she'd actually had contact already in order to clarify that he was the *right* Arthur Maitland. Not that it should matter, after all, she'd withheld her number and had been vague; nothing specific to link her call to Alarcon. 'But how long should I hold off for? After all, even if Dario Alarcon isn't linked to the hitman, Maitland could give us valuable information on Isabel's ancestral link with Alarcon – or indeed tell us what happened to Isabel's father the day of his accident. Did they have any meaningful conversations on the phone about that ancestral background before that planned visit, for instance?'

'I see what you're saying.' Christina could sense Melanie's combination of enthusiasm and frustration the other end, and understood it. After all, she'd fired herself up to find and contact Arthur Maitland, and now she was being told to *wait*. 'Hopefully, it won't be long. Mauricio finishes his shift mid-afternoon, and I'll speak to him again then. I think he just wants to get a feel for things in Alarcon – read the mood there, see if anyone else in town has heard anything else about this Larry Gilbert; or *Tobias Mercer*, as he signed himself in as at the Miramar.'

Melanie got the hint. Mauricio obviously wanted to speak to people directly at this local hotel, get the inside track on what the police might know. But there was only so much Christina could share at this stage over the phone. 'Okay, I'll hang on.'

Melanie tapped her fingers again after hanging up. She glanced at her watch. A few hours to wait, maybe more. There was another call she should make; in fact, it was a call she should have made days ago, but she'd kept putting it off.

She picked up her phone again and dialled Terry and Barbara Haines's number in Valencia.

42

Lapslie and Bradbury, now

'I'm sorry to call you out of the blue like this, and what I'm going to say might come as something of a shock . . .'

'Who *is* this?' Terry Haines's voice pointed, insistent.

'It's Melanie, Melanie Taylor. Isabel's old schoolfriend. I don't know if you'll remember me.'

'Of course, I remember you, Melanie. How are you?'

'I'm fine . . . but it's Isabel I'm calling about now. She asked me to call you.'

'*Asked* you? What's going on, Melanie?'

'She asked me to call you, because she knew you'd be worried about her. But she wanted to let you and Barbara know that she's fine.'

'Well, she's got that right. We've been worried sick about her. The police have been looking for her and everything . . . they even found some bloodstains out at Alarcon.'

'I know . . . I *know*. But believe me, she's fine.'

Heavy pause. *Doubting*. 'And why isn't Isabel making this call herself, if she's fine?'

'It's a long story. But she just needs to get everything clear in her mind about what's happened.' Another deep breath, as if drawing strength. 'You see, there *was* an attempt on Isabel's life. And she's afraid that if she surfaces, they'll try again and finish the job this time.'

'Why doesn't she just go to the police with all this? I know I've often had my differences with them – but this is more their quarter. She's out of her depth with things like this.'

'That's why I'm helping her. Isabel thinks they've got it all wrong. The police suspect this hitman from Malaga and a connection to Vic Denham – but she thinks it stems from someone in Alarcon.'

'*Who?*'

'She's not a hundred percent sure yet. But once she's tracked down one last lead in England connected to her father's death, she'll know for sure. Then she should be able to surface without any problem.' There was a long silence, no response from the other end. 'But, please, no mention of this to anyone in the meantime.'

'I . . . I suppose. If it's only a matter of a few days.

It's a weird one this, I must say.' Tired sigh. 'But you're sure she's fine?'

'Yes, I'm sure. She'll be in touch when everything's clear.'

Lapslie sat back as the recording came to an end, looking into the middle distance. He'd exchanged a number of questioning looks with Emma Bradbury and Bernardo Ruiz as the recording played, but now he wanted a moment to let his thoughts solidify.

They were in Ruiz's office in Madrid, the information seen as too sensitive to play at even the local Guardia Civil station in San Clemente. News might filter back to Alarcon, or someone might tip off Enrique Navarre: 'Hey. *Some higher-up department in Madrid has approved a phone tap on your client, Mauricio Reynes, without you knowing.*'

At the end of the table was a translator who Ruiz had introduced as Paco Grijalba, busy on his own laptop translating into English a transcript of the last brief recording picked up from Mauricio Reynes's mobile phone late morning.

'Okay, first thoughts?' Lapslie asked. He had his own, but he wanted to get the general consensus first.

'Could be just as it sounds,' Ruiz said. 'That Isabel is still alive. After all, we haven't found a body so far.'

Bradbury held a palm out. 'Or could be that now we've found Larry Gilbert's body, Vic Denham fears the net is closing in on him. So, he's trying to suggest that either Isabel is alive or point things more towards problems in Alarcon.'

Lapslie grimaced. 'Except we don't know if or how Vic Denham picked up on Isabel having problems in Alarcon.'

'Well, he made sure the hit was there,' Bradbury said.

'Yes. But that might have been more to keep things away from the Valencia–Marbella area than anything else,' Lapslie offered. 'Which, with being home turf, Denham might have felt pointed the finger more squarely in his direction.'

Ruiz nodded thoughtfully. 'It wouldn't have taken long for this Larry Gilbert to pick up on Isabel's problems in Alarcon and report back to Denham. We all know how small the town is and how gossip spreads.' He gestured to his laptop. 'Partly why we're all here now listening to these recordings.'

'Good point,' Lapslie agreed. 'But pointing things away from Vic Denham and towards Dario Alarcon has been more Mauricio's forte so far. So, if it is a put-up call, my main money would be on him.'

Bradbury shrugged. 'Except Mauricio isn't really our prime suspect in Isabel's disappearance or death anymore, so there's little or no pressure for him to do something like that.'

'True.' Lapslie looked keenly at the two of them. 'Unless Mauricio is guilty and fears we might know more than we actually do.' There was silence for a moment as Lapslie observed Bradbury and Ruiz grapple with what that *more* might be. Then he gestured towards the translator at the end of the table. 'But perhaps, if that transcript's now ready of his last call, some clues might be gained from that.'

'This is the first chance I've had to call you back, Christina. What is it?'

'I've had Melanie on the phone again from England. She's finally located this Arthur Maitland.'

'But she hasn't made contact yet?'

'No. You said not to. Not for now, at least. But she sounded impatient to get in touch with him.'

'I can't blame her.' (Heavy sigh). 'But I have to check a few things first in Alarcon – then she can go ahead once I'm ready.'

'You're still concerned about the link to Marbella with this Larry Gilbert?'

'Yes. Part of that makes no sense. So, I want to speak to a few people again – particularly Sara at the Miramar. Sara and her mother would probably have been the last people to see Gilbert that night.'

'I understand your thinking. But let's not keep Melanie waiting too long.'

'We won't. I should know which way to play things by tonight.'

Lapslie looked up from reading. 'Some new names to check from between the two conversations. This Christina – she's obviously a good friend of Mauricio's.'

Ruiz nodded. 'Yes. But then everyone knows everyone in Alarcon at some level, so doesn't mean that much.'

'The advantages and disadvantages of a small community,' Bradbury commented.

'You could say.' Ruiz shrugged. 'One Christina Escajeda worked as a secretary in Gabriel and Dario Alarcon's office up until eighteen months ago.'

Lapslie raised a brow. 'Any allegiances still there?'

'No,' Ruiz said. 'She left under a bit of a cloud, according to others in the village we spoke to.'

Lapslie was thoughtful for a second. 'So, that old axe to grind could be quite useful.'

'Especially if you were planning a break-in,' Bradbury offered after a moment. 'She'd know many of the internal workings of their office.'

'Dario Alarcon denies there was a break-in,' Ruiz said. 'Certainly, he didn't report anything.'

'Yes. But it's a possibility we should keep an open mind to.' Lapslie sank into thought again for a moment. 'And it certainly looks as if they're using this Christina as a hub. So, it might be worth monitoring her calls as well.'

Ruiz nodded slowly as Lapslie's gaze rested on him. 'I'll arrange it.'

Silence for a moment, then Lapslie looked towards Bradbury. 'But for this old schoolfriend of Isabel's in England, Melanie Taylor, and this researcher, Arthur Maitland, we'll have to get some help from Chelmsford HQ.'

'Maybe DC Kempsey and Rebecca Graves,' Bradbury suggested.

'Yes. Or possibly Dereck Bain too. He's also good with digging up names and research.'

Bradbury nodded. Something struck her as familiar

about the name Arthur Maitland, but she couldn't place it.

'Another thing we haven't considered,' Lapslie said after a moment. 'If these calls have been set up in any way – whether to angle us away from suspicion of Denham or more towards Dario –'

'Or to convince us that Isabel is still alive,' Bradbury cut-in, 'if Mauricio fears still being in the frame.'

'Yes, that as well.' Lapslie smiled tightly. 'Then it means they might already suspect that we're monitoring them.'

43

Christina and Melanie, now

'You still looking to be more or less on time? Where are you now?'

'Still on the A20.'

'How far from the A252 turn off?'

'Uh, four or five miles.'

'Okay. And don't forget, not long after taking the A252, you then take the Canterbury road, which takes you all the way into Challock. I daresay you'll be with me in twenty minutes or so.'

'Yes. As long as I don't get lost or take any wrong turns.' Light chuckle from Sebastian. 'Thanks for the directions. See you shortly.'

Melanie tapped her fingers thoughtfully on the table as the recording came to an end. The last words accessed from Sebastian Alarcon's mobile phone from a call made by Arthur Maitland. Sebastian had been late picking up, possibly because he was driving, and it had started to go into voice message, which had then recorded the remainder.

Fifteen minutes later he'd had his fatal accident, a head-on collision with a lorry while overtaking a slow-moving trailer truck. The police surmised that he'd misjudged the speed of the truck he was overtaking, as well as the sharpness and blindness of the upcoming bend. For the police there was no suspicion on their part that it was anything other than an accident.

As soon as they'd discovered the significance of that final meeting with Maitland, through a cousin of Christina's who was with the nearby Albacete Guardia Civil, they had accessed the records on Sebastian Alar-con's mobile phone; one of the last things they'd got before that night's fateful confrontation on the Parador ramparts. There had been another call logged from Maitland's mobile an hour beforehand, but obviously that hadn't been recorded.

Could Maitland have possibly been involved in, or even orches-trated, Sebastian's accident?

They'd hit on the subject when Melanie spoke to Christina earlier in the day. 'One thing that strikes me as a bit strange is Maitland calling back again so quickly to check on Sebastian's progress. It's almost as if he wants to know exactly where Sebastian is at that moment.'

'Oh, I don't know,' Christina said. 'Maybe he was just being helpful, in case he was getting lost. Some of the country roads in that region probably get a bit tricky.'

'Yes. You're probably right,' Melanie said. 'I'm just getting paranoid. Starting to see demons and shadows where there aren't any.'

'I don't blame you. It's been a nightmare for us all.' Christina sighed. 'And, after all, that is your main job now – digging and *sleuthing*.'

44

Southend, now

Sleuthing. Sunglasses, woolly hat pulled down hard, she waited until it was dark before going out. She'd suddenly realised late in the day, waiting on Mauricio's final nod of approval to make contact with Arthur Maitland, that she needed to take some cash out at some point.

She tried to avoid the busier streets, and she kept herself tight into the buildings one side or the other so that she wouldn't be noticed. As a final precaution, she didn't use the cash machine closest to where she was staying; she'd choose one at least three or four blocks away.

She finally came to the machine she'd decided upon, keeping her gaze straight ahead as a couple of people passed by. She looked around: nobody else approaching. She slid in her card. Then seconds later tapped in her PIN.

At first, the message that appeared on-screen, she didn't understand: *PIN not recognised. Please try again.*

She tapped in the number again; and she'd only just hit the last digit when she realised what she'd done, gasping and biting at the back of one hand as the message appeared again. She ejected the card, looked at it. *Oh, God!* Wrong card. She'd been so caught up with her churning thoughts about Maitland and Sebastian, she hadn't paid attention. She hoped that mistake wasn't going to come back to bite her.

She slid in the right card, tapped in the number again, and was just twenty yards away with the hundred pounds tucked into her pocket when her mobile rang. A couple on the other side of the road appeared to be looking at her curiously. *Had they been looking at her long?* She hadn't really been paying attention. But she waited until she was further along before answering. 'Hi, Mauricio.'

'You were talking earlier about following-up with this Arthur Maitland and . . .' He broke off. 'Are you okay?'

'Yeah, fine. Why?'

'You sound a bit out of breath.'

'Oh, I came out to a cash machine, and I was just making my way back quickly.' She didn't want to tell him that she'd used the wrong card momentarily, and that's why she'd been flustered and out of breath.

'I know you're keen to follow up with him, but I'm still waiting on some news this end. Probably nothing, but you can't arrange to meet him until tomorrow now anyway. So, it's worth waiting.'

'I see your point,' she said hollowly. 'Just that with the long wait already to get to the bottom of Alarcon's dark secrets, it feels frustrating to wait longer.'

'Know what you mean.' Mauricio fell silent the other end for a moment. 'Christina also said you had some concerns about Maitland.'

'Yes, but only minor. Not worth holding things up over.'

'Still, it might be worth using that time to put some precautions in place for when you do meet Maitland.' Mauricio took a fresh breath. 'Okay, this is how I think we should play it with him.'

45

Lapslie and Bradbury, now

Bradbury and Bernardo Ruiz observed as Pepe Romero explained the reason for their visit to the owner of the neighbouring warehouse, Rubio Coria. Romero had told them that he'd been happy to make that offer, 'Because having already been through this myself, I can more easily explain it, and it will help put Rubio's mind at ease that he's not in any sort of trouble.'

When they'd left Romero the last time, Ruiz had left his office number and asked him to call urgently the minute his neighbour showed up, then to immediately go next door and tell the neighbour that the police wanted to see him.

After Romero's initial explanation to Coria, Ruiz spoke directly on the phone with Coria for a moment. At first Coria had just seemed perplexed, then had asked, 'How long will it take?'

'About an hour or two.'

'Trouble is, I don't have an hour or two spare right now. The materials my men are loading the truck up with now has to go out to a site in El Cabanyal.'

Ruiz said that he too needed time to get down from Madrid – so the arrangement was made for 6 p.m. 'When I arrive, it will be with a British detective, Emma Bradbury, who has an interest in the case.'

Coria led the way to his office. 'I don't check the security videos that often, I'm afraid. First of all, I'm only here a few times a week. Secondly, there's no point. If there's nothing missing from my stock of planks and steel, what's the point of checking?'

'Are there any occasional exceptions to that rule?' Bradbury asked. Ruiz translated.

Coria sat down at his desk and opened up the first of the tapes, thoughtful for a second. 'The only times might be if I suspect one of my own staff of stealing stock, or there's word of a gang in the area targeting scaffolding companies.'

Bradbury had to wait for Ruiz to finish the translation, by which time she could see that Coria had brought up on-screen three distinctively different images.

'What are the three angles we're looking at?' Bradbury enquired.

Ruiz spoke to Coria briefly, then translated. 'These are the three cams live now: two at the back flanking the car park, the other on the side looking at the driveway approach.'

Coria did a bit more juggling with the video boxes, then started winding back through images. 'What date did you say you were looking for?'

'The nineteenth,' Ruiz said. 'Almost two weeks ago now.'

'And what sort of time?'

'Twelve twenty-four to twelve twenty-six.' They had the time pinned down precisely now from Romero's cameras. 'It's a white Seat Leon we're interested in – particularly its driver.'

Coria wound forward rapidly until he got to 11 a.m. of the day in question, then ran them through slower. At one point he sat forward more keenly.

'Might that be the Seat Leon you're looking for?'

They watched on the screen showing the side drive, a white Seat Leon approaching. As it got closer, Ruiz said, 'Yes, looks like it.'

Too many shadows to discern who was inside,

Bradbury thought. They watched it move out of that cam's field of range and into view of the two at the back. They already knew from watching the footage on Romero's cameras that where the Seat parked would be out of range of the furthest cam – so then came the tense wait for its driver to come back into view, *if* indeed he did.

Bradbury noticed that the driver seemed to take a wide berth of the first two cams, the view of him was at best only partial, from the chest down. But on the third cam it was different: covering only a narrow side drive, there was no possibility of avoiding it, and the view of him as he turned the corner was quite clear.

'Stop it *there!*' Bradbury held one hand up. She moved closer to the screen. 'Now release the frames very slowly, until I tell you to stop again.'

There was a short exchange between Ruiz and Coria, and the frames started running again at a third of their normal speed.

Bradbury half-raised her hand again in anticipation. *Maybe a second or two more will give us the best shot.* But from the look fired at her from Bernardo Ruiz, already he'd worked out who it was. She shot the hand all the way up. 'Okay, there! *That one!*' The image froze on-screen, and she prompted. 'And if you could zoom in a bit closer?'

Ruiz translated, and they both watched as the image of Mauricio Reynes filled the screen.

Bradbury smiled tightly as she muttered, 'Now, what might you be doing dropping off Larry Gilbert's car?'

46

Chelmsford squad room, now

The squad room was in a spin. Three or four strands of information, all of them arising in the last few hours. But the question was, how might they link together? DC Dereck Bain cradled his head in one hand as he tried to make sense of it all.

The first thread had in fact come from their end: a local Southend bank had alerted them to the attempted use of the debit card of Isabel Alarcon, a British subject reported missing fourteen days ago. Lapslie had put out an all-banks alert when he'd started his investigation in Spain; apparently, Inspector Ruiz had done the same with banks in Spain. This was the first use reported in all that time.

Bain called out to DC Rebecca Graves on the far side of the room. 'How long before the bank say they'll get the corresponding video footage for that "attempted-user" to you?'

'Forty minutes or so, an hour at the most.'

'And any joy yet in speaking to this Melanie Taylor directly?'

'No, the two times I've tried, her mother has said that Melanie is bedridden and simply too ill to speak to us.'

Bain grimaced. 'So, we don't even know for sure if she is at home. Her mum might simply be covering for her.'

'True.' Graves nodded reluctant accord.

Bain turned to Pete Kempsey. 'And what about this Arthur Maitland character – the researcher?'

'I tracked him to a new address near the Kent coast. But Lapslie said to hold off until we know for sure whether Melanie will be planning to see him or not.'

Graves raised a brow. 'Certainly won't be the Melanie I've been trying to contact, if her mother is to be believed. I pressed that it was about Melanie's cash card being used at a bank branch three miles from their home, and her mother was quite insistent: "Won't be Melanie, then. My daughter hasn't left the house the last four months without me pushing her in a wheelchair. She's got multiple sclerosis".'

Bain nodded sombrely. The cash withdrawal made seconds after the attempted withdrawal on Isabel Alarcon's account had been £100 from Melanie Taylor's account, so they were convinced the two were linked. But Bain was perplexed: why use someone in England to track down these leads, when that person was clearly crippled? Unless, again, Melanie Taylor's mother was lying, covering up for her daughter?

They hoped that the cash point video might throw more light on the issue, so when it arrived half an hour later, they huddled around Rebecca Graves's computer as the segment began to roll.

'Okay, woollen hat, dark glasses, bit of a rock-chick thing going on,' Graves commented. 'Bit strange, given that it's already dark. But I suppose we've seen stranger things . . .'

At the point that the user appeared to look directly ahead at the machine, slightly startled – as if suddenly aware they'd done something wrong – Graves froze the frame, then zoomed in closer. 'Hopefully, it will now be clearer what's going on,' she said.

'Yes, as clear as mud,' Dereck Bain agreed hollowly, as he reached for the phone to call Spain.

47

Isabel, then

Falling into the abyss . . .

Mauricio's heart was in his mouth as Isabel slipped from his grasp. He felt sure she would fall into the abyss below after the large man.

'No . . .*no!*'

But as the last echo of his cry died, he heard a faint mumble; and with his eyes finally adjusting in the darkness, he could see Isabel clinging to a rock outcrop fifteen feet below.

'Don't move,' he called out. 'I'm coming down to get you.' He could see that her position was precarious; that if she moved or leaned back, she could fall.

He edged down cautiously; and, as he got closer, he ventured, 'Are you okay?'

Faint groan in response.

'You're conscious, at least. Are you able to talk?'

'I . . . I suppose.' Tremulous, tentative. '*Just.*'

Mauricio could see some blood on the rock from where she'd collided with it, but hopefully her injuries wouldn't be too severe. 'I'm almost with you. I'll get you back to safety.'

Arms clamped tight around Isabel, he hoisted her back up the rock face a foot at a time. For the last few feet it was tougher going, by then his energy was flagging. 'You're going to have to help me with this last part. Push up and clamber against the rock as I pull – otherwise, we won't make it.'

'Okay.' Shaky, quavering. 'I'll try.'

They were breathless as they finally got onto the firm slab of safety of the rampart wall. They took a moment to catch their breath, then Mauricio asked, 'Can you walk?'

'I don't know. I can try.'

Mauricio observed that she could walk, but she'd done something to her left ankle, so it was with an unsteady hobble, with Mauricio partly taking her weight, that they made their way along. There was a bloody graze on her forehead and another on her shoulder.

'Let's get you to Christina's to get cleaned up.'

'Thanks, Mauricio,' she muttered. 'I don't know what I'd have done without you.'

'That's okay. The question now is: what do we do next?'

48

Lapslie, now

Stone silence in the room as Mauricio related his account.

They were back in the interview room at nearby San Clemente: Mark Lapslie, Emma Bradbury, Bernardo Ruiz, and Mauricio's mousy lawyer, Enrique Navarre. Lapslie stroked his forehead for a moment.

'And did anyone see you on the way to Christina's with Isabel?'

'Only Betina. One of the young maids at the Parador, on her way to work. But I know Betina well, so I swore her to secrecy.'

'As you did no doubt with Sara at the Miramar,' Lapslie commented sharply, 'when you came to pick up Larry Gilbert's belongings that morning.'

Mauricio smiled meekly. 'One advantage of small towns. Some people can be depended upon for support. Even more so when Dario Alarcon is the suspected adversary.'

'You still suspect he was behind everything?'

'Yes, I do.'

Lapslie held Mauricio's stare for a moment. Certainly, the young man had the courage of his own convictions, even if they were misplaced. Little visible shadow of doubt. Lapslie shook his head.

'But why not just go straight to the police – why all the subterfuge?'

'Because Isabel and I feared we might be guilty of something with the man's death.'

'That surely would have been viewed as self-defence, with no charges to follow,' Lapslie said.

'We weren't sure of that. Especially in a country like Spain. We feared that we might still be facing manslaughter charges – which can carry six to eight years here.' Mauricio shrugged. 'Lapslie nodded slowly; not full acceptance, by any means, but at least a tame understanding.

Mauricio took a fresh breath. 'Also, Isabel feared that as soon as Dario discovered she was still alive, he'd simply hire someone else to try again – and next time be successful.'

'You're still convinced that Dario hired Gilbert?' Lapslie said. 'Despite the Marbella gangland link and the problems uncovered between Isabel's godfather and his old rivals?'

'Yes, I do. I think that Dario found out about those past problems, and that's why he hired someone like Gilbert from that world – so it would direct suspicion away from himself.'

Lapslie nodded thoughtfully. That too made perfect sense; but he was also keenly aware of the bitter rivalry between Mauricio and Dario, so had to take that into account and not let his judgement be swayed.

Mauricio sighed. 'Finally, Isabel needed time. Time to prove all these final things we'd uncovered about Dario Alarcon. So, her remaining missing, or dead, served a purpose with that also.'

'Including tracking down this Arthur Maitland – a researcher Isabel's father was due to meet the day he died,' Lapslie commented.

'Yes, that was the main thing. But Isabel simply couldn't appear as herself in tracking down and meeting Maitland – so she got the help of an old schoolfriend, Melanie Taylor.'

'Melanie wouldn't be able to help much in that regard,' Emma Bradbury interjected. 'Our team in Chelmsford spoke to Melanie's mum. She's got multiple sclerosis.

Hasn't been able to leave her house in four months without the aid of a wheelchair.'

'I know. I know.' Mauricio cradled his head in one hand. 'Isabel didn't know about that initially – Melanie had hidden her illness from Isabel. So that came as a total shock to Isabel when she found out.' Pained smile. 'But nevertheless, when Isabel told Melanie what had just happened to her, almost getting killed, Melanie was keen to help in whatever way she could. The first thing was her passport. Melanie said, "I'm not going anywhere, so you might as well use it. Driving licence and some debit cards too." They arrived a few days later by express post. Christina meanwhile worked on Isabel's hair colour and length, and make-up, so Isabel looked as close to the passport photo as possible.'

'That's quite a favour to call on a friend for,' Lapslie said.

Mauricio held one hand out. 'You don't understand. Stuck in her bedroom the past few months, suddenly this was some excitement for Melanie. Some activity. She felt *involved*, Isabel said. And meanwhile Christina would wire to Melanie's other account – a building society – any money that Isabel was using from her main account. So, she was never going to be out of pocket.

Besides, it was only going to be for a couple of weeks. Once we'd nailed Dario, Isabel would have surfaced.'

'So, what happened next?'

'Isabel initially lived at Christina's, so her injuries had time to heal. Then, when she was all cleaned up and the make-up right, I ran Isabel to Barcelona. And from there she hired a car in the name of Melanie Taylor to take her to England.'

'And where's she staying?'

'I don't have the exact address – but I suppose not far from that cashpoint you picked her up on in Southend.'

Lapslie wondered whether Mauricio was telling the truth, or whether in fact Isabel had withheld her actual address to protect everyone.

'I suppose Isabel's first port of call will be seeing this Arthur Maitland?'

'Yes. But she had some concerns, so I advised her not to go to his house. To meet him somewhere public.'

'So, they've already arranged to meet?' Lapslie pressed.

'Yes, apparently.'

'And where exactly might that be?'

'I'm afraid I don't know. All I know is it's some service station not too far from where he lives.'

Again, Lapslie wondered whether Mauricio was purposely being cute and holding back what he knew. But at least 'nearby service station' would narrow things down a bit.

49

Isabel, then

'You should have told me,' Isabel said.

Sat on the edge of her bed, Melanie wafted one hand towards her painfully thin legs, already half-wasted away. 'I didn't want you to see me like this.'

'I'd have understood. You're my oldest friend.' Isabel shook her head. 'After all, isn't that what good friends are all about? If you can't get them to understand with things like this, who can?'

'Well, I daresay you'd have understood.' Pained smile. 'But all those *understanding*, sympathetic looks – all those *"OMG poor you"* looks – I wasn't sure I could take those. It would have changed things between us.'

'I see.' Isabel wasn't sure what else to say; she still felt numbed by it all. Her old friend suddenly crippled by a debilitating disease.

'Oh, don't worry. It's not just with you – I hardly see

anyone else for the same reason. I just figured it would simply remind me of my plight. I'd see it reflected in each visitor's eyes.'

Isabel nodded. She could relate to that, *understand* that. 'When did you first know you had it, the MS?'

'I already had it when we last met for that murder-mystery weekend. That's why I invited you on it. I knew that might be one of my last chances for some "normal" time together with you.'

Isabel held a hand out. 'But *still* you didn't say anything?'

Melanie smiled tightly. 'That would have spoilt the "normality", wouldn't it?'

'Yes, I suppose it would have.' They were silent for a second, then Isabel commented with a smile, 'That murder-mystery weekend certainly was fun.'

'Yes, it was.'

'And if you think you're getting rid of me that easily, you've got another think coming. Do you recall those times when we used to race the train to the end of the pier?'

'Yes, I do.'

Isabel saw Melanie's face light up with the memory.

'Well, we can do the same again now – with me pushing your wheelchair.'

'Are you serious?' A sly leer from Melanie.

'It will make the race even more of a challenge. And the main shopping lanes of Southend – watch-out! We'll be as much a force to reckon with as all those don't-give-a-shit pavement cyclists put together.'

'Oh, Isabel.' Melanie was openly beaming. 'I think that near-death experience has somehow got to you.'

'Maybe.' Isabel nodded thoughtfully. 'Maybe it took getting close to losing my life to fully appreciate that it wasn't being lived to the full. But, for now, let's see if we can recreate the magic and excitement of that murder-mystery weekend with some good old-fashioned *sleuthing* . . .'

50

Lapslie and Bradbury, now

'Is my client under arrest?' Enrique Navarre asked.

'Not immediately,' Lapslie said. 'But I need to confer with my colleague, Inspector Ruiz, on what charges might arise, if any, from the information he's just given us. Which might also give rise to some further questioning . . .'

Emma Bradbury excused herself from the interview room for a moment, and as soon as she got outside of the Guardia Civil station at San Clemente, she dialled Dom in England on her mobile.

With all the talk about this Arthur Maitland and Isabel planning to meet with him, she suddenly thought she knew where she'd heard his name before.

As he answered, 'Dom. Emma. Does the name Arthur Maitland ring a bell?'

'Yeah, why?'

Bradbury felt her pulse quicken. 'It was *you* where I'd heard the name before. I couldn't recall at first.' She took a fresh breath. 'His name has come up in this investigation with Isabel – Terry Haines's goddaughter. Apparently, he's some sort of researcher who was involved in looking into her family's ancestry.'

'*Researcher?*' Dom chuckled. 'That's a good one. Arthur, or 'Awth' as he's known in the criminal fraternity, might have been a researcher while in the Navy, and a good signals man too – but his main trade is as a hitman. A bit like Larry Gilbert, who you found washed up the other day.'

Bradbury's stomach sank. 'Are you sure?'

'Yep. I'd bet the fort on it.'

'But why doesn't he come up on any police records? Why is there nothing on him anywhere?'

'Because he's been too careful. None of the hits he's been involved in have ever been recorded as anything other than either natural causes or accidents.' Dom sighed. 'No crime to start with . . . so no possible record.'

'*What?* Not a trace on a single one?' Bradbury was incredulous.

'You got it. That's why his nickname's AWTH – Accident Waiting To Happen. It's Arthur Maitland's main stock in trade.'

'Thanks, Dom. Gotta go . . .'

Bradbury raced back into the interview room and quickly brought Lapslie up to speed on her conversation with Dom. 'We must stop Isabel meeting up with Maitland! She's in danger. He's a hitman.'

Lapslie had just been finishing up with Mauricio, Navarre and Ruiz. Across the table, Mauricio looked suddenly alarmed, the colour draining from his face.

'Jesus!' Lapslie clutched at his head. He looked sharply across at Mauricio. 'Look! Try to get hold of Isabel urgently – tell her not to meet with Maitland under *any* circumstances.'

As Mauricio started dialling, the rest suddenly hit Lapslie in a rush. He led Bradbury back outside again.

'You know what else this means, don't you?'

'I . . . I'm not sure, sir.' There were a score of things it could mean, but she wasn't sure which specific one her boss might be thinking of.

'Two remote hitmen, hired years apart. The first after Sebastian Alarcon visits the town, the second when his daughter follows in his footsteps . . . Lapslie sighed. 'Mauricio has probably been right all along. From the outset, it *has* been about Alarcon.'

51

Sebastian Alarcon and Arthur Maitland, then

'You still looking to be more or less on time? Where are you now?'

'Still on the A20.'

'How far from the A252 turn off?

'Uh, four or five miles.'

'Okay. And don't forget not long after taking the A252, you then take the Canterbury road, which takes you all the way into Challock. I daresay you'll be with me in twenty minutes or so.'

'Yes. As long as I don't get lost or take any wrong turns.' Light chuckle from Sebastian. 'Thanks for the directions. See you shortly.'

As soon as the call was finished, Maitland left the phone on a side table, slipped on a jacket in which he had a fresh pay-as-you-go mobile, then drove four miles west, turned and stopped in a lay-by on the A252, a half-mile from the Canterbury road turn-off. Halfway along, he'd passed the long-trailer truck pulled into a similar lay-by on the Canterbury road.

He now took out his mobile to phone that truck driver. 'He should be passing me in just a few minutes. I'll let you know.' Then he phoned the driver parked in a heavy truck four miles further along the Canterbury road and said the same. 'Wait for my call.'

It had been dusk when he left home, now it was fully dark. Early November, it was dark by four-thirty. He knew Sebastian Alarcon's car-model, a grey Audi 80, and registration number, having asked it so that he could get him a resident's parking sticker when he arrived. He kept his eyes peeled at the passing cars, and finally he saw the grey Audi approaching. He pulled out straight after, then took out his mobile.

'He just passed me now,' Maitland announced to the truck driver. 'I managed to pull in right behind him. Steady forty-five miles an hour, so we should be with you in just a few minutes. I'll keep the line open . . .'

Maitland tapped out the next two minutes anxiously on his steering wheel, hoping that nobody came in between them in the meantime. He kept the gap between them as small as possible without appearing to press too close, or alarm the Audi in any way. With his headlights on full, he doubted that Sebastian Alarcon could see much beyond that glare, if he looked in his mirror.

'Okay. Pull out now,' he instructed the truck driver. 'Keep to just twenty to let the one car ahead of Alarcon pass you, then edge up to thirty . . .'

A double-length trailer truck, it was a formidable obstacle. Maitland watched it pull out ahead, the Audi and the Ford Mondeo ahead of it having to cut their speed drastically. Maitland watched the Mondeo wait for one car passing the other way, then he went for it, accelerating hard past the truck and pulling in ahead of it. He watched the Audi tempted to do the same, but then the truck picked up speed and another car was approaching . . .

Maitland phoned the other truck driver. 'Okay, set off now. Slow at first, then speed up as you see us approach.' Then he switched back to the first driver. 'Cut it back gradually to twenty again . . . then speed up again as he starts to overtake . . .'

At the 22 m.p.h. mark, Maitland watched the Audi swing out and go for it. He followed straight after, so that he was overtaking just behind the Audi. The truck was powerful though, and immediately started to pick up speed ... thirty ... forty ... fifty. The Audi tried to put on an extra spurt, but was still only two-thirds past the double trailer when the lights of the oncoming truck became visible swinging around the bend ahead.

There was a split-second when it looked like Sebastian Alarcon might just make it, but the truck simply edged up its speed to compensate, now touching sixty ... and the fall-back became the only option. The Audi frantically beeped its horn, perhaps at the truck to slow down, or at Maitland behind to pull back. But the truck didn't slow, and Maitland held his position firm just behind the Audi.

The oncoming truck lights filled their vision, a last frantic beeping from the Audi – perhaps this time to also warn the oncoming truck – but Maitland held his position till the last second, the point of no return for the Audi. Then he braked hard and tucked in sharply behind the double-trailer truck, watching the oncoming lorry hit the Audi with a sickening rending of metal as it swept the tangled wreck past him.

The double-trailer truck pulled in twenty yards ahead, and Maitland simply kept on driving, as if he'd never been present in the first place.

Which is the account that the two truck drivers would

give to the police: *no, no other vehicles were involved*. The Audi simply tried to overtake the double-trailer truck on a blind bend, and the oncoming truck driver didn't stand a change of avoiding him.

52

Isabel and Arthur Maitland, now

They'd arranged to meet at Park Farm, a nondescript retail park near Folkestone with the prerequisite sprinkling of brand-name stores, and a few others not so readily recognised. The main options to talk over tea or coffee were Sainsbury's or McDonalds, so they agreed on the Sainsbury's café.

Arthur Maitland had given her a description: late-fifties, sandy-haired, with a small beard and moustache, wearing tweed. 'I suppose I might look like an ageing sergeant major.'

She said she'd be wearing a green woollen hat, and she noticed a sandy-haired man lift one hand from the front window as she walked towards Sainsbury's. He'd obviously taken a seat by the window so that he could see her approach.

As she moved towards his table with a smile, he stood

up in greeting and held out one hand. 'Melanie Taylor, I assume. Pleased to meet you. Arthur Maitland.'

She took the hand and Maitland shook it vigorously, beaming. Though not that tall, she noticed that Maitland was quite stocky; he was strong, his grip firm. He was quite old-fashioned looking in many ways, even had a tweed waistcoat with a gold pocket watch on a chain.

'Ah, some teas or coffee? I'll get them.' No sooner had they sat down and Maitland was on his feet again. Maitland said he was having tea, and Melanie followed suit. She was generally a coffee person in the morning, tea in the afternoon.

Maitland beamed back at her halfway along the order counter, watched her smile meekly in return. *Melanie Taylor?* He wasn't fooled for a moment. He could see her father's resemblance strongly in her.

'Shame Isabel's father couldn't make it last time,' he said with a bittersweet smile as he set the tray down with their teas. 'Because I had something important to show him.'

'Oh, what was that?'

'Well, long time ago now . . . but I'd dug it all out ready to show him when he arrived. Got it with me in a folder in the car, if you want to see it?'

'Yes, that would be great.' She looked at him expectantly, but his face dropped slightly as if there had been a misunderstanding.

'Oh, I was thinking I would give it to you when we made our way back to our cars. If we break off now, our teas will get cold in the meantime.'

They sipped their teas in silence for a moment, then Isabel asked, 'Do you recall what this particular folder concerned? The one you planned to show Isabel's father?'

'It was to do with Joaquim Alarcon – Isabella's suspected son. The one they packed off to Madrid to study art. It appears Isabel's father was on the right track following that thread.'

'In what way?' Isabel sat forward keenly. 'Do you recall the details?'

'Long time ago now, and quite detailed . . . that's why I put it all into a report at the time. But it seems there was an extra element to all of that which Isabel's father appeared to have missed.' Maitland took a sip of tea. 'Still, it's all there in black and white. Nothing removed or embellished since. I'll show it to you in just a minute . . .' Maitland's gaze and thoughts drifted for a second. 'Must say, that apple pie on the counter looks tempting. I was tempted to grab a bit while I was there, but thought it impolite if I didn't ask if you wanted a slice as well.'

Isabel was a bit slow picking up the social cue. 'Oh, right. Don't worry – I'll do the honours this time, get some for us. After all, you got the teas.' She suspected he saw this as part-payment for going to the trouble of meeting her and giving her all the details on the Alarcon family history. *Small graces and mercies at his age.*

'That's very kind of you. Thank you.' Maitland smiled at her as she made her way towards the counter.

As she was preoccupied ordering the tart, Maitland slipped the pill into her tea. She didn't notice, nor did anyone else nearby. He'd disguised the action as he'd folded out his newspaper on the table to read. Concealed by the newspaper was the other thing she hadn't noticed: a small black call-jammer, busily blocking any mobile signals for two yards around. She wouldn't be able to receive any calls, nor make any out. He made sure to cover it again a moment before she returned with their apple pie.

'This is good,' he said, savouring a spoonful halfway through eating. 'Thank you.'

'No problem. My pleasure.'

'There was another name I recall from the file I had

for Isabel's father,' he commented after he watched her sipping her tea. '*Felicia*. Another missing link in the Alarcon family tree he didn't appear to have.'

'Not Magdalena?'

'No. From what I recall, he had that name already. But Felicia was Magdalena's half-sister. Her name didn't appear much, but she was also a descendant of Joaquim Alarcon, so equally important.'

'I see.' Melanie took another swill of tea. She couldn't wait to see this file. It appeared to be full of information they didn't already have. Seeing Arthur Maitland appeared to have paid off.

'I must say, Isabel's father sounded very nice on the phone.' He looked into the distance for a second. 'Such a shame . . .'

'Yes, he was.' She closed her eyes for a second, the memories too close, *too poignant* for a moment. She didn't want to break down in front of this Maitland and half a Sainsbury's café and make a spectacle of herself. She knocked back the last of her tea, grimaced tautly, as if to say: *Okay. Can we see this marvellous file now?*

Maitland was looking at her curiously, as if he was waiting for something, or perhaps was simply lost in thought. He snapped to after a moment. 'Sorry, my thoughts were drifting with the reminder of that almost-meeting years ago.' He slapped his hands on his thighs. 'So, yes if you're all finished, we can go get this file.'

Maitland stood up and she followed him. As they got outside, the thought suddenly hit: *his* car! But there were a fair few people around, ambling to and from their cars, and more still looking on from the café they'd just come from. It would be too obvious for him to suddenly cosh and bundle her into his car.

When Isabel saw the direction they were headed, she realised he couldn't have parked that far from her own car.

Sudden spasms hit her legs – and as she straightened, she felt everything swimming around her. She held onto the nearest car for support.

Her breath fell short, rasping – her first instinct to pull away as she saw Maitland reaching towards her. But then she realised she was collapsing completely, her legs giving way under her, and Maitland was trying to support her, carry her weight so that she didn't fall like a sack of potatoes onto the tarmac.

The car park continued spinning around her, then the tarmac below seemed to be moving past her without her even moving her legs.

And as Maitland hobbled along with her, through her spinning haze it hit her what had happened. When she'd gone to get the apple pie, he'd slipped something into her tea! Obviously, he seemed to know the exact time for it to take effect. Now to anyone looking on, it would look like she was simply drunk or unsteady, and this man was helping her to her car. *Her* car! They weren't heading to his own car at all. And now as she thought about it, she had no idea where his car even was . . .

53

Lapslie and Bradbury, now

'I can't get through to Isabel.'

'Try again,' Lapslie said.

'Still nothing,' Mauricio said after a moment. And this time he held his mobile screen out and looked at it curiously, as if it had caused him personal injury.

'What's happening when you phone? Simply ringing out, engaged?'

'It sounds engaged at first, then just dies. As if she's got her phone switched off.'

'Maybe she *has* got it switched off,' Lapslie commented.

'No, no.' Mauricio shook his head. 'We agreed that she wouldn't, that she'd keep her phone switched on throughout.'

They both sank into thought for a moment. Lapslie was first to look up.

'Let's see if we can get someone there – a local squad car. Where was it they were meeting?'

'A service station close to Maitland's home. She mentioned the name once – but I can't immediately remember it now.'

Bradbury had her laptop open and spun a few names from her Google search: 'Shell garage, Tesco, Gulf Station, Park Farm, Malcolm Waite . . .'

'Park Farm . . . yes, *yes*. That's it!'

'Are you sure?' Lapslie pressed.

'Absolutely.'

'Okay, Emma. Phone Chelmsford and get them to raise two squad cars from the Dover–Folkestone squad to visit Park Farm pronto.'

Bradbury brought back the Skype screen used for her previous contact, and within seconds was speaking again with DC Graves in Chelmsford. 'Dark-blue Barcelona-plated VW Polo, a Europcar hire car. So hopefully it should stand out a bit.'

Then the anxious wait to see what came back in.

Bernardo Ruiz had felt at a bit of a loose end with the current interplay, so had gone a few doors along to the nearest café to grab a coffee. And he was just walking back in when the news came back from Chelmsford.

'Nothing, I'm afraid.' Rebecca Graves sighed on the Skype screen. 'No sign of Isabel's car.'

'Okay, let's think, *think*,' Lapslie said 'Where might they have gone?'

'Perhaps his house,' Ruiz suggested. 'Especially if it's not that far away.'

'No, don't think so,' Lapslie said. 'If he's planning an accident of some type, that puts it too close to his doorstep.'

'Maybe he's slipped her some pills that would make it look like a natural-cause death,' Bradbury said. 'In which case, she could be slumped over the wheel in any lay-by or public car park.'

Lapslie gave this suggestion longer consideration. 'Possibly. But she's very young for a natural-cause death. Would take a lot to get it past a coroner without suspicion being aroused.'

As they exchanged suggestions, Mauricio tried Isabel's number again. 'Still no response from her,' he said as the same quickly dying engaged tone sounded the other end.

Silence for a moment in the room.

'Would he try and make a run for it to France with her?' Ruiz suggested. 'After all, the Channel Tunnel is right there.'

'Doubt it,' Lapslie said. Too much chance of getting stopped. Besides, he'd still have to plan an accident of some sort the other side.' Lapslie was suddenly hit with the thought; the mention of *accident* and *right there* bringing it to the forefront of his mind. He blurted out, '*Beachy Head!* That's right there too – only a few miles away.'

'What's that – Beachy Head?' Mauricio asked.

'It's one of England's prime spots for committing suicide,' Lapslie said.

54

Isabel and Arthur Maitland, now

Isabel could feel the breeze playing across her hair, teasing it, and heard the swell and crash of surf somewhere nearby, seagulls crying overhead. But she felt unable to move. It was as if it was all happening remotely, to someone else.

Someone else? And at a moment like this, she supposed, all subterfuge went too. She was no longer 'Melanie', no point in subterfuge anymore, her cover appeared to be blown in any case. So she was Isabel again, her thoughts drifting to other days on the beach with seagulls overhead. So many happy days and memories flooding in: with her father and mother when she was no more than eight or nine, then later with Terry and Barbara on Spanish beaches; although then it had been hotter, with hardly any seagulls in sight, and the smell of Ambre Solare and Nivea heavy in the air.

Other noises now, beyond her side vision: a dog barking, some people calling out. Then after a moment, they were suddenly in view, about forty yards ahead. A couple throwing a stick for their dog, calling out to it as it fetched, a hazy blue sea backdrop behind them, white cliffs to one side.

She wished she could raise a hand and call out to them, but her voice felt trapped in her throat, her body frozen. But then, after a few moments of helplessly watching them playing with their dog, as if through a hazy, opaque screen, she felt a fresh tingle in her fingers – she could suddenly move them! Her toes too when she tried. She made sure to keep the small motions hidden from the man next to her, and she felt the tingling start to spread to other parts of her body.

Maitland watched the couple playing with their dog ahead with mounting impatience. He didn't like it when things came up which might possibly interfere with his plans. Sure, if the couple looked back at them, it would look simply like a daughter with her father or uncle enjoying the view. But he should have had the car rolling forward relentlessly towards the cliff edge by now; if he left it too long, her pill might start to wear off.

She'd been completely immobile, her body lifeless, as he'd swapped their positions and put her behind the steering wheel. Hardly had he finished than the couple with their dog came into distant view; until that time, there'd been nobody in sight.

So now he simply had to wait it out.

They seemed to be taking forever. The stick thrown, the Labrador – or was it a Golden Retriever? – running and grabbing the stick, then dutifully returning with it, dropping it at their feet and looking at them expectantly, panting, excited for where they might throw it next.

Please, not another throw, Maitland mumbled to himself. *Or just throw the stick over the cliff.*

But they turned and threw it the other way along the cliff path this time. *Oh, variety wasn't dead after all.* Maitland closed his eyes momentarily, losing the will to live.

Two more stick throws before they finally gave up the ghost, decided it was time to head off. But they were slow moving away, and he had to wait until they were fully out of sight before he could set the car rolling towards the cliff edge.

*

As the figures ahead drifted out of her view, Isabel felt the movement fully back in her hand, and in part of her arm!

Though she didn't want to move her hand or arm fully, and give the game away that she could move now. Maitland might simply give her another pill or inject her with something.

A few moments later she saw him reach for the handbrake and open his door a few inches ready to leap out, and she realised she couldn't hold back any longer. She had to see how far she could reach out – whether she could get out of the car herself before it was too late.

Maitland let the handbrake off and they started to roll forward. Slowly at first, but as they started to gain momentum, his passenger door was pushed wider, ready for the jump.

As soon as she felt him tense for the leap – the car doing 20 m.p.h. now and steadily gaining speed – she went for it herself, reaching out for the door handle and flinging the door wide open.

But *too early!* He'd seen her trying to make the leap, and clutched at her, desperate to pull her back in. And he was strong. She had to wrench her body away from him once, twice . . .. *three times* before she finally broke free from his grip and was tumbling out.

As they'd grappled, the car had built up to 35 m.p.h. – one shoulder and her head banging against the car side as it rolled relentlessly past.

Maitland looked up, startled, as he realised she'd rolled clear, the cliff edge now only fifty yards away and the car now doing over forty.

He tried desperately to make the leap out his side, hoping that he didn't get too mangled by the rolling car – but then realised something seemed to be holding him back. His watch-chain had looped and caught around the handbrake as he'd frantically reached over, almost supine at one point, to grab her and hold her back.

Handbrake! His last possible saviour. He pulled up on it hard. Hopefully, it would stop the car before the cliff edge – only twenty yards away now!

But rather than stop, the car seemed to go into a lazy sideways slide, before finally tilting on its side and starting to roll.

'No . . . *no. No!*'

In her side vision, Isabel watched her VW hire car go into a roll and tumble over the cliff edge, Maitland's screams fading as it disappeared, the screeching of sea-gulls becoming prominent again.

She didn't have enough strength for a fist thrust fully skyward in victory, but she did manage a half-hearted, half-mast effort.

Then finally another screaming noise in the air; no, more a *wailing* as the sirens of two police cars wound their way towards her.

55

Lapslie and Bradbury, now

Dario Alarcon parked his red Ferrari at the furthest point of the Parador car park, close to the rampart edge.

It was a position he'd parked in many times before. It gave one of the best views over the town and the surrounding landscape. Not only a grand vista, but an overview of all his family owned. All *he* would soon own; after all, his father and uncle couldn't have too many years left.

And today the view seemed even better than normal; there had been a cloudburst a few hours ago, the first in days, and it had cleared the air. Usually at this time of year, a faint haze from the heat and dust would build up and partly obscure the view, restricting it. Now it was crystal clear.

He tapped his fingers on the steering wheel. When on earth was Maitland going to call? Over two hours since he was meant to have phoned with news about the girl. *What could have happened?* Maitland had said that it would be an easy hit; especially compared to the more complex hit arranged by his father on Sebastian Alarcon all those years ago.

That was another reason he'd swung up to the Parador car park. There were points in the town, a combination of closely encroaching buildings and the surrounding hills, where mobile reception wasn't a hundred percent; especially with calls from abroad. And Dario had started to worry that he might be in one of the town's signal 'blind spots'. That Maitland had been trying to reach him, but had been unable to get through. So, he'd headed up to the Parador car park, where signals were never impeded.

After fifteen minutes with nothing, he tried Maitland's number. No answer. It went to a voicemail service; he didn't leave a message. Then after another twenty minutes, he tried again. The same voicemail, but this time he left a message: 'I expected your call by now. Phone me back urgently to let me know how everything went.'

He waited, his impatience building, his finger-tapping on his steering wheel becoming increasingly anxious.

Beautiful girl *and* a long-lost relative. He'd actually felt a pang at having to get rid of her, whereas with her father he'd felt nothing. He hardly knew the man; most of her father's meetings had been with his own father. Whereas he'd personally met her and actually started to feel some genuine fondness for her. *Why did she have to go digging?* Once that started, the process became inevitable. His family had far too much to lose.

But as with Maitland and her father, he'd chosen hitmen remote from himself and any connection to Alarcon. Once he'd found out about the colourful background of her godfather, Terry Haines, it hadn't taken that long to track down a local Marbella–Malaga hitman, Larry Gilbert.

He hadn't in fact been sure of Gilbert's failure to get rid of Isabel until she'd surfaced again as Melanie Taylor in England, trying to make contact with Maitland. It had taken Maitland only a few hours to discover that Isabel's old schoolfriend Melanie Taylor had been wheelchair-bound the past four or five months. There was no way she could drive. So, Isabel had entered the spider's-web herself; they hadn't even needed to reach out and grab her.

It seemed to be a day of missed calls. The final confirmation from Maitland after he'd met the girl and was driving away from Park Farm with her drugged in the passenger seat beside him had gone into his own voicemail: *'Yes. I can confirm it's her. Positive match with the photos you emailed me. We're heading to Beachy Head now. Should all be wrapped within half an hour, forty minutes at most. I'll call you straight after.'*

Dario had been free of his meetings soon after, but no call back as yet. And now over two hours had passed since that first call!

Dario's fingers suddenly paused their drumming – a movement in his side vision catching his attention: two police cars pulling up in front of the Town Hall, Inspector Ruiz getting out of the lead car. Then a third unmarked car, the English Inspector and his assistant getting out. As they walked towards the Town Hall entrance, they were gone from view: the archway at the end of the main square obscured part of the view on each far side.

What was going on? Dario found himself torn between waiting for Maitland's call and finding out what this police entourage were up to at the Town Hall.

Finally, after a few more minutes, his curiosity was too

much. He tucked his mobile back into the side-partition of his glove compartment, fired up, and wound his way down the two hundred yards towards Place Marie.

'What's the meaning of this?' Dario Alarcon blustered as he walked in and took in the scene: a row of stacked files spread across the long council boardroom table, a young policeman at his father's computer in the adjoining office, two more at computers each side. 'We answered all of your questions at now two separate interviews and . . .'

Lapslie held one hand up, cut him short. 'You can spare us the faux-outrage. We've already had all of that from your father.'

Two yards to one side, Gabriel Alarcon flushed slightly at the put-down. Dario's eyes darted around anxiously a second longer.

'I trust you've got a warrant for all of this?'

'We most certainly have,' Bernardo Ruiz said, stepping forward and passing Dario four stapled sheets of paper.

Lapslie noted that Ruiz kept to English out of respect to himself and Bradbury. Certainly, both Dario and Gabriel Alarcon's English was good enough to perfectly comprehend. Although the warrant itself was in Spanish, and considerably longer than its English counterpart, Lapslie observed.

'As you'll see,' Lapslie said, 'it gives us full access to all your files and records, paper and electronic. Now, your father's already been kind enough to give us his password – so if you'll be kind enough to give us yours?'

'Ah, one minute,' Dario said, looking flustered as he glanced up from reading the warrant.

'Or, if you don't wish to give it, in half an hour or so the technicians will have hacked it.' Lapslie smiled tightly. 'But that might later add an "obstruction" charge when it comes to Court.'

Dario glared back. Then he reached for a pen and pad to one side, jotted his password down and passed it across.

'There you are, Inspector. Supplied without hindrance.'

Lapslie in turn passed it to Ruiz, who instructed the technicians in Spanish. One of them broke off and went to give it to the technician checking Dario's office computers a few doors away.

Dario took a deep breath, as if he was summoning strength. 'And what is the supposed charge?'

'The charge is that you and your father hired a certain

Arthur Maitland, a UK national, to murder Sebastian Alarcon. And that you hired another hitman, Larry Gilbert, and later Mr Maitland *again*, in the attempted murder of Sebastian Alarcon's daughter, Isabel.'

Lapslie noticed Dario's faint flinch at the mention of 'attempted'. Obviously, he'd expected that to be completed by now.

Dario smiled lopsidedly, as if shaking off the accusation. 'That's ridiculous! And what earthly evidence?'

'We have some files and evidence already.' Lapslie waved one hand towards the files on the boardroom table. 'And I'm sure we'll find more here.'

Dario's eyes continued darting for a second, searching for escape routes. 'And we have to ask ourselves just how you might have gained those earlier files, Inspector?' Dario smiled slyly. 'As we both know, anything gained through criminal means, such as a break-in, would be inadmissible.'

'A *break-in*?' Lapslie's brow knitted. Dario had made his first mistake. 'I don't recall any report of a break-in being made by yourself or your father.' He turned to Ruiz. 'Anything recorded to your department or local police?'

'No.' Ruiz shook his head. 'Nothing reported.'

Dario's face reddened. 'I . . . I wasn't sure there *had* been a break-in.'

'So, did you want to report that break-in now, along with its timing?' Lapslie pressed.

'I . . . I don't know. I have to think about that.'

'You see, this is how it works: no reported break-in, so officially it doesn't exist. Difficult to then later claim inadmissibility on files that were never stolen in the first place.' Lapslie watched Dario wither under his intense stare. He took a fresh breath. 'But I think we all know why you didn't report that *alleged* break-in. Because if you suspected Isabel Alarcon was behind it, that then supported a strong motive for you arranging her murder.'

'That's ridiculous,' Dario spluttered. 'As I told you before, I liked Isabel.'

Lapslie nodded slowly. 'I concede that you probably did. But, in the end, the protection of your position in Alarcon's hierarchy took precedence. You had too much to lose.' Lapslie held his hand out. 'Your mobile phone, please.'

The request had been tacked so quickly onto the end of the sentence that it took a second for Dario to snap to, take his mobile from his pocket and hand it over. Lapslie in turn handed the phone to Bradbury to check.

Lapslie gestured towards the files piled on the boardroom table and the technicians working on the computers. 'Apart from the semantics of any possible "inadmissibility" of our current evidence – I'm sure we'll find more than enough from this lot in any case.'

Bradbury had linked Dario's mobile to her computer. After a moment of scanning through call records and making comparisons, she looked up.

'I'm afraid there's nothing we don't already know from our past call monitoring.'

Lapslie noticed another small twitch of anxiety from Dario at the mention of 'call monitoring'. 'Which I suppose indicates the use of another mobile,' Lapslie said to Bradbury, before turning to look at Dario. 'Care to enlighten?'

Dario just shrugged, but a second later Ruiz moved in on him, waving a four-inch square black plastic device up and down in front of him.

'Nothing registering on him,' Ruiz said. 'And we've already checked the boardroom here and his private office a few doors away.'

'What is that?' Dario asked.

'Mobile phone signal scanner,' Ruiz said. When earlier Lapslie had asked if they had such a device, Ruiz had checked with his Madrid technical team and confirmed that indeed they did. Since then, it had been Ruiz's new toy, scanning at every available opportunity.

Lapslie noticed Dario's eyes fall to their own mobiles all laid on the boardroom table, so that the signals weren't confused. Lapslie was pensive for a second before looking up again and holding out one hand.

'Your car?'

Dario's hand went protectively to his key fob. 'I'm sorry, Inspector, I don't just hand my car keys to anyone.' They stood for a moment in an awkward Mexican stand-off before Dario offered hesitantly, 'But ... but I'll open it up for you if you wish.'

Lapslie followed Dario out the boardroom and down the Town Hall steps to his car, Ruiz and Bradbury with her laptop close behind. Ruiz would scan, Bradbury would check the calls if a mobile was found. But Lapslie noted that Dario's step was heavy, hesitant, and a faint lemon and creosote taste hit the back of his throat. *Deception.* Dario was hiding something.

Dario pressed his automatic key and the Ferrari's lights flashed.

Ruiz opened the passenger door and started scanning. He quickly picked up a signal from what looked like the glove compartment, but when he opened it, there was nothing but papers inside: no mobile phone.

Ruiz looked up. 'Is there another compartment here?'

Dario just shrugged, and it took a few more minutes of Ruiz fumbling before he managed to locate and press open a side compartment and fish out the mobile there. Ruiz looked curiously at the clip-on grill on its front for a second, then got out and handed it to Bradbury. She plugged the mobile into her laptop and started scanning.

A couple of non-related calls, and then she hit gold with the earlier voicemail message:

'Yes. I can confirm it's her. Positive match with the photos you emailed me. We're heading to Beachy Head now. Should all be wrapped within half an hour, forty minutes at most. I'll call you straight after.'

Then, two hours and forty-three minutes later, a return call logged to that same mobile number; obviously, Dario following up on that earlier call.

Examining the clip-on front grill, Bradley commented, 'Probably some sort of voice-masking.'

The Ferrari's car door closing broke their concentration. They'd been so absorbed with listening to the phone messages two feet to its side that meanwhile, obviously knowing the game was up, Dario had slipped into his car.

As the engine fired up, Ruiz reached out desperately to the car – but shiny metal slid quickly from under his hand as, with a throaty roar, the Ferrari sped away.

56

Lapslie and Bradbury, now

It was quickly determined that Ruiz had the fastest car. Lapslie jumped into the passenger seat, Bradbury in the back, and they set off. But the Ferrari had a good hundred and fifty metres on them, and gaining.

'We'll have trouble catching him,' Ruiz said. 'We'll have to radio ahead for some other cars to try to head him off.'

'But that will depend on which way he heads when he hits the main N111,' Lapslie commented. 'Whether he heads for Madrid or Valencia.'

'True.' Ruiz began to worry that the Ferrari might be out of sight by the time they reached the N111 themselves, especially if there were any nearby curves in the road. But a smile slowly rose on his face as they approached the main road junction and he heard the roar of the Ferrari off to their left. 'He's heading to Valencia.'

Ruiz got on his radio and put out an alert to cars within ten to thirty kilometres east of the N111 Alarcon junction. He gave a description of the Ferrari and its registration. 'Set up a road block to stop the car. It's unlikely you'll catch it in a straight pursuit.' Ruiz checked his speedometer: touching 150 k.p.h. on a flat stretch. 'And be careful not to set it up too close to the junction. He'll be travelling at one-sixty to one-eighty kilometres an hour – so he'll have covered twenty kilometres in just six or seven minutes.'

The first to pick up the alert was a single Seat police car parked at the small village station of Motilla del Palancar, sixteen kilometres east of Alarcon, and a Nissan Highway Patrol car travelling another eleven kilometres east of the town. Given the speed of the approaching Ferrari, they worked out the best place to convene to set up an effective roadblock was two kilometres east of Motilla del Palancar. The road also narrowed down slightly at that point, with a rock face one side and gulley the other. An approaching car wouldn't simply be able to sweep around them, as it might do on flat ground.

*

Dario knew every inch of the roads surrounding Alarcon. So, apart from his faster car, with his local road knowledge, it wasn't anywhere near a fair contest. He knew that Ruiz had little chance of catching him.

His mind turned to options, his possible escape routes. He'd headed to Valencia because the options were broader. Not just an escape by private plane, as would be the case with Madrid, but also various points along the Valencia coast; he knew a number of people with private boats as well as planes.

The only thing then would be contact. He'd have to stop off at some stage to buy a pay-as-you-go mobile. And while his Ferrari was fast and he could lose most if not all Spanish police cars, it was also easily spotted and recognisable; he might at some point have to change for a slower but more invisible car. Perhaps a Seat that would blend in with thousands of other Spanish cars. But to do that, he'd first have to create enough distance from any pursuing police cars to lose them completely.

He put his foot down harder. Already Ruiz's Alfa Romeo was just a blip in the distance behind him, only barely visible on flat stretches. Within a couple of minutes – Dario meanwhile flashing past a Renault barely doing ninety k.p.h. – the Alfa had completely gone from view.

Dario smiled thinly. But then it as quickly faded as peering into the distance ahead he could see faint flashing lights, becoming clearer as he got closer. A road block!

He slowed, his mind frantically spinning for other options. *A turn-off!* He recalled passing the turn-off for the CM220 just over a kilometre back. But that would also mean heading back towards Ruiz.

Not ideal, but the only remaining option! He slowed and braked, did a sudden spinning U-turn two hundred metres short of the roadblock, and sped back the way he'd just come.

He spun back past the Renault, who beeped and flashed his lights at him, obviously perturbed by Dario's erratic driving. Then five hundred metres on he could see Ruiz's Alfa approaching, blue light flashing on its roof.

Ruiz appeared to slow, obviously confused for a moment by his approach. But Dario was also faced with a dilemma: the CM 220 junction was fast approaching on his right. Did he let Ruiz swing past, or put his foot down harder and try and make the turn before Ruiz got to it?

Ruiz was slowing even more and attempting to play chicken by swaying into his lane, which made the decision for him. He put on an extra burst, swinging in with a wild tyre screech just twenty metres ahead of Ruiz.

'What the *hell* is he doing?' Lapslie exclaimed, thinking for a second the Ferrari was aiming straight for them before realising he was aiming for the turn-off.

Ruiz had already braked slightly to avoid a head-on collision and slammed them on hard as he realised Dario had taken the turn off, coming to a halt finally thirty metres past the turn. He quickly did a U-turn and swung back, noticing that the two road-block cars – the Nissan Patrol and a Seat – had also picked up on what was going on and were fast approaching as he swung into the CM220 turn off, trailing about a hundred metres behind him as he started along the narrower side road.

Dario checked in his mirror. Ruiz was a good three hundred metres behind, but he'd be able to outrun him on this road also; Dario knew the country well, and his Ferrari was built for these narrower, winding roads.

He put his foot down hard, felt the wheels gripping each turn, as if his car and the road were one. The turns were slight at first, but then became steeper and sharper as the road wound its way up through the hills and the mountains approaching Almodovar del Pinar.

In many ways, it reminded him of the hills and valleys around Alarcon. *Familiar ground.* He felt not only part of the road, but also the surrounding scenery; whereas in contrast, he doubted Ruiz had ever been on this road before.

He glanced again in the mirror: Ruiz was now almost five hundred metres behind, completely out of sight on the sharper turns, and slipping further behind by the minute. A sudden thought was sparked, and he tried to recall what turn-offs there were on the road ahead. Even a small farm track would do. He'd get enough distance from Ruiz that he was completely out of view, then take that turn quickly and duck down out of sight behind the nearest farm building, rocky outcrop or hedgerow. And immediately kill his engine. Hopefully, Ruiz and the police cars behind would sail straight past, thinking he'd simply continued on the CM220.

But he'd need more distance between himself and Ruiz to achieve that, and he put his foot down more. A sign flashed by: *Almodovar del Pinar, 8km.* Or maybe in the village itself. There'd be a number of turn-offs and buildings he'd be able to duck quickly behind. At this rate, averaging at over 120 k.p.h., he'd be there in only four minutes – and certainly would have created enough distance from Ruiz by then!

His thoughts suddenly ground to a halt, along with his car, with a bus looming ahead. Only one of six buses to Almodovar del Pinar a day – one every three hours – it chugged up the slope towards the town, belching diesel fumes as it went, barely doing forty. But to Dario, cutting back from 120 k.p.h., it felt like coming to a virtual halt.

He looked frantically ahead, but the bend ahead was completely blind, and as the road straightened and he started to edge out, a Seat Ibiza was coming towards him, lights flashing – only the fourth car that had so far passed the other way – he had to hastily pull back in again.

Another blind bend ahead. He looked anxiously in his mirror: Ruiz was only 250 metres behind now, and closing fast. He'd have to go for it soon, otherwise Ruiz would catch him!

A flat stretch again ahead, but another blind bend at its end – though he was sure he could make it. He swung out and put his foot down hard, distracted halfway through overtaking by the bus beeping its horn at him.

What on earth is he beeping at? Then he suddenly saw it: a camper van swinging around the bend ahead towards him. He had a sudden flashback to the dilemma Sebastian Alarcon must have faced that night with Maitland's arranged accident. But this was different. He had a powerful Ferrari, and he was sure he could make the gap.

He put his foot flat down, touching 120 k.p.h. again, and swung sharply back in the gap between the bus and the approaching camper with only a split-second to spare.

He smiled to himself at his driving skills and the Ferrari's power. But it quickly died as he felt the back end of his car still drifting away with the sudden swing back in.

While he knew the road, one thing he hadn't taken account of was the earlier rain. Eight dry days, the first rain had lifted all the oil and tyre rubber stuck to the road meanwhile, so that now it was a slippery film.

Dario braked and swung his steering wheel the other way to compensate, but his wheels were locked, his back end continuing to swing inexorably towards the side barrier at over 100 k.p.h. The barrier crumpled on impact, Dario holding his hand up defensively as the air bag burst against him.

There was a suspended moment when it looked like the barrier might hold him teetering on the edge, but then the last part gave way and the Ferrari rolled down the rocky slope three hundred feet into the ravine below.

The bus pulled in just behind where the Ferrari had gone over the edge, and a few people, including the driver, got out to see. This was obviously quite a dramatic local event.

Ruiz edged past the bus, blue light still flashing, and, as he got out, he asked the crowd to keep back a bit, making it clear this was now a potential crime scene. The Nissan and Seat parked just behind the bus, three uniformed policemen getting out and walking up.

'If you've got some marker cones and tape,' Ruiz directed them, 'can you mark the area off from here?' He pointed five metres back from where the barrier had been broken through.

Lapslie and Bradbury were only a yard from where the barrier had broken through, looking at the crumpled Ferrari far below. Ruiz was already on his mobile, calling for an ambulance along with back-up recovery vehicles – but Lapslie knew, looking at the wreckage

below, there would be no chance of Dario Alarcon sur-
viving such a crash.

Lapslie sighed. 'Usually when things like this happen,
there's a bulldozer emerging from a tunnel pushing the
car over the edge.'

Bradbury's brow knitted. 'What was that, sir?'

'*The Italian Job*. It's okay. Before your time, Bradbury.'

57

Isabel, Melanie and Mauricio, now

Isabel's breath started to catch, the wind-rush against her face and hair bracing, exhilarating, as she ran full-pelt along Southend pier pushing Melanie in her wheelchair in front of her.

'We're ahead of it now!' she exclaimed breathlessly. 'A good ten yards at least!'

Melanie joined her in glancing to the left at the mini-train that trundled the length of Southend Pier – at one mile, Britain's longest.

'Yes, we've done it, *we've done it!*' Melanie joined in excitedly. 'We've beaten the train! But let's see how much more of a lead we can get on it.'

'I don't want to go too fast. If we hit a bump, you might tip out.'

'Don't be silly,' Melanie admonished. 'I can get in and out of a wheelchair. How do you think I got in it in the first place? Faster, *faster!*' she exclaimed, slapping the side of her wheelchair as if she was whipping a horse.

'Okay.' Isabel put on an extra spurt, gaining an extra eight yards on the train over the next two hundred yards. But looking ahead, she could see that they were only just over halfway, and already she could feel herself flagging. As she became tired and her legs weakened, the train might start to catch up. It was equally important that she pace herself so that they were still ahead at the end of the pier – not just in the lead for a short while.

Isabel managed to get another two yards' lead before she felt the peak of her energy go, and they started to slide back, able to only keep the same lead on the train for the next hundred yards – then the train started to chip away at that lead. Eighteen yards behind . . . *seventeen!*

'It's catching us!' Melanie exclaimed worriedly, mock-whipping the side of her wheelchair again, as if that might help.

Isabel's chest was aching with the effort of drawing breath, her legs throbbing and feeling like rubber – but she pushed on regardless, determined to beat the train as they reached the pier-end.

Fourteen . . . twelve . . .

Still a hundred and fifty yards to go, and the train was catching up fast – it didn't look like they would make it.

Nine . . . *seven* . . .

The end of the pier jolted in Isabel's sweat-dappled vision, her whole body trembling with tiredness and exhaustion, the train now only a few yards behind pulling level with them. *Impossible*, Isabel thought, no strength left . . .

But then in the last fifty yards, the train began to slow in preparation of the stop ahead, and Isabel managed to reach the end with Melanie just two yards ahead of the train.

'We did it . . . *we did it!*' Melanie shouted excitedly. 'We beat the train!'

Isabel just nodded, gasping for breath, unable to speak for almost twenty seconds, and only then between heavily-drawn breaths. 'Yes . . . *yes* . . . we did it!'

Isabel imagined that she could still feel that exhilarating breeze against her face now as she opened her eyes to look out at the hills and valleys surrounding Alarcon. Standing on the Parador rampart edge not far from where she'd almost lost her life twenty-odd days ago, her eyes had closed for a moment with the memory – a warm breeze rising up from the valley floor and playing across her body.

'It's good that you did that with Melanie,' Mauricio said as she finished telling him about her day out with Melanie in Southend. 'It shows you've got a good heart.'

Stood at her side, enjoying the view – one he'd seen countless times before – Mauricio affectionately clutched her arm before letting go. Not quite the fully fledged touch or embrace of a boyfriend but getting there.

Isabel lightly touched his arm back, making it clear his affection was reciprocated. What she'd have done without Mauricio's help, she didn't know. *I'd be lost in the void below, for a start.*

'It was the least I could do. Melanie and I go a long way back – and I feel guilty now that we lost touch when I came to Spain.' She grimaced tautly. 'So I'm making up for lost time.'

After the Pier run, they'd had fish and chips at a seafront café, then made a day of it among Southend's shops and pedestrian lanes.

Her first call from the Dover Police Station had been to Terry and Barbara to let them know she was alive and well.

'We did have a call from your old friend, Melanie, so

we began to wonder,' Terry commented. 'But we did as told and kept schtum with the police.' Terry no doubt smiling to himself his end, knowing that the police in Dover would be listening in on the call.

Then four hours later she spoke with Inspector Mark Lapslie of Chelmsford police who told her about Dario Alarcon's accident and brought her up to date with the status of his investigation with Inspector Bernardo Ruiz from Madrid.

'It does appear as if the claim originally made by Mauricio Reynes, that Dario Alarcon and his father were behind your attempted murder and the murder of your father, is in fact true. Though we have a couple more days searching through files and records to be able to determine the full extent of Dario and his father's involvement. No doubt you will want to spend that time with your family in Valencia before we meet with you and Mauricio to share the final outcome of the case.'

They arranged to convene on Inspector Lapslie's last night in Alarcon before he had to fly back to the UK. And Isabel did indeed spend that time with Terry and Barbara in Valencia. Having left Melanie with the promise that they'd make their days out together a regular thing, she took the first flight out, spending much of her time by the pool while Barbara brought her endless teas or lemonades, asking her every other hour, 'Are you sure you're okay?', and cooking gigantic fry-ups, BBQ's or curries, as if she hadn't eaten for a year.

Mauricio swept one arm out at the view and the town to one side. 'Seems that much of what you see before you will now be yours.'

'Don't get carried away now. There's an awful lot of paperwork to sift through to get anywhere near that being determined.' She smiled tightly. 'And you won't be doing so badly, either. Not only your mother's property, but the way your family was historically sidelined might see other property granted to you too.'

Mauricio nodded thoughtfully. 'Probably there are a fair few others in a similar position to my family. Their rights and property chipped away by the Alarcons over the past few centuries.'

'*Exactly*,' Isabel said, smiling. 'By the time that's all sorted out and put to rights, I'll be a pauper again.'

They chuckled lightly, Isabel reminded that self-deprecation worked equally well in Spanish. Isabel peered more intently at the view ahead.

'Mixed memories,' she said. 'But I think I need to follow through wherever my family's fortunes lead for my father's benefit as much as my own.' She sighed heavily. 'After all, he lost his life pursuing my family's bloodline.'

'And you almost lost your own.' Mauricio lightly gripped her arm again, as if reassuring her, *You're safe now*. 'And I'm sure he'd approve of your decision. It's almost as if you're finishing what he started.'

Isabel nodded sombrely, feeling in that moment as if an invisible thread linked her to her father. She'd felt it at moments during her own family-history search but, looking out across the town and the view beyond, that link felt stronger now. *Everything coming full circle from the search her father had started all those years ago.*

She noticed Mauricio look back at the sound of a car approaching, pulling to a halt in the Parador car park.

'Looks like they're here,' Mauricio commented, as two men and a younger woman got out of the car.

'Oh, right,' Isabel said, a second slow in responding. She'd never seen Mark Lapslie or Bernardo Ruiz before, only heard their names mentioned.

They walked towards the Parador entrance to greet them.

58

Lapslie and Isabel, now

They just indulged in light conversation while their orders were placed, speaking of nothing specific to the case.

'I must say, it's good to see you finally in person,' Lapslie said to Isabel as he handed his menu back to the waiter. 'And most importantly, given all you've been through, to see you well and all in one piece.'

'Scrubbing up well,' Isabel commented, smiling.

Lapslie nodded, returning Isabel's smile. Mauricio's brow knitted faintly again; clearly another English expression still lost on him.

Lapslie turned to Mauricio. 'I think I should start by apologising for initially doubting you about Dario Alarcon's involvement – putting it down to just bitter rivalry between the two of you. But the main reason for my involvement and that of my colleague Emma Bradbury was a suspected gangland feud with Isabel's godfather. So we were duty-bound to pursue that lead first.'

Bradbury interjected, 'It seems that Dario also picked up on that possible link, which is why he chose Larry Gilbert as a hitman.'

'Pointed suspicion as far as possible away from himself and Alarcon.' That had been one of Lapslie's toughest conversations so far with Rouse back at Chelmsford HQ: telling him that in the end there'd been no involvement at all with Vic Denham. With Beneyto drawing a blank on any alternative places Larry Gilbert might have his old 'insurance policy' mobiles stashed away, it looked like Rouse's old nemesis would get away clean again.

'Are you *certain*?' Rouse had pressed.

'Yes, absolutely. We've acid-tested every possible remaining angle, sir. Vic Denham wasn't involved at all . . . But look at it this way: if it wasn't for us pursuing that Vic Denham link and coming out here in the first place, the real culprit behind Isabel's disappearance might never have been uncovered.'

'I suppose.' Reluctant acceptance of that silver lining. Rouse would obviously have far preferred to nail Denham.

'It's also, if I may say, been a great feather in our caps for striking a good working accord with the local Spanish police. Not only nailing the right suspect in Dario Alarcon, but also those other major collars in Marbella that Inspector Beneyto has been able to make.'

'Yes, I suppose there is that.' Rouse sighed. 'Still would have been nice to have the cherry on the cake of finally getting Denham, though.'

Rouse was still clinging to that hope of justice for his old nemesis, Denham; and Lapslie could hardly blame him. But hopefully that shining example of international cooperation – when so often British liaisons with police abroad had gone disastrously wrong – would go some way towards salving it. 'Also, there's one final factor we should consider.'

'What's that?'

'Well, if it's any consolation, sir. Having seen Denham in person, he's old and frail now. Legs thin and doddery. His days of kicking anyone to death are long gone. He'd have trouble kicking a cockroach to death.'

'Yes, I daresay there's some sort of solace in that.' Heavy sigh. 'But it still seems somehow wrong that Denham should finally escape justice.'

Hanging up, Lapslie thought to himself: *Is that how*

every copper saw it? They couldn't mentally close the book on anything until justice had been 'seen' to be done?

'It will take some while to sort everything out with this case,' Ruiz was saying to Isabel and Mauricio. 'A lot of old files and records to sort through. The main case alone against Gabriel Alarcon and his brother could take a year to come to court, and all the connected property and rights issues with Alarcon another eight months to a year after that.' Ruiz grimaced. 'The wheels of justice in Spain move slowly, I afraid. So, it could take you a while to see any reward from it.'

Isabel smiled tightly. 'It's okay. I'm a student. I'm not meant to be rich.'

Lapslie noticed Mauricio reach across and lightly clasp Isabel's hand, reassuring. Clear affection between the two of them.

'One thing that's perturbed me about this case, though,' Lapslie said to them. 'Why did you "play dead" for a while after Larry Gilbert's attempt on your life? Why didn't you come straight to the police after that?'

They looked at each other for a moment. Mauricio answered. 'Because we were unsure how much of a grip

Dario had on the town. We thought that if he discovered Isabel was still alive, he'd simply try again.'

Isabel added, 'I was also worried about being implicated in the man's death.' She shrugged helplessly. 'Also at that point, we had no idea who he was and why he might have tried to kill me. I thought I might have more chance of finding all of that out, as well as chasing the last links my father had pursued, if I was invisible for a while.'

Lapslie glanced at Ruiz before looking back directly at them. 'While I can't speak fully for how the Spanish justice system works, I would imagine that your actions would be seen as self-defence. Gilbert was trying to pull you to your death, and if you hadn't kicked him free, he'd have been successful.'

Ruiz nodded. 'I think that's very much how the courts will look at it. But there are also the slightly stickier points of misleading us, possibly "perverting the course of justice" with assumed identities, collecting Gilbert's belongings and removing his hire car.' Ruiz's eyes rested keenly on Mauricio as he finished before easing into a strained smile. 'You'll both need a good lawyer for that. But if he argues the case strongly and convinces the judge of the fear and threat you felt under at the time, the first indications from my bosses are that the courts will look leniently upon that. At most, six months to a year, suspended sentences, if not completely cleared.'

Lapslie noticed another brief hand-clasp between Isabel and Mauricio. They'd already been through a lot together, but still a residual strain of that journey remained.

Ruiz took a sip of his red wine. He still seemed troubled by something. 'I must also take issue with you thinking Dario Alarcon and his father might have any influence over the police. Those days are long gone in Spain. In fact, going all the way back to when Paloma Picasso was prosecuted for tax fraud. That sent a clear message within Spain: that even those at the heart of the establishment were not safe from the law.'

'I accept that,' Mauricio said, grimacing. 'But often towns like Alarcon are insulated from that. It can take a while for the justice in the power centres of Madrid and Barcelona to make it all the way out here.'

So, they were back again to Alarcon's insulation from the world outside, Lapslie considered. What on one hand, clinging to a medieval past, was its main attraction, on the other hand was its downfall.

Looking at Isabel Alarcon, Lapslie wondered whether

a new era might now await the town. A fairness, justice with property and other rights for its inhabitants that so far hadn't been evident. Hopefully, its only remaining link to the past would be in visual terms.

'And are you sure Arthur Maitland was guilty of killing my father?' Isabel asked Lapslie.

'Yes, we're sure,' he answered, glancing briefly at Bradbury. 'Maitland in fact had a past MO for arranging accidents, which he'd been so careful and meticulous in handling that it was only known on some criminal grapevines. Nothing had ever appeared on past police records.'

'I see.'

Lapslie could see the pain etched in Isabel's face; the bitter pill that her father might have died in a car accident – which she'd accepted and believed for many years – far easier to swallow than the fact that he'd been intentionally murdered.

'But it was in fact that connection with Maitland,' Lapslie added, 'which led to us nailing Dario Alarcon. Two quite specific hitmen hired years apart, both far removed from Alarcon. And then of course the final element of Maitland trying to arrange your "suicide", and Dario's calls to him. The last nail in Dario's coffin.'

Isabel nodded thoughtfully, and soon after their meals arrived, the atmosphere lightening.

As they ate, Lapslie reflected that it had probably struck Isabel in that moment how her father's murder had reached a hand through the years to bring about justice for Dario and Gabriel Alarcon. *Karma*, even if in such a roundabout way.

Lapslie raised his glass in a toast. 'To the future of Alarcon, and whatever good I'm sure you two will now bring to the town.' Lapslie's eyes rested warmly on Isabel and Mauricio before turning to Bernardo Ruiz. 'And to Spanish justice for finally reaching *nether regions* like this.'

Isabel and Emma laughed. Ruiz shrugged, smiling. 'I asked for that.'

Both had been a long time in coming, Lapslie thought as they settled back to finish their meals, reminding him of a home truth from his long years of police work: *justice often took a while*.

In the case of Isabel Alarcon and her family, it looked like it had taken several hundred years to arrive.

59

Lapslie, now

A small glint. Hardly noticeable halfway down the rock face.

Mark Lapslie perhaps wouldn't have noticed it if he hadn't been taking one last look at the crime scene – the spot where Largo had tumbled to his death – before he left Alarcon.

He'd gone out to his favourite look-out spot just as the sun was going down over the surrounding hills. His favourite times to stand there were sunrise and sunset, feeling the surrounding peace and grandeur suffuse through him as he took steady breaths. A last recharging of his batteries before his flight early the next day and returning to face the more hectic cut-and-thrust of London and Chelmsford HQ.

He squinted but couldn't make out clearly what it

was. He went into the hotel, asking reception, 'Do you have such a thing as a pair of binoculars?'

The girl at the desk grimaced hesitantly. 'I'm not sure. Let me ask one of the maintenance men.'

She came through a door at the back after a moment with some binoculars, with a man in overalls talking in Spanish a yard behind her.

'It appears you're in luck,' she said, passing them to Lapslie. 'Apparently, we use them to check the castle roof for damage.'

'I'll let you have them back in just a minute,' Lapslie said, and headed back out.

It took him a moment to get the object in focus: it looked like a key attached to a small leather fob. He lowered the binoculars for a second to gauge the relative position on the slope – just over midway down the rock face – then looked through them again at the object.

Why hadn't the forensic team spotted it during their exam-ination? But then he reminded himself that they'd concentrated on only two sections: higher up, and then close to the river, where blood stains had been visible. Also, looking through the binoculars, he could see a small rocky outcrop just above the key. Lapslie lowered them again, looking at the sun's position now. Low and shining straight at the rock face, so the key glinted with reflected light. Whereas, when the forensic team had been on the rock face, the sun had been high. The key would have been in total shadow under the outcrop.

It was in a direct line from where Largo had fallen, and it would have to have been dropped recently; it didn't appear weathered or dirty.

The only question now remaining was how to retrieve it?

Lapslie watched as the climber was slowly lowered down the rock face by his two co-climbers at the top: one operating the main rope-winch, the other providing extra guidance and resistance with the rope – feeding it out more gently at points where the winch might jolt slightly.

The climber, in his early thirties, had clambered down most of the first part. But as the rock face became steeper, he was hanging free, reaching out to touch and brace against the rocks at points so that he didn't start spinning. He also signalled more towards his colleagues at the top now, Lapslie noticed; directing both the speed and direction of his descent.

At first, Lapslie had been stuck for how to raise a

climbing crew quickly, but Mauricio had come to the rescue. He recalled that there was a keen climber in town, Ramon; he'd seen Ramon board his bus with all his climbing gear on a couple of occasions to meet up with other climbers in nearby La Almarcha.

It turned out that Ramon was part of a dozen-strong group of keen local climbers. Most of them were un-available at such short notice, but Mauricio pressed him, stressing the urgency: 'But you said yourself – you only need two others to assist you.'

Ramon managed to raise two others during the morning, and they met at midday by the Alarcon Parador. Lapslie had also had to delay their flights and put in a call to Rouse about the extra delay. 'We have found an item of evidence connected to Larry Gilbert that we previously missed. Shouldn't hold us up long, sir. If it's not significant, obviously we'll head straight out.'

As Lapslie looked on at the climber's progress, he saw that his theory about the key being in heavy shadow as the sun rose higher was correct. He'd had to visually guide them to the spot where he'd seen it earlier that morning, 'Just under that small nub of rock jutting out,' he'd pointed. 'It will hopefully become evident as you get closer.'

Lapslie watched keenly as Ramon got closer to the small outcrop. Resting one hand on the nub of rock to steady himself, he looked underneath, holding his other hand up to signal that he'd seen it; then, using the same hand, he picked up the key and fob and held it proudly aloft with a smile.

Vic Denham awoke slowly at first; in that trapped moment between the last vestiges of nighttime and dawn. Then with a *'What the hell'*, he sat up sharply as it hit him that some of the light was swinging around and moving like strobe lighting. He'd barely registered the time on his bedside clock, 3.14 a.m., as one of the lights swung fully onto his body, the red dot just beneath it aimed squarely at his chest.

Two other GEOs – *Grupo Especial de Operaciones*, the Spanish equivalent of a SWAT team – quickly joined their colleague, their MP-5 red dots hovering inches to each side. Denham held both arms up hesitantly as he saw Inspector Mark Lapslie walk in just behind them with a self-satisfied smile.

'Okay. Out of bed, so we can get you cuffed!'

Denham swung himself out of bed, but sat there for a

second, blinking slowly. Lapslie noticed that Denham's spindly legs were shaking.

'Give us a chance to get my legs steady and working, will ya,' Denham said with a heavy scowl.

'Maybe that's not such a good idea given your history,' Lapslie said, his smile rueful before dropping sharply. 'Come on, shift it!'

Between the four locksmiths contacted in the Marbella–Malaga area, the key was quickly identified as a Banco de Santander safety deposit key; and with only two branches in the area offering safety deposit facilities, within another hour the right branch had been located. The next process – getting a notarised death certificate for the bank's lawyers to allow the police entry to that specific safety deposit – took longer, eating up the next forty-eight hours.

During that total three-day process, Lapslie flew back to England, caught up with other Chelmsford squad activity, informing Rouse on the final day – having just got the latest update from Bernardo Ruiz about the key – that it might be good news regarding Vic Denham, then he had a pleasant dinner that same night with Charlotte before flying back out again to Marbella.

Lapslie wanted to make sure he was alongside Javier

Beneyto and the Marbella GEO squad for their raid on Denham's villa.

Inside Largo's safety deposit box were more gold chains and sovereigns with a total value of £28,000; although the accompanying papers, three old mobiles and numerous recorded telephone conversations on a flash stick proved to be the main prize; the rest of Largo's 'insurance policies' where he'd recorded hit instructions to offer up as plea-bargains: *If we can do a deal, I can give you a much bigger target than me. A real kingpin.*

Vic Denham was one of those kingpins; he'd hired Largo for three hits, one of which was the failed attempt on the Haines villa in Marbella. From the recording and notes, it appeared Largo had offered to go back to complete the contract, but two things had happened in the interim: Haines had upped-pegs with his family and gone to Valencia, and Denham had meanwhile heard that another local villain, Danny Blake, had been responsible for the raid which cost his son's life.

Denham bided his time for four months, then got Largo to target Blake's son, Callum. Particularly fitting, according to Largo's notes, because rumour also had it that 32-year-old Callum had been the main driving force urging his father to expand his drug-dealing empire and get rid of any rivals. Vic Denham also hadn't bothered to tell Terry Haines that his family were 'out of the frame', *'because that then might point the finger at him being behind the Callum Blake hit,'* Largo concluded.

Apart from Denham, the safety deposit 'gold mine' also led to the arrest of Danny Blake and two other major Marbella gangsters. More 'feathers in the cap' for Javier Beneyto and his team, as well as Ruiz, Lapslie and the Cheltenham force for their collaboration.

Vic Denham appeared even more unsteady on his feet as he was handcuffed and marched out of the villa at rifle point. His two 'minders' were already being loaded into a black van as Lapslie came out to join Javier Beneyto on the villa's front terrace.

One had been in a bedroom at the far end of the corridor, and quickly gave up reaching for the handgun on his bedside table when he saw the amount of firepower massed against him. The other had been in a room by the villa's gatehouse and had half-raised a pump-action shotgun before recognising the foolhardiness of such a move; two red dots were already aimed squarely at his body.

'Went well, by the looks of it,' Lapslie commented to Beneyto.

'Yes. Always good when there are no shots fired, no injuries.' Beneyto lit up a cigarette. 'We've got one more raid to finish things, just a mile down the road from here. You coming along to that one too?'

'No, it's okay.' Lapslie shook his head with a tight smile. 'I just flew out for this one.'

'This one special to you?'

'You could say.'

Lapslie watched Vic Denham being led down the villa pathway lined with Roman statues, gait unsteady, shoulders slumped in defeat. He looked far from a Roman emperor now.

Lapslie took out his mobile to phone Rouse.